HOW TO KISS YOUR BEST FRIEND

JENNY PROCTOR

AF516773

Srishti
PUBLISHERS & DISTRIBUTORS

Srishti Publishers & Distributors
A unit of AJR Publishing LLP
212A, Peacock Lane
Shahpur Jat, New Delhi – 110 049

editorial@srishtipublishers.com

First published in India by
Srishti Publishers & Distributors in 2023

First Published by Jenny Proctor Creative

Copyright © Jenny Proctor, 2022

10 9 8 7 6 5 4 3 2 1

This is a work of fiction. The characters, places, organisations and events described in this book are either a work of the author's imagination or have been used fictitiously. Any resemblance to people, living or dead, places, events, communities or organisations is purely coincidental.

The author asserts the moral right to be identified as the author of this work.

All rights reserved. No part of this publication may be reproduced, stored in a retrieval system, or transmitted, in any form or by any means, electronic, mechanical, photocopying, recording or otherwise, without the prior written permission of the Publishers.

By arrangement with Jenny Proctor

This edition is for sale in the Indian Subcontinent only

Printed and bound in India

to Misty and Brian
whose love story inspired this one

Chapter One

Brody

I STARE AT MY phone like it's about to sprout legs out of the speaker port and dance across the coffee table.

Kate Fletcher sent me a text.

Today.

Five minutes ago.

And I have no idea how to respond.

Look, I realize better than anyone that pining after my childhood best friend is a dangerous game. I have three brothers, and they have reminded me more times than I can count (and that's saying something because I am very good with numbers) that I am only setting myself up for heartbreak. They say if anything were going to happen with Kate, it would have by now.

Logically, I get that. I understand we aren't ever going to be together.

But I can't let her go completely.

Kate is my favorite bad habit. The impossible wish. The dream I can't shake.

It's been one thousand, four hundred and thirty-three days since we last had a conversation. That streak ended today. At least it will once I text her back.

I stand up and start pacing, my fingers tapping against my leg. There are so many things I want to ask her. But I can't launch into an inquisition when all she said was hello. She's the one who reached out to me. I'm a mature adult, and a mature adult would say hello back and let her make the next move.

I am seventeen laps into my pacing when my oldest brother, Perry, knocks twice before pushing into my house, a backpack slung over his shoulder. "You . . . do not look ready to go."

I pause next to the fireplace, halfway through lap eighteen. "I'm . . . *close*."

"Right. Yeah. It looks like it." Perry surveys the room and sighs, but he's overreacting. My living room may look like an outdoor outfitter threw up all over my furniture, but I know where everything is, and I know exactly where it's going to go when I stash it all in my pack. I'm only waiting to finish packing because I just cleaned my tent, and it's still in the backyard drying off.

And also because Kate Fletcher just sent me a text message.

"What's up with you?" Perry asks as he discards his pack and drops into the chair by the window. "You look all weird and stressed and stuff." He pulls out his phone and reclines into the chair like he expects to be waiting a while.

"I, um, I just got a weird text, and it threw me off."

"Aww, did Taylor Swift finally respond to all the messages you've sent her fan club?"

I grab the bundled merino wool socks sitting on the arm of the couch and chuck them at his head.

He deflects the socks without even cracking a smile.

"Honestly, hearing directly from Taylor Swift herself would be less surprising."

Perry looks up, his expression morphing into actual concern.

"I got a message from Kate," I say.

His eyes go wide. "High school Kate? Your Kate?"

I nod and lean forward, resting my head in my hands.

"What did she say?"

"Nothing. She said hi. Said it's been a while."

The thing is, I do not hold Kate accountable for our friendship falling apart. We did a decent job of staying in touch after graduation even though I headed to college, and she headed to Europe to live with her dad full time. We saw each other once or twice a year, whenever she was back in the states, and we texted regularly.

Until we didn't anymore.

It didn't make me mad. It just made me worried about her.

My brothers, on the other hand, were thrilled when Kate dropped out of my life. *Now you can move on, they said. Now you can stop waiting for something that's never going to happen.*

I know that at some point, I'm going to have to take dating other women more seriously. I'm twenty-eight years old. I don't *really* want to spend the rest of my life reading Kate's articles—she's a travel writer—and stalking her Instagram feed. I know precisely how pathetic that makes me look.

Don't get me wrong. I date.

Just not *seriously*. A three-month relationship here. A six-month relationship there. I even made it a year with a woman named Jill my senior year of college. But nothing ever sticks. Because somewhere in the back of my mind, I can't let go of the hope that at some point, Kate will come back into my life and this time, things will be different.

"It's been a while?" Perry repeats. "How kind of her to acknowledge."

"Don't do that," I say. "You can't play it both ways. You were pissed at her when we were still in touch, now you're pissed at her because we fell out of touch?"

"I'm not pissed at *her*," he says. "I just don't like what she does to your head. She's been messing with you for a lot of years, Brody."

I push a hand through my hair. "But that's on me. She didn't do anything on purpose. I can't blame her for what she doesn't feel."

Perry lifts a shoulder in the sardonic way that makes my oldest brother so annoying. "I won't argue with you about it. But I think you're being generous by saying she's never strung you along on purpose."

"Strung me—? Geez, Perry, do you even know what a real friendship looks like?"

He looks at me over the top of his phone. "I don't need friends," he says dryly. "It's bad enough I have so many siblings. Friends and all their *neediness* would make my life even more unbearable than it already is."

It's arguable that the last four years of Perry's life have been hard enough to justify his attitude. An ugly divorce, settled in court, that nearly cleaned him out. Then all the stuff we've dealt with at home. Dad had a stroke and was forced to retire early, leaving Perry to step up and take over daily operations of Stonebrook Farm, the working farm and event center that's been the family business for almost thirty years. As soon as our only sister, Olivia, finished her MBA, she moved home to help out, but Perry is still juggling a lot.

All that aside, Perry has never been particularly . . . jovial? Happy isn't the right word. I've seen him happy. He just doesn't smile much. He's Roy Kent minus the swear words. Stanley Hudson minus the indifference. Dr. House minus the cutting insults. He perpetually looks like he's carrying the weight of the world—or at least our family—on his shoulders.

"Your life isn't unbearable," I say.

"And you aren't in love with Kate," he responds without missing a beat. His eyes are back on his phone now. "See? Saying something out loud doesn't necessarily make it true."

"I'm not in love with Kate."

I say it mostly out of habit. Like it's an affirmation I'm trying to will into existence. I don't love her because I *can't* love her. Because it's fruitless to love her.

"Right. Sure. Should I get Lennox on the phone so he can jog your memory? I bet Flint remembers that night out at the ledge. Should I call him up, too?"

Perry is playing dirty.

I shouldn't be held accountable for things I said nearly nine years ago, the one time in my entire existence I allowed myself to get completely wasted.

I was with my brothers, up behind the orchards on our family's property, on a cliffside we brothers dubbed *the ledge*. It isn't truly a cliff. Had one of us ever fallen, we wouldn't have done more than tumble a few yards into a grove of rhododendrons.

But it still provided great views of the valley, was a short hike from the house, and an even shorter one if we took one of the Gators, the 4x4s we used to get around the farm, to the orchard edge. From the time we were old enough to brave the shadowy, Western North Carolina woods alone, the ledge was our escape whenever we were mad, sad, angry, or in trouble. It was also where we took dates when we wanted to impress them with the view and make out without the risk of our parents catching us. That night nine years ago, all four Hawthorne brothers were on the ledge together, beverages provided by the two oldest. Perry and Lennox wore their older age like a badge of manhood me and Flint, the brother younger than me, were still aspiring to.

I was exhausted after finishing freshman year finals and bemoaning the fact that my high school best friend had gone off and started traveling the world with some guy.

Preston was her long-distance boyfriend all through our junior and senior year, so I shouldn't have been surprised. But traveling together, visiting far-off countries, staying in Preston's family villas and seaside condominiums. It felt so . . . permanent. So *adult*.

I don't remember much of what I said out on the ledge that night. But my brothers seem to remember every last word of my miserable tale of unrequited love. They must, because even nine years later, they remind me of it every chance they get.

They also remind me that, with tears streaming down my face, I poetically claimed I'd been in love with *two* women in my nineteen years of existence. Kate Fletcher and Taylor Swift.

"Are you going to respond?" Perry asks.

"Sure. Eventually. I just have to figure out how."

Perry breathes out a heavy sigh. "Brody. How many minutes have you been staring at your phone?"

The number pops into my head as quickly as they always do. "Seventeen and a half."

"You gotta snap out of it, man. Finish packing. Tyler will be here soon. You can respond in the car."

I nod, knowing Perry is right. I've wasted too much time as it is.

It was a last-minute decision to join Perry on his annual two-week trek on the Appalachian Trail. We're all big hikers, my entire family, but Perry is the only one into the long-distance stuff. He says he'll thru-hike it one day—tackle the entire 2,190 miles in one uninterrupted trip—but I'll believe it when I see it. He likes working too much to take six months off to go hiking. I hesitated to take even two weeks off, but after the volatility that dominated the last month of the school year, I need the break. Even if it means hanging out with Perry.

I stand and start gathering my gear from various places around the living room.

"Did you read Kate's last piece in *The Atlantic*?" Perry is behind me now, rummaging around in my kitchen. "On the impacts of tourism on the Maasai tribe in Zimbabwe? It's brilliant."

I stop and stare at my oldest brother. It does not surprise me that, after all the traveling she's done, Kate has turned herself into an accomplished travel writer. It does surprise me Perry reads her stuff. "You read Kate's articles?"

Perry walks back into the living room with a to-go container of leftover chicken fried rice in his hand. "Not as a rule. But I read *The Atlantic*. If she's in it, then I read it."

I, on the other hand, read everything Kate writes. And buy hard copies, whenever there is one, for safe keeping. "Yeah, I read that one too," I say noncommittally.

Perry takes a bite of the rice and winces. "How old is this? The rice is crunchy."

"Old. Why are you eating that for breakfast?"

"Why didn't you throw it out?" He frowns but doesn't stop eating. "Does it ever seem weird that you know so much more about Kate's life and what she's up to than she does about you?" He nudges the socks I threw earlier with the toe of his shoe. "Don't forget these."

I grab the socks and add them to my pile of gear, then move toward the back door to retrieve my tent. "I don't know. She lives a pretty public life. I only know the stuff everyone else knows too."

At least that's how it's been the past four years. I used to know everything.

I disappear into my backyard long enough to collapse my tent and fold it up. Back inside, I put it, and the rest of my remaining gear, into my bag. "Kate might know some stuff. I don't post anything, but Olivia does. I'm pretty sure they still follow each other."

"Olivia's feed wouldn't tell Kate anything but how much Olivia loves the farm. And Tyler."

"True." I glance at my watch. "Speaking of Tyler, shouldn't he be here by now?"

"He's coming," Perry says. "He had to help Mom with something in the goat barn, but he said he'd be here by nine-thirty."

"I swear she likes him better than the rest of us." Olivia's husband, Tyler, who will drop us off at Springer Mountain, the Southern terminus of the Appalachian Trail, made fast work of convincing Mom he was her favorite.

"Only because he loves her goats," Perry says grouchily.

"And helped make her a grandbaby." It's not lost on any of us that the youngest of the five Hawthorne children, and the only girl, managed to find a husband and get pregnant before any of her older brothers have even come close. With the way things are looking, Olivia's baby, due at the end of the summer, may be the only grandchild Mom and Dad get.

Perry swore off women after his divorce and despite our best efforts to resuscitate whatever part of his brain controls desire, he's still uninterested. A vegetarian in the meat aisle of the grocery store.

Lennox, the next brother down, has the opposite problem. He desires *too much*. His problem isn't finding a woman, it's wanting to settle down with only one.

The brother right under me, Flint, has an acting career that isn't exactly conducive to normal relationships. Last time I saw his face, it was plastered to the front of one of my AP Chemistry student's notebooks—a cut out of the photo that made the cover of People magazine's latest "Sexiest Man Alive" edition.

If it isn't yet obvious, I'm the only Hawthorne brother who's even remotely normal, at least when it comes to relationship stuff. I'd love to get married. Settle down. Have kids. Be the son who takes the kids over to have dinner with their grandparents every Sunday afternoon. It's what I want. I just need to meet the right woman.

My eyes dart to where my phone is still sitting in the center of the coffee table.

Step one? Convince myself Kate is not the right woman.

I'll get right on that. Make it my top priority.

Just as soon as I respond to her text.

Chapter Two

Brody

I WAS NINE YEARS old when Katherine Anne Fletcher—Kate—climbed onto the school bus just after the three o'clock bell, looked at the empty seat beside me, and said, "If I sit here, will you promise not to be stupid?"

She dropped onto the narrow bench, nudging me over with her hip, and pulled her overlarge backpack onto her lap. Her hair was long and dark, hanging over her shoulder in a thick braid, and her face was covered in freckles. We didn't get new kids in Silver Creek very often—it's too small a town for people to move in with any regularity—so everyone on the bus was sitting up and taking notice of the new girl. And the nerdy kid she'd chosen to sit beside.

As for me, I couldn't even manage a word. I just sniffed and pushed my glasses up from where they'd slipped onto the end of my nose.

"The thing is," she continued, "experience has taught me that most boys are dumb with a capital D." She eyed me, her gaze shrewd. "I watched you when you got off the bus this morning. You're nicer to your sister than the other one."

I looked toward the seat directly in front of me where my

younger brother Flint and our little sister Olivia were sitting together. Our two older brothers were already at the middle school and rode a different bus. Kate was observant. Flint was always tougher on Olivia, but Olivia was tougher on him too.

I lifted a shoulder. "I'm older," I said, like that explained everything.

She shook her head dismissively. "Some kids use that as a reason to be meaner. Are you good at math? I'm terrible at it, so it would be excellent if you are."

Was I good at math? Even with my limited experience, I understood that I was being interviewed. Kate Fletcher was deciding if I was friend material or not. And that question? It was a winning lottery ticket. I wasn't just good at math. I was a genius at math. The kind of next-level nerd who tested out of every math class our elementary school offered by the middle of my fourth-grade year. The kid who, two years later, would go onto the Ellen DeGeneres Show as a twelve-year-old "human calculator."

"Did you just ask if he's good at math?" Flint said, turning around in his seat so he could look over the back. He was a faithful and competent wingman even back then. "He's the best there is at math. Give him a math problem. Any math problem. Something with a billion numbers in it." Flint tapped the side of his temple. "He can do it in his head."

It was a slight overstatement. There were limits to what I was capable of computing in my head, but I usually did all right when it was kids coming up with the problems.

"Really?" Kate asked, her eyebrows arching high on her forehead.

I shrugged noncommittally even as my heart started racing and a thin sheen of sweat broke out across the back of my neck.

"Any math problem?"

I nodded.

"Two-hundred forty-five thousand, five hundred fifty divided by twenty-five."

"Piece of cake," Flint muttered under his breath. "He can always do the ones with fives." Olivia was watching now too, her eyes hopeful as her gaze darted from me to Kate and back again. She seemed to sense the gravity of the moment just like I did.

The answer tumbled into my brain with measured certainty. I can't explain how it all works, though as an adult, it's easier to recognize the patterns that back then just felt like magic. "Nine-thousand, eight-hundred twenty-two," I said.

It's been eighteen years, and I still remember how her eyes lit up when she checked my answer with a calculator she pulled out of her backpack.

Our friendship was a done deal after that.

Kate decided we would be best friends—a very Kate move I recognize in hindsight more than I did at the time—and we were.

But now? I don't know what to call what we are now. We aren't estranged exactly. But we aren't talking either. At least we haven't been until today.

Kate: Hi, Brody. It's been a while.

I don't need to have my phone in front of me to see her text. The words are floating in my mind's eye, even as I move around the room and pack up the last of my gear. I force myself to focus, mentally cataloging all the items in my bag, double and triple-checking that I've remembered everything. Perry's list was comprehensive. The only thing I adjusted was how much water he suggested I bring. His estimates shorted me sixteen ounces.

"You've got all your food packed?" Perry says, eyeing my bag. "Everything I suggested?"

I nod. We'll be on the trail three days before we can resupply, so we'll be carrying everything we'll need to eat until then. "I've got everything. Plus a little extra water, which you're going to need too. How heavy is your pack?"

"Brody." Perry levels me with a glare. "If you run the calculations for how much water I'm going to need one more time, I'm going to tell Dad about the time you stole the Gator and drove it to Kate's in the middle of the night. He never did figure out who caused all four tires to go flat. I bet he'd like to know."

My words stop, even if the numbers keep moving through my head. Exactly how much water we'll need on the trail depends on a lot of factors. How fast we're walking. How hot it is outside. Our body weight relative to how much weight we're carrying. The distance we have to travel before we can resupply or find potable water on the trail. Perry ought to be glad I can run the calculations in my head. Dehydration is a big problem for long-distance hikers.

"Stop it," Perry says.

"Stop what?" I say as I shoulder my pack.

"Stop calculating." Perry grabs his own bag and follows me to the front porch.

"I'm not calculating anything."

"Yes, you are. Your eyes are doing that thing where they dart around. I promise we'll be fine. There's water all over the trail."

We will be fine. I know this. People hike the Appalachian Trail every summer without coming close to the kinds of ridiculous calculations that keep my brain occupied. Best guesses, rough estimates, those are good enough. Especially when there are so many unexpected variables with long-distance hiking that can't be calculated.

That doesn't mean I won't be doing the math anyway.

Sometimes I forget that constant number-crunching isn't normal. That all drivers aren't calculating exactly when they'll reach their destination based on slight fluctuations in their speed. That people on walks aren't estimating the number of steps they'll take before they reach some landmark in the distance. But it's how my brain works. It's actually why I decided to teach chemistry instead of math. There are still a lot of numbers in chemistry, but the science part gives my brain a break from the constant calculating.

Tyler pulls up minutes later, and we load up our gear. I take a deep breath and climb into the back seat of Tyler's SUV, content to let Perry take the front.

I need this trip. The decompression. The time in the mountains. The time away.

I settle into my seat and tap my cell phone into my palm. We won't be without service while we're hiking, and I've got a solar charger in my pack, but coverage will be spotty in places. If responding to Kate starts a conversation, I'd rather have it now, when I've got hours to kill in the car, than later, when I'm on the trail and Perry is watching my every move.

But what do I say? And how do I say it?

No exclamation points. That's important. I want to seem chill. Not overly exuberant. The fact that it's already been an hour since she first texted is a good thing. I won't seem over-eager, *annnnd* now I sound as bad as the girls in my freshmen environmental science class stressing about how long they can leave guys *on read* without responding. I have to just do it. Respond. Adult this situation once and for all.

I pull up my texting app, but a new message pops up before I make it to Kate's thread, this one from Monica, a fellow teacher at Green River Academy and the woman I sort of dated a few months back. I may or may not appreciate the delay. Even if it *is* caused by Monica.

Monica: Hey! Wasn't sure you'd check your email before leaving. Confirmation just came through that the next school board meeting is delayed until you're back in town. I'm glad they're seeing the benefit of having you there to defend the program. In the meantime, enjoy your trip!

I close out the text thread and pull up my Green River Academy email. Sure enough, there's the form email addressed to the entire district pushing back the date of the next school board meeting, plus a separate message addressed only to me. It's brief, relaying what Monica has already told me.

Brody–The school board agreed you deserve the opportunity to speak for the program. I can't make any promises, but we'll give it our best shot. -John

It's more encouragement than I've gotten from John Talbot, Green River Academy's principal, in weeks, so I'll take it.

Green River Academy is a charter high school focused on integrating experiential outdoor learning with regular classroom experiences. When they hired me to teach Chemistry and Environmental Science, they already had enrichment programs that covered rock-climbing, backpacking, horseback riding, and swimming.

What they didn't have—weirdly, because the academy sits less than a mile from the Green River—was whitewater kayaking. It took a little bit of maneuvering. Okay, *a lot* of maneuvering. I wrote grant proposals, begged for donations and support from local businesses, completed layers and layers of safety certifications. All total, it took thirteen months for me to get the Green River Academy whitewater kayaking program officially off the ground. The first year, six kids enrolled, which was good because I'd only managed to acquire seven kayaks. Five years later, the program is maxed out at twenty-five high school students, with another twenty on a waiting list.

And now the whole thing is under attack.

I force my jaw to unclench and take a long, slow breath. The whole point of this trip is to get *away* from the stress of all this.

Another text from Monica pops up.

Monica: Would love to get together as soon as you're back in town. Without the teachers' lounge, I'm going to miss you! She ends the message with a kissing emoji that makes me roll my eyes.

Monica is very nice. But she's also not taking the hint. And by hint, I mean a very specific conversation in which I told her I'm not attracted to her and only want us to be friends. I don't know how I could possibly be more clear.

Monica started working at the academy two years after I did, and since we sort of knew each other in high school, she glommed on quick, using me as her go-to guy for questions about the school. Everything from teachers' lounge politics to what cafeteria meals ought to be avoided. I never minded her questions that first year. She's a genuinely good person. Great, even.

That doesn't mean I feel any spark when I'm around her.

I can almost hear Perry's voice in my head. *You'll never feel a spark with someone new until you get Kate out of your head.*

Getting Kate out of my head might be easier if I didn't still live in Silver Creek. Reminders of her are everywhere. All over my parents' farm, in all the places we used to hang out.

Every square inch of this place holds a memory with Kate in it.

Still, even if there is truth in what Perry is saying, that isn't what's happening with Monica. There's just nothing there.

I type out a quick response to her first text.

Brody: Thanks for the heads up about the school board meeting.

I completely ignore her second one. I've already said everything I could possibly say on the subject.

I switch over to my messages from Kate, my heart rate climbing. There's absolutely no reason to freak out. I have no idea what triggered her message, but it's probably something inconsequential.

I have a long history of trying to turn things Kate says or does into more than they are, but I'm too old to do that now.

I finally type out a response as friendly and generic as her message was and send it before I can spend even one extra second thinking about it.

Brody: Hey. Nice to hear from you. How are you?

Her response pops up almost immediately, like she was waiting for me to respond.

Kate: A simple question with a complicated answer. I'm okay, I think. But . . . I'm coming home. I'd love to see you.

The words hit like a punch to the gut.

She's coming home. To Silver Creek. Weird to hear her call it home because she's done pretty well at staying away. She's passed through a few times, but she never stays long enough to even unpack. She used to joke about how different we were when it came to our life plans. How I was the guy who would never leave Silver Creek, the guy who would always play it safe and stay close to home, while she dreamed of traveling to every country on the map. I wouldn't exactly call whitewater kayaking the Class V rapids in the Green River Narrows playing it safe, but still, she wasn't wrong. I *was* the guy who came back to Silver Creek the minute I graduated college. When I landed a job at the academy, it felt like hitting the jackpot. I've never wanted to live anywhere else. Meanwhile, she's got more stamps in her passport at twenty-eight than most people have in a lifetime.

I key out my response, trying my best to keep things neutral.

Brody: That's crazy. It's been a long time.

Again, her response comes through lightning fast.

Kate: It has been a long time. I know I owe you an apology, Brody. But I want to do it in person. There's so much to explain.

Relief washes over me. I don't know her reasons for going dark, but I know her well enough to trust that she has a good one.

Brody: You don't owe me anything. How long are you in town?

Kate: I don't know, actually. A while? Mom has finally decided to sell Grandma Nora's house. I'm coming home to clean it up and get it ready. I was hoping you might be able to pick me up from the airport tomorrow night.

Kate grew up living at her grandmother's, a two-story farmhouse with a big wraparound porch, right down the street from where I live now. Nettie, Kate's mom, hasn't lived there full time since right after Kate's grandma died four years ago, though she's in town every couple of months checking on the place. I've always wondered if she planned to sell.

A pulse of excitement skitters through me. I'm going to see Kate again. And *soon.* For a split second, I consider bailing on my trip with Perry so I really can pick Kate up at the airport.

But that will not go over well with a brother who is already convinced she has me completely whipped.

Brody: Actually, I'm out of town for a couple of weeks. Heading to the Appalachian Trail with Perry.

Kate: WHAT. That sounds amazing! Don't worry about me then. I'll figure out a ride. Or just rent a car. But two weeks?! That's so long.

I run a hand through my hair, the knot in my stomach tightening. How am I ever going to handle two weeks on the trail when I know she's at home waiting for me?

No. Not waiting for *me,* exactly. But she *is* wanting to see me. And that . . .

"You okay back there, Brody?" Tyler asks, eyeing me through the rearview mirror.

I've been half-listening to their conversation, but I must have zoned out. "What? Yeah. I'm good."

"I thought you might be carsick," Tyler says. "You look a little green."

I feel a little green, but it doesn't have anything to do with being in the car.

"Did you respond to Kate?" Perry asks, turning in his seat to glare at me over his shoulder.

"Yeah. We've been texting back and forth. She's um," I clear my throat. "She's coming home."

"To visit?" Perry asks. "Or for good?"

I measure my next words carefully. I don't need a lecture about Kate, and knowing she'll be around awhile will absolutely make Perry lecture. But I won't lie to him, and I can't ignore a direct question. I clear my throat. "Not for good. But she'll be around all summer."

"Living at her grandma's house?" Perry asks.

"Where else would she live?"

"The house that is exactly three doors down from *your* house?"

I sigh. "Perry, just say it."

"I'm not saying anything," he says, his tone cautious. "I'm just wondering how you feel about it."

"I feel like it'll be great to spend some time with her." I'm immediately proud of how chill my voice sounds.

"Um, I hate to butt in," Tyler says, "but who's Kate?"

"Brody's high school best friend," Perry says. "She moved away years ago, but she sure loves to swoop into town once or twice a year and stay just long enough to keep Brody obsessing over her."

"That's not what she does," I say, immediately defensive. "I haven't seen her in four years. And I'm not obsessed with her."

Perry shoots Tyler a droll look. "He's totally obsessed with her. He's been in love with her since middle school."

"Please let it go, Perry." I can't do this with him. Not when we're about to spend two weeks hiking together.

He turns his attention back to me. "Fine. But two months from now, when you're even more in love with her than you are now, and you're brokenhearted when she leaves again, I'm going to say I told you so."

"You won't be saying it because you're wrong," I say, hopefully ending the conversation. "Nothing is going to happen."

I turn my attention back to Kate's messages. Perry doesn't know what he's talking about. I can handle this. I'll be fine with Kate back in town. Everything will be *fine.*

Brody: Two weeks will be long for you? While you chill in Silver Creek? I'm the one hiking with Perry.

Brody: We're going to be alone on the trail, Kate.

Brody: All day.

Brody: Every day.

Kate: Do we need a safe word? Something you can text if you need me to come rescue you?

I grin. It's nice that after four years, we drop right back into our friendship like nothing has changed.

Brody: The word is TACOS.

Kate: A man after my own heart.

Ha. If she only knew.

Brody: Nah, I'll be all right. Perry won't admit it, but he's glad I'm coming along. He needs me more than he likes to admit.

Kate: Some things never change.

Kate: I can't wait to see you.

Brody: Me too.

Me freaking too.

Chapter Three

Kate

Fine. Yes. When I first hatched the plan to hike in and surprise Brody in the middle of his two-week trek with Perry, I vastly underestimated the logistical nightmare I was taking on. It isn't like the trail runs from town to town, complete with paved walkways and cell phone charging stations. The Appalachian Trail is *wilderness.*

The section Brody is hiking crosses through a few different towns close to the Georgia/North Carolina border, but pinpointing which one and when? It feels like one of those word problems you find on elementary school math tests. If train A enters a tunnel at three p.m. traveling fifty miles an hour, and train B enters a tunnel at six p.m. traveling forty-two miles an hour . . .

I could have used Brody and his math brain with all the calculating I've had to do. How far do people usually hike in one day? How many days will it take me to get to one of those trail-crossing towns? Is it even possible to time it so that Brody and I are in the same town at the same time?

Possible? Yes.

Easy? Absolutely not.

Risky because Brody doesn't have any idea I'm here and might not want to see me? *So much yes.*

Worst-case scenario, I spend a gorgeous weekend hiking and hanging out in a quirky mountain town with my cousin Kristyn who flew down from Chicago to help me get started on Grandma Nora's house. Kristyn was unexpectedly enthusiastic when I suggested we change our plans and spend half our time tracking Brody through the woods instead. But it might feel like less of a wild adventure, as she called it, if we never even find him.

"Are you sure this is the right place?" Kristyn asks.

I drop my bag at my feet and stretch my back. "There's a plaque right here that says Siler Bald. It's the right place." The metal plaque, bronzed and weather-worn, sparkles in the afternoon sunlight, marking the latitude and longitude of the mountain's peak.

Kristyn steps up beside me, her hands on her hips, her gaze on the horizon. "You were not lying about these mountains."

"I think I forgot how beautiful they are." I've seen a lot of amazing views over the past few years, and I've hiked to the top of a lot of mountains. But this is different. These mountains feel like home. My gut tightens, an unexpected pulse of emotion radiating out to my fingertips.

I focus on a distant lake nestled in between the rolling hills that stretch out in front of us. *Lake. Trees. Sky. Breathe in. Breathe out.*

I'm going to get through this summer if it's the last thing I do.

The Siler Bald trail is about two and a half miles one way. It only took us an hour or so to hike in, but the last quarter mile, a steep climb through knee-high grasses to get to the top of the knoll was more of a quad workout than I expected. The view from the top is worth it though. Three hundred and sixty degrees of rolling blues and greens, mountains as far as the eye can see in every direction. The Blue Ridge Mountains are the only mountains I've ever seen that melt into the horizon. On a clear day, when the sky is a brilliant blue overhead, it's hard to tell where mountains stop and sky begins.

Kristyn nudges me with her shoulder. "It's been a while, right? How does it feel to be home?"

I'm not home, exactly. But I'm closer than I've been in a long time.

I tamp down the discomfort still pulsing in my midsection. I did not hike all this way to have a meltdown on the top of a mountain. I have done *hard* things over the past eight years. Traveled to every continent. Survived on a shoestring budget and a healthy side of gumption. I have met people whose lives make my own complicated history seem like a children's book. I can handle this. I can master my emotions.

"Good, I think? Maybe a little weird."

"Are you nervous about seeing Brody again?"

I *should* be nervous. Brody was my north star growing up. When the rest of my life felt impossible, he was the one who was steady and constant. When I missed my dad, who divorced my mom and moved away when I was little, when my mom resented me for reasons I couldn't pinpoint, Brody was reliable like only a best friend could be. But we haven't seen each other in a long time, and I was the one who stopped responding to his messages.

He says I don't owe him an apology, but I *really* do.

"A little," I finally answer. "But I'm more anxious than anything else." Even if Brody isn't interested in rekindling our friendship, I at least know him well enough to trust he will still be kind.

"It's been what, four years since you've seen the guy?" Kristyn asks. She pulls a couple of bananas out of her bag and offers me one.

"Four years since we've talked, but more like four and a half since we've seen each other."

"What if it's totally weird?" she says around her banana. "You know it could be."

I shoot her a look. "Thanks, K. I appreciate your positivity."

"I'm just saying. Do you even know anything about what his life is like right now? He could be married and have kids for all you know."

"In four years? He would have had to work fast." A pulse of uneasiness skitters through my belly. I don't think Brody's married. His presence on social media is basically nonexistent, but I follow his little sister Olivia. If any of her brothers had gotten married, she would have posted something about it. At least a picture or two.

"I met and married Jake in eighteen months," Kristyn says. "If we decided to have a baby right now—"

I shoot her a look.

"*Hypothetically,*" she adds. "I promise I'm not making an announcement. I'm just saying if we *did,* we could totally have met, gotten married, and had a kid in four years."

I pluck the fabric of my tank top between my fingers and lift it a couple inches, relishing the breeze as it rushes past and cools my skin.

"There's no way," I say. "I would have heard something from someone. Or Brody would have told me himself."

"Engaged, then," Kristyn says. "He could be engaged."

I hold my shoulders back and suck in a deep breath of mountain air. "So what if he is? I'm just here as his friend. That's all we've ever been. A lot of time has passed, yes, but my friendship with Brody is bigger than time or distance. Just because we haven't seen each other in person doesn't mean things will be different." Even if I basically ghosted him.

Kristyn shoots me a skeptical look. "Are you trying to convince me or yourself?"

I crack a smile. "Oh, definitely myself. But it's working, so don't ruin things for me."

She shakes her head and chuckles. "I just don't want you to get hurt, Kate."

"I know. But Brody won't hurt me." I lift my shoulders. "He's my family."

I walk to a spot on the knoll that will give me the best view of the bottom of the hill. The Appalachian Trail doesn't climb the spur trail that comes up to the bald, so theoretically, Brody and Perry could hike across the field and not come close enough to see us. But knowing Brody, the potential view will be worth the climb.

"So what's our plan?" Kristyn asks as she drops onto the grass beside me. "Are we just going to wait? What if we missed them?"

"We didn't miss them. When I texted him last night, he said they were in Winding Stair Gap. That's close enough that unless they started before the sun rose this morning, they haven't been through here yet."

I started texting Brody questions about his whereabouts and how many miles they were covering per day right after Kristyn and I arrived in Franklin, the nearest town to this section of trail. I called it "research" for a potential article on the Appalachian Trail, and as far as I could tell, Brody bought it. Last night, I didn't even have to ask him where he was. He just sent me a screenshot of his GPS location, followed by a smiley face.

Some internet sleuthing also taught me most thru-hikers stop to resupply in Franklin. There's even a shuttle that picks people up at the Siler Bald trailhead and drives them into town. The hope is we'll be able to convince Brody and Perry to leave the trail and head into Franklin with us instead.

Hopefully.

If Brody wants.

But he will. Of course he will. Won't he?

I wrap my arms around my stomach. "Okay. I think I lied before. I maybe am a little nervous."

Kristyn eyes me, a grin playing around her lips. "What was he like in high school?"

I immediately smile. "He was the sweetest. Tall. A little gangly, but still so cute. And he was one of those guys who was just so genuine. Literally nice to everyone."

"That sounds too good to be true. Are his brothers the same way?"

I huff. "His *mom* is the same way. I mean, they're all great guys. But in high school, his brothers—at least the two closest to us in age, were total hotshots. Lennox was a player—he looked like he was twenty-five when he was seventeen, so girls were always all over him—and Flint was always hamming it up and making people laugh. Sometimes I think Brody stayed a little more chill because he felt like he had to balance them out."

"Flint was funny?" Kristyn stretches her arms high over her head, then leans back on her hands. "That feels so weird because he's such a serious actor now."

"Right? I mean, he's great at the serious stuff. But yeah. He's also a really funny guy."

"I can't imagine having Flint Hawthorne as a brother," Kristyn says. "Talk about pressure."

"I don't know. The rest of the Hawthornes hold their own. It isn't fair, honestly. The amount of beauty and brains in that family is completely ridiculous."

"Did you and Brody ever hook up?" She nudges my shoulder and raises her eyebrows, a teasing gleam in her eye.

"Is that what it's always about with you?"

"Yes. Yes it is. I always want the dirty details, Kate. You know this about me."

I roll my eyes. "I promise there are no dirty details with Brody."

"Really? You never looked at him and thought making out might be fun?"

Something flickers low in my gut. "I mean, maybe? He has these amazing brown eyes, and sometimes, the way he looked at me made me feel like he could see all the way in, you know? A couple times, when he looked at me like that, I maybe *considered* the possibility."

Kristyn claps her hands giddily and smiles wide.

"Stop it," I say. "I know what you're thinking, and that's not what's happening here. I'm pretty sure Brody has always seen me more like a sister."

"Uh, I know you don't have any siblings, Kate, so you can't know this from personal experience, but my brothers *never* look at me in ways that make me want to kiss them."

"I didn't say he looked at me to *make me* want to kiss him, I just said sometimes the thought popped in my head. That doesn't mean he wanted it too."

"Whatever. You're missing the point." She turns sideways and crosses her legs, her hands resting on either knee, and levels me with a glare that feels way too serious for the situation. "The point is, Brody sounds totally hot with brains to match. *And* he has a fantastic family, *and* he has a steady job."

She grows more and more excited the longer she talks, and I start to laugh. "What are you getting at?"

She shakes her hands like she's just made some amazing discovery. "I'm *getting at* Brody sounding like a first-class catch." She lets out a gasp and reaches out to grab my knee. "Kate! You could have a friends-to-lovers romance!"

I roll my eyes. "With Brody?"

"Of course with Brody. You already know each other incredibly well. You're here for the summer, he's hot and brooding . . ."

"Brody does not *brood.* And you read too many romance novels."

"And all those novels have taught me a lot," she says matter-of-factly. "In friends-to-lovers, the hard work is already done. You already know each other. You already *love* each other. All you have to do is crank up the heat."

"You're completely ridiculous." I toss my banana peel at her, and she smirks as she catches it.

"You say that now, but—"

Her words cut off when I reach over and grip her arm, my eyes locked on a pair of men climbing the hill below us. "Look. I think that's them."

The figures at the foot of the hill are too far away for us to see discernable facial features, but there's still something familiar about the man in front. Familiar because . . . it's Perry. I'm sure of it. The dark hair, the set of his shoulders. I haven't seen any of the Hawthorne brothers in years, except Flint who I've at least seen in movies, but they all have a very distinct look.

Which means the guy behind Perry . . . cannot possibly be Brody.

The hair is right. Light brown, a little wavy. But he's so . . . *broad.* He looks up, and my breath catches. It *is* Brody.

Kristyn blows out a slow breath beside me. "Um, which one of those guys was gangly in high school?"

"The one in the back. It's him. Oh my gosh, Kristyn, it's him."

I stand up and spin around, away from the trail. But it's not like I can hide. I'm standing on top of a grassy mountain top. They call it a *bald* for a reason. There isn't a tree, bush, or boulder I could crouch behind if my life depended on it.

Kristyn pops up beside me, setting a calming hand on my shoulder. "Just breathe. This isn't a big deal. He's your friend. He's going to be happy you're here."

Her words are simple, but it's just enough of a pep talk to help me refocus. I nod. "You're right. I can do this. No big deal." I turn back to the trail, watching as Brody finishes the climb.

His eyes are on the uneven terrain beneath his feet, his hands hanging onto the straps of his backpack as he leans into it. His t-shirt is stretched across his generously muscled chest and equally defined shoulders, clinging to biceps he one hundred percent *did not* have the last time I saw him in person.

Still, it's Brody. *My* Brody.

My heart squeezes at the sight of him, and a little laugh bubbles out of my chest. I've been a fool for staying away so long. Without thinking, I take a few steps forward into the path, my hand shielding my eyes from the sun. Whatever this summer is going to bring, however Brody is going to respond to my sudden and unexpected appearance on the Appalachian Trail, there's no turning back now.

Chapter Four

Kate

"Brody!" I call when he's twenty or so feet away.

He stops in his tracks, his gaze jumping to the top of the ridge where I'm standing. The shock that overwhelms his features quickly melts into a wide smile. He shakes his head and starts to laugh, even as he makes fast work of the remaining distance between us. It's the steepest part of the climb, but it seems to give him no trouble, not that I'm noticing the flex of his quads with every single step.

Okay. I'm totally noticing. But Brody almost looks like a different person. He's the same, there's just . . . more of him.

As he walks, he unbuckles the chest straps of his backpack and shrugs it onto one shoulder. At the top of the rise, he drops it onto the ground and takes two large steps until he's standing right in front of me. In one fluid motion, he pulls me into a giant hug, lifting me off the ground and spinning me around.

He is warm and solid under my hands, and a surge of emotion floods to the surface, pricking my eyes with tears.

This moment, Brody's arms around me, tears streaming down my face like I'm some ridiculous teenager hugging her first crush, it's an emotional gut punch I'm not prepared for.

I am a capable, independent woman. I have traveled to twenty-seven different countries. I have lived with indigenous tribes in the heart of the Amazon. I have hiked in the Himalayan mountains with Tibetan Sherpas and eaten live honey pot ants with the aboriginal people of Australia. I haven't had an actual *home* in almost a decade.

But that's what Brody feels like.

He feels like *home,* triggering a craving for something I didn't think I'd ever want again.

The moment is only slightly diminished by the smell which, honestly, it's . . . not great. Exactly what you'd expect from a man who's been hiking for three days with no shower.

"What on earth?" he says as he finally sets me down. "What are you doing here?" He hugs me again, my hands pressed up against his chest, and I start to laugh.

"I wanted to surprise you," I say, finally stepping back and wiping the tears from my face.

"I . . . you . . . I can't believe you're here," he says, a hand still pressed to his head. "This is why you were asking so many questions about where we were."

I lift my shoulders and grimace. "Guilty."

He laughs. His expression is warm, his eyes fully engaged in our conversation. He's already doing it again, looking at me with that intense, brown gaze, his attention wholly on me.

"I'm just seeing you, Kate," he would always say.

And he did see me. All of me. Saw my sadness, my frustration, my loneliness whenever I was particularly annoyed with my mom. And he always reacted accordingly, taking care of my emotions like no one else ever has.

I suddenly wonder what he sees when he's looking at me now. Kristyn's suggestion pops into my mind. *Could* I see Brody as more than a friend? The way my body is buzzing, it doesn't feel like such a crazy leap to make.

That doesn't mean it's a leap I *should* make.

Brody looks over his shoulder at Perry, and my eyes follow.

"Hi, Perry," I say.

Perry nods in his usual stoic way, no trace of a smile. "Kate."

I almost laugh at the predictability of his response. All these years, and Perry is the same curmudgeon he's always been.

Kristyn clears her throat beside me, and I step back, motioning her forward. "This is Kristyn. My cousin from up in Chicago."

Brody extends his hand. "It's nice to meet you."

"Yeah. You, too. I've heard a lot about you," Kristyn says.

Brody holds my gaze for another long moment, his hands propped on his hips. "You look good, Kate. The same, but . . . better."

"Thanks. *You* look like you were dosed with the super serum that turned Steve Rogers into Captain America." I playfully push against his chest. "What is all this? I had no idea any of this was going on."

"What would you have had me do? Send you shirtless selfies?" His grin is teasing in a way that feels very Brody, just a little more confident.

My eyes involuntarily drop to his chest, and I imagine, for a split second, what a shirtless selfie from Brody might look like.

The idea is as foreign as it is enticing.

I take a giant step backward, nearly colliding with Kristyn. "Fair point," I say as I awkwardly regain my balance, one arm on Kristyn's shoulder. "Though honestly, most guys who have all . . ." I wave my hand awkwardly toward his body. ". . . this going on would definitely be sending shirtless selfies. Or at least posting them on Instagram." My voice is higher and breathier than it should be, and I clear my throat.

What is going on? There are two very different reactions happening inside my body right now. If my brain is the middle-aged mom at a Harry Styles concert, wearing earplugs and holding her purse in her lap, my body is the college sophomore in the front row, screaming through happy tears as she throws her bra onto the stage.

But this is *Brody*. My body shouldn't be *reacting* in any sense of the word. I should be joking about this. I *have* to joke about this. Because the alternative?

Fantasizing about Brody shirtless or anything else-less is completely unacceptable.

"You okay?" Kristyn asks quietly.

"Mm-hmm," I mumble under my breath. "Totally good. Fine. Good."

She only chuckles. She ought to apologize. Had she not planted the seed in my head, I wouldn't even be feeling any of this.

Brody stretches his arms over his head, and his shirt lifts, revealing a brief glimpse of an inch of smooth skin above the waistband of his shorts.

Fine. Probably I'd still be feeling something without Kristyn's suggestion. But I still blame her for starting it.

"So what are your plans?" Brody says, looking from me to Kristyn and back again.

"We're staying in Franklin," I say. "We just hiked up for the day hoping we'd catch you."

He shakes his head. "I still can't believe you figured out we'd hit Siler today."

"Your last text made that part easy. We were already in Franklin, hoping you were close. When you responded, it was only a matter of leaving early enough this morning to beat you here."

"What would you have done if I hadn't responded?"

"Hiked in and camped, probably. And just hope you'd eventually show up. But trust me, we were happy to give up the campout for another night in our comfortable hotel beds."

"Says the woman who's slept on more mountainsides than I have."

I tilt my head. His awareness of my travels sends an unexpected burst of warmth right to my heart. "Yeah, well, Kristyn isn't quite as adept at roughing it as I am."

"I heard that," Kristyn calls from where she's kneeling over her daypack, digging through it like she's looking for something. "I was perfectly willing to sleep on the ground, thank you very much."

"Are you going into Franklin to resupply?" I say, not even trying to keep the hope out of my voice. "We could give you a ride, then maybe we could hang out for a night before you get back on the trail?"

"We're definitely in need of a resupply," Brody says. "And a shower." He pinches his shirt and lifts it away from his body. "We haven't left the trail in four days. In case you haven't noticed, we stink."

"Oh, I noticed," I say, my nose wrinkling. "You smell terrible."

He steps forward and wraps his arms around me, pinning my own arms to my sides. "What was that?" he says. I can't see his face with the way he's holding me against his chest, but I can hear the smile in his voice. "Something about me smelling bad?" I shriek in protest—he really does smell potent—and lean away, but who am I kidding? If I wanted to get out of his arms, I totally could. Instead, I stay pressed up against him, loving that he's here, that we're together.

I haven't been looking forward to a summer in Silver Creek. Facing my mistakes, making things right, it isn't easy work.

But Brody will be in Silver Creek too.

That can only mean I'm going to be okay.

Chapter Five

Kate

SOMETHING IS DIFFERENT.

First of all, sweaty, smelly trail Brody is . . . delicious.

I don't know how I feel about this. I have loved Brody as my closest friend nearly as long as I can remember. And in all that time, I have never felt that visceral tug deep in my gut, the spark of attraction like I did on the trail this afternoon.

The new muscles help. He's broader than I've ever seen him, and he seems more comfortable in his body. But it isn't just that. There's something else that's different about him.

Or could it be that the person who's different is me?

When Brody steps through the doors of the Mexican restaurant just up the street from the tiny hotel we're staying in, a small noise sounds in the back of my throat.

If sweaty, smelly trail Brody was delicious, freshly shaven and showered Brody is glorious. The kind of glorious that inspires poetry. I'm not a poet by any stretch, and even I feel like writing some. There should be angels singing right now. At least a pair of violins serenading us from the corner.

Wait. Hold up. Not *us.*

There is definitely not an *us* that needs serenading.

These are strictly platonic, entirely physical observations I'm making right now.

Kristyn offers me a napkin, her expression dry. We're already seated, having gone ahead to the restaurant to get a table and satisfy my craving for chips and salsa while the men showered and cleaned up. "You're drooling, Kate," Kristyn says, shaking the napkin. "Might want to take care of that before he gets to the table."

My hand flies to my chin before I realize she's kidding, and I scowl. "That was mean."

She only grins. "You're being incredibly obvious. Maybe dial it back a bit?"

I sigh and sink into the booth. "I'm just . . ."

"Feeling attracted to a really attractive man who is also a great guy? I know. It's so surprising."

"Shut up. We aren't talking about some random attractive guy. We're talking about Brody. This is entirely different."

She cocks an eyebrow. "Why?"

"Because we're friends."

"We went over this earlier, didn't we? That's how all good relationships should start."

"We're *just* friends."

"Adding a *just* doesn't make my observation any less true."

"But *he* doesn't see me that way. And even if he did, our lives are totally different. Totally—" My words cut off as Brody and Perry slide into the booth across from us.

I give Kristyn's knee a nudge under the table, hoping she understands it to mean, "Don't you dare say a word about *attraction,*" and smile at Brody. "Feel better?"

He nods. "Much." He eyes the empty basket on the table between us, then smirks. "Hungry, Kate?"

I immediately grin, recognizing the cadence behind a question he used to ask me every day at lunch. I was usually hungry, and him asking turned into a game. He would ask, then pull out some surprise he'd brought from home to share. His mother cooked way more than my mother ever did, and by the time we were in high school, Brody's older brother Lennox, a chef, was already baking and experimenting with recipes.

I grin. "Always," I answer, just like I did back then. We share a look that makes my heart squeeze. "The waitress is bringing us more."

"And some queso," Kristyn adds, totally oblivious to what's happening between Brody and me.

Brody glances around the restaurant. "Google reviews said this place was good. I hope it checks out."

I follow his gaze. I've been too hungry to notice much before now. The place is . . . festive? Kitschy might be a better word. The walls are covered in enormous sombreros and life-size cacti made out of paper mache. A mariachi band is tuning up in the corner, but the musicians look more like a country group who got lost on the way to their real gig. One guy is wearing a flannel underneath his traditional mariachi ensemble, four inches of shirt hanging below the hem of his suitcoat.

If I hadn't already blasted my way through an entire basket of chips, I might suggest we try and find something a little more authentic. Except, the chips were really good. Clearly homemade. And the salsa was legit.

I lift my shoulders in a shrug. "So far, so good. But the music hasn't started yet, so we'll see how things go from here."

Brody eyes the mariachi band and grins. "Are they in the right place?"

"I wondered the same thing."

We fall into easy conversation as the meal progresses. Perry even livens up a bit, contributing to Brody's story about their run-in with a bear a few days before.

"She wasn't more than ten paces away from my tent," Perry says, "and was even closer to Brody's."

"Close enough for me to smell her," Brody says casually.

"Oh sure. Close enough to smell her. That's not a big deal at all." I shake my head. "Who are you, and what did you do with the guy who hid behind me when we ran into a raccoon in the apple orchard?"

Perry chuckles.

"Listen," Brody says, folding his arms. "Raccoons have very scary teeth. And I swear that thing was hissing at us. It was ready to charge."

"Which totally justifies you using *me* as a human shield."

"Come on," he says with an easy grin. "We both knew you were tougher than me. You probably still are."

I eye his muscled torso. "I'm not so sure about that."

He takes a long drink of water, and I watch his Adam's Apple bob up and down with each swallow. Did he have one of those when we were in high school? I feel like the answer is no because it feels impossible that I could have been around him and *not* noticed.

Kristyn nudges me with her elbow and I startle out of my stupor. Was I staring? I *was* staring. Oh, I am in trouble if I even think his *swallowing* is sexy. What is happening to me?

I clear my throat. "So what are you going to do with the rest of your summer?" I push my half-eaten burrito into the center of the table. The thing was legit the size of a football. I'm proud I managed to finish as much as I did.

"First, I'm going to eat the rest of your burrito," Brody says, fork poised over my plate. He lifts his eyebrows in question, and I nod, nudging it even closer to him. He takes an enormous bite, and a wave of nostalgia washes over me. Somehow, it feels both achingly familiar and like an entirely new thing.

We have done this so many times. Shared meals. Passed plates between us without a second thought.

"Once I'm off the trail, I'm working an eight-week season at Triple Mountain, then I'm back at the academy the second week of August."

"Triple Mountain?"

He nods. "It's a paddling school on the Green River."

"Oh, right. The kayaking thing. I remember you mentioning something about that."

"Back then it was just a hobby. Now, I'm teaching."

"How to kayak?" Kristyn asks. "Don't you just sit in the boat and paddle down the river?"

Perry scoffs, but Brody only smiles, his expression kind. "It *can* be that simple. But I teach whitewater kayaking. It's a little more complicated."

"Oh, right. Of course," Kristyn says. "Jake and I went whitewater rafting down the Menominee River in Wisconsin once. His idea," she says, lifting a hand to her chest. "I was terrified. I guess that's not where my brain went when you said kayaking. We were in these enormous rafts."

I'm grateful to Kristyn for keeping the conversation going, because my brain is still functioning in slow motion. I'm only just blinking away the image of Brody's bobbing Adam's Apple, and now I have to think about him in a kayak, paddling through whitewater? There is little doubt in my mind that were I to happen across a random man, a stranger, and he mentioned he was into whitewater kayaking? I would immediately find him sexy. My taste for adventure, and for men who *also* love an adventure, has always been strong.

Whenever we talked about our plans, *I* was the one who was going to leave Silver Creek in search of adventure while *he* was the one who only ever wanted to stay in the mountains. In my head, that meant staying *home* and doing the things he always did when we were in school. He studied. He worked on the farm. Occasionally he would race the 4x4s with his brothers, but that was the most adventurous thing he ever did.

Brody says something else that I miss, but then Perry cuts in, snapping my attention back onto the conversation. "He's being modest." Perry looks at me with an intensity that almost feels like he's trying to tell me something. "He's a level five whitewater kayak instructor. The best Triple Mountain has. He also runs a whitewater kayaking program at Green River Academy that's getting statewide attention for how well it's doing."

"That's where you teach?" I ask Brody, and he nods.

He's sitting with his elbows resting on the table, his fingers steepled together in front of his face. His shoulders are slightly hunched, and I can tell by his body language that he's uncomfortable with Perry's praise. But when he meets my eye, there is something else there, too. A glimmer of pride? And . . . a question. He wants me to know about his kayaking. And he cares what I think about it.

"That all sounds really amazing, Brody," I say.

His mouth lifts in the smallest of smiles. "It's not a big deal."

Perry scoffs. "It is a big deal." He turns his attention back to me. "He likes to downplay it, but he's really good."

Brody makes a noise that sounds so similar to the one Perry just made, I almost giggle. Brody and Perry are the least similar of all the Hawthorne brothers, but there's a common thread that runs through all four of them. Gestures, and sounds, apparently, that they all share. "Dane Jackson is really good," Brody says. "I do fine."

Perry rolls his eyes. It's kind of adorable how enthusiastically he's talking up his baby brother. "Dane Jackson is a professional athlete. Kayaking is his job. It's not a fair comparison. Plus, what you've done at the academy is impressive." He shakes his head and reaches for his drink. "No matter what idiots like the Carsons say." This last part feels more like a general complaint than something he's saying to anyone in particular.

I look at Brody, and he meets my gaze with a new heaviness in his expression. It ignites a flare of worry in my gut. "Who are the Carsons?"

"Parents of a student," Brody says, his jaw tight. "There was an incident that happened at the end of the school year, and now they're complaining about the safety of the program. But it's not a big deal. It'll all work itself out."

The expression in his eyes says it's a *really* big deal, but I don't feel like I can push him. Not five hours into our newly reestablished friendship.

"An incident?" Perry's tone is thick with disdain. "Some punk kid ignored Brody's instructions and got in the water when he wasn't supposed to. His kayak flipped over, he couldn't get out, and it took Brody twenty whole seconds to jump in and save him."

I look back to Brody, and he nods. "That's the gist of it. Except I'm not even sure he was under water a full twenty seconds. Had he been listening instead of sneaking away and trying to skip ahead, he would have learned how to get himself out of the boat when he flipped upside down. For beginners, it's a question of when not if you're going to flip. But that didn't stop him from whining to his parents that he almost drowned."

"I don't understand," I say. "He flipped over, but he stayed in the boat? Was he strapped in?"

Brody shakes his head. "Not exactly. In a whitewater kayak, you wear this thing called a spray skirt around your waist. Then, when you're sitting in the boat, the skirt stretches over the rim of the boat opening, sealing you in and keeping your kayak from filling up with water when you hit rapids."

"Got it. Which works great until you flip upside down?" I might have a tiny bit of sympathy for the punk Carson kid. The idea of being trapped in a boat while hanging upside down in the water? I'm more adventurous than most, but that sounds terrifying.

"Only if you aren't prepared. You can do a wet exit—that's when you exit the boat while you're underwater—in about four seconds. You just have to learn how."

"Which the Carson kid didn't do," I say, finally connecting all the dots.

"And now his parents are passing around petitions and going to the news and making a big stink about Brody *and* the program," Perry says. He swears under his breath, and I stifle a laugh.

I didn't spend a ton of time hanging out with Perry when we were growing up. By the time Brody and I were in high school, he'd already left for college. Still, I'm positive this is the most I've ever heard him say at once. I shouldn't have expected anything different though. That's the way the Hawthornes are. Connected. Fiercely loyal. They've *always* been that way.

Somehow, I both crave that level of closeness and feel terrified of it at the same time.

"So what's going to happen?" Kristyn asks. "Surely his parents aren't getting any real traction. It was their kid's fault for not listening."

"They can't necessarily come after me," Brody says. "Or the school. Not legally. They signed the waivers and knew the risks involved. But they're doing their level best to shut things down. I have to appear before the school board in a couple of weeks."

"But they'll listen to you, right?" I ask. "Hear your side?"

Brody nods. "I think so. But the bad press is hard for the district to ignore. We're a charter school that depends on public funding. Negative attention like this stirs up people who think their tax dollars are better spent in more traditional schools with typical classroom settings."

"But Green River Academy uses traditional classrooms too, right?" I feel my own anger rising. If this is something Brody cares about, I want to care too. "They can't shut the whole school down."

"Not the whole school. I spend most of my time in the classroom. I'm only on the river with students twice a week. But the district *can* shut down the kayaking program."

I am of course furious that anyone is trying to end something that Brody feels so passionately about. But mostly, I'm just in awe of his passion. So much of him is the same. He was always an amazing teacher. I should know since he's the only reason I passed high school calculus. But he's different too. More confident. More . . . settled.

"When did you start kayaking?" I blurt out, not realizing until the words are out of my mouth that I've interrupted something Kristyn was saying. "Sorry," I say sheepishly. "I didn't mean to interrupt."

She eyes me, her look saying she knows exactly why I wasn't

paying attention. "That's okay. I was finished." She looks to Brody, and he clears his throat.

He holds my gaze for a long moment. "That first summer, right after you left." There's something else he isn't saying. I see it in his eyes, I just can't make out what it is.

"We were all positive he'd die on day one," Perry says. "He didn't even have biceps enough to hold up a paddle."

My eyes fly to Brody's biceps. Those things could definitely hold up a paddle now. A paddle and a boat. A paddle and a boat with me in it. Actually, let's forget the boat altogether. How about his biceps just hold me up?

I grab my water and take a long drink. That feels slightly less obvious than holding the cool glass to my flushed cheeks.

"Hey now," Brody says, but his eyes are smiling. "So I was a late bloomer. There's no shame in that." His gaze shifts to me, and he looks at me with that same familiar intensity. "There's a lot about me that's different now."

He's trying to tell me something. Or maybe I just *want* him to be trying to tell me something?

Do I *want* to want him to be telling me something?

Oh, good grief. I have never been this upside down over Brody. Or any guy, for that matter. We're together, just like we've been thousands of times before. But even though all the same pieces are here, nothing is fitting together like it always has. It's like I'm wearing my shoes on the wrong feet. Or my bra on the outside of my shirt. I almost feel like I need to strip everything off and start over just to figure out what I'm feeling.

Annnd probably I should not use metaphors that involve stripping when I already can't stop noticing all the new contours of Brody's body. I reach up to my neckline and make sure my bra strap is covered by my shirt, like my discomfort *must* be obvious to everyone else. "I bet you're still the nicest guy anyone knows," I say. "You're still looking out for your siblings. Still taking care of your friends."

"Trying to," he says with an easy shrug.

Perry reaches over and wordlessly pats his younger brother on the shoulder.

"You should go and see Mom as soon as you're back in town," Brody says. "Don't even wait for me to get home."

I bite my lip. I would love to see his mom. I loved Stonebrook Farm growing up. All of it. The apple orchards. The strawberry fields. The baby goats. And of course, Brody's parents and the rest of the Hawthornes. But it's more complicated than that. "I'm not sure she'll want to see me," I finally say. "She has to be upset that I didn't come home for Grandma Nora's funeral."

There it is. The proverbial elephant in the room.

Except, it hasn't really *felt* like there's been an elephant in the room. I told Brody via text that I owed him an apology, and I do. But we haven't been alone yet, and we've been so caught up in, well, *catching up*, I haven't even thought about it.

But I've brought it up now, and there's no turning back.

The elephant has finally reared its head. Stomped its foot? Trumpeted its . . . trunk? Whatever elephants do to get attention, it's happening, and I can't ignore it.

Despite the trumpeting elephant, Brody's face softens. "She won't care about that, Kate. She's always loved you. She still does."

His lack of judgment, or at least his confidence in his mother's lack of judgment, does a little to soothe my guilty conscience, but only a little. When my grandmother died four years ago, I wasn't in a good place. Mentally, emotionally. But it shouldn't have mattered. I should have tried harder to get back.

Brody was at the funeral, of course. And his mama, who tended my mother and helped her take care of all the details.

"I should have been there," I say softly.

Brody nods. "Okay. So you should have been. That doesn't mean Mom won't love you anymore. Or me," he adds.

My breath catches, and I stare at my hands. I'm pretty sure if I look at Brody right now, I'll start to cry. The certainty and unwavering acceptance of his friendship are doing strange things to my heart. Despite my hesitation, my eyes lift to his. And yep. There it is. That intense gaze that says I see you, I understand you, *I know you* all at once. This man and his tenderness are going to end my life this very moment.

Here lies Kate Fletcher. Melted by tenderness. And amazing biceps.

When I open my mouth to speak, Brody gives his head the slightest shake, his eyes darting over to his brother.

Not here, his eyes tell me.

I nod my understanding. We need to have this conversation, but we don't need to do it here, with Perry and Kristyn as a captive audience. The thing is, I *would* have the conversation. Say the hard things no matter who is listening in. The discomfort of doing so would be a small price to pay to make things right between us. But all these years later, Brody is still looking out for me.

"I'll go see your mom," I say. "I promise."

I look over at Kristyn, who has been observing our exchange with raised eyebrows. "I'll take you with me. I'd love for you to see the place." For the first time in as long as I can remember, I'm actually looking forward to going *home.*

Chapter Six

Brody

I CAN ALREADY SENSE the struggle it's going to be to maintain perspective with Kate around full time.

It's only been a few hours, and already, for every ounce of control I hold onto, two more ounces slip away. I feel like I'm on a tilt-a-whirl at the county fair, trying to keep a mug of coffee from spilling over the sides. The coffee is my resolve, and it's splashing all over my shoes.

Logically, I know the likelihood of Kate suddenly growing feelings she's never had before is slim. Kate loves me like a brother. She always has. But remembering that was easier when she was thousands of miles away.

Now she's back.

Here. Present.

Sitting right across the table from me, laughing and smiling over chips and salsa.

In her short cargo shorts and tank top, Kate looks like she should be modeling for an outdoor catalog. Her shoulders are toned and tanned, freckles speckling her skin just like they used to whenever she spent time in the sun. It's the strangest thing to look at her and simultaneously see the little girl she was—the one who quizzed me with math problems on the school bus—and the woman she is now.

Perry and Kristyn have both gone back to the hotel, leaving Kate and me to have dessert just the two of us. The waitress's eyes go wide when I ask for two servings of churros in addition to the one Kate ordered for herself, but I could probably eat fifteen churros and still be under my caloric need. There's no way to ever eat enough when you're hiking sixteen or seventeen miles a day.

"He just got off the Appalachian Trail," Kate says to the waitress. "He'd eat everything in the restaurant if you let him."

The waitress nods knowingly. "Ah. Got it. I'll be right back."

Kate shakes her head at me, and I grin. "You're lucky I only ordered one extra."

"What you probably ought to be eating is extra protein. Or some carbs with a little more substance to them."

"Okay, *Perry*."

She scoffs playfully. "You did not just call me Perry."

I smirk. "I've been eating oatmeal cooked in a Ziploc bag for three days, Kate. Let me enjoy my dessert."

Her eyes dance as she smiles, her expression bright. "When I hiked Kilimanjaro, my guides were constantly making me eat. Even more than I thought I needed to."

"When you hiked Kilimanjaro, huh? You're going to just throw that out there like it's something anyone can relate to?"

She rolls her eyes. "Shut up. I'm not the only person who has ever hiked it. We're relating here, Brody. You hike. I hike. I'm making conversation."

"I loved the piece you wrote about Kilimanjaro."

"You read it?"

That, and everything else she's ever written, all the way down to the responses on her Instagram comments. “I read it,” I finally say.

She breathes out a sigh. “It was a great trip.” Her gaze shifts to the window behind us. We have a clear view of the rolling blue and green mountains in the distance. “What about the Appalachian Trail?” she asks. “Would that make a good story?”

“Absolutely. There’s a lot you could write about. It’s so much more than people hiking. There’s a whole culture that has grown up around the experience, especially for thru-hikers. You’re good at telling the stories that are under the surface. There’s a lot of those along the AT.”

She tilts her head to the side and studies me. “Do you read all my stuff?”

Heat creeps up my cheeks, but I don’t have a good reason to deny it. A *friend* would read all her stuff. There’s nothing wrong with that. “Of course I do.”

The smile she gives in response warms me all the way to my core. It feels *so good* to make her happy.

“How’s your dad? Is he still in Paris?”

“He’s all over, really. You know how Dad is. But yeah. He’s still got a place in Paris. That’s mostly where I stay when I’m in Europe.”

“He’s still working for the same company? Overseeing . . .?” I wince and shrug. I don’t actually remember what her dad does.

“Mergers and acquisitions. And yes. Same job. Same company. Same crazy travel schedule.”

“It runs in the family then.”

A shadow flickers behind her eyes, but then she smiles. “Yeah. I guess so.”

“Tell me about Kristyn. I don’t remember you being close with any of your cousins when we were growing up.”

"We weren't close until recently. We saw each other every once in a while, when Dad would take me to family reunions. But then I got stranded in Chicago during this freak snowstorm five or six years ago, and I couldn't find a place to stay. Kristyn took me in like a stray puppy and decided to keep me."

"I bet you loved that."

"I resisted for all I was worth. But Kristyn wouldn't budge. She insisted I needed her, and I eventually caved. Now, whenever I'm passing through the states, she lets me crash at her place."

"So you've been in the states then? Recently?"

Her shoulders drop, and her expression shifts. Finally, she nods. "A few times."

Disappointment pings around in my chest. It would be easier to understand if her mom hadn't left Silver Creek. She's always been pretty good at avoiding her mother. But her mom moved four years ago, right after *her* mother's funeral.

"I wasn't avoiding *you*, Brody," Kate says gently, clearly sensing my unease. "I was avoiding Silver Creek. Avoiding . . ." She breathes out a long sigh. "Guilt, I guess?"

That, I can understand. But why didn't she talk to me? Why didn't she explain? "You know I didn't judge you for missing the funeral. We could have—"

"But you should have judged me," she says, cutting me off. "That's what I'm trying to say. I didn't have a good reason not to be there, except that I was so *angry* at my mother, and I knew skipping it would hurt her."

"So you weren't really stranded in Manila," I say, remembering the excuse Kate gave for not being there.

"No, I was. There was terrible weather, these huge storms that lasted for days, and all the flights were grounded. But I knew about the funeral before the bad weather hit. I had two solid days when I could have left. And I didn't do it." She gives her head a little shake. "You want to know the worst part? I don't even remember what Mom and I were fighting about. Probably something about her wanting me to move home. Settle down." She huffs out a laugh. "Last time we talked, she said, and I quote, 'Katherine, when are you going to realize you're ruining your life just like your father did?'"

I can't hold Kate's decisions against her. My life experience is so colored by the unwavering support my family has always given me. I know what a privilege that is. If I had to deal with the criticism Kate has over the years, I can't say I wouldn't have done the same thing.

"Regardless," she continues, "it was wrong of me to shut you out, and I'm so sorry. I turned my back on anything I thought might remind me of home. Then enough time passed that I wasn't sure you'd even *want* to hear from me again. Staying away felt so much easier."

"I always want to see you," I say. "There's nothing you could do, Kate. We're family." Maybe not in the way I want to be family, but I'll take whatever I can get.

She sniffs. "I knew you'd say that."

I offer her a small smile. "And you stayed away anyway?"

"Don't try and understand. You'll never succeed. I'm just a mess. That's all there is to it."

I chuckle and hold out my hand, and she slips her fingers into mine. "You aren't a mess. You're here now. We move forward from here."

Her expression softens. "Thanks for not being a jerk about it." She pulls her hand away, and I squeeze my fingers into a fist, immediately missing her warm skin against mine.

"Can I ask you one question?"

She quickly nods. "Ask me a dozen if you want. I owe you the answers."

"What changed?" I shove my hands into my lap, hiding them under the table. It's the only way I know how to resist the urge to reach for her again.

Just friends. Just friends. Just friends. I repeat the mantra in my head like it's the combination to a safe holding a million dollars. If I'm going to get through this summer, it has to stick.

"What do you mean?" she asks.

"What made you come home now when you haven't for so long?"

Her eyes drop to her napkin. She picks it up, creasing it over and over.

"The house, mostly," she says without looking up. "I left Mom to handle everything when Grandma Nora died, so when she asked for my help, I didn't feel like I could tell her no." She shrugs, disappointment clouding her expression. "But I'm also in a better place mentally. I've been working on owning my choices more and paying attention to my motivations. Yes, Mom always made me feel terrible for wanting to leave Silver Creek, but that doesn't make it okay for me to stay away only because I wanted to make *her* feel terrible back. I don't want transactional relationships like that. I just want to do the right thing. And coming home to help is the right thing."

"I bought a place right up the street from your grandmother's house," I say. "You remember the trail we cut through the woods? From your grandma's house over to the back orchard at Stonebrook?"

"That was so much work," she says through her grin. "Worst afternoon activity ever."

I chuckle. "Come on. You loved using the machete."

She wrinkles her nose. "Okay, true. I definitely loved the machete."

"Anyway. The trail is still there. And now it's wide enough for a four-by-four. It wraps right behind my house. I use it all the time when I need to get to the farm quick."

"Brody, we were literal trail blazers," she says. "I feel so proud!"

"I think of you every time I use it."

Her eyes jump to mine, an unspoken question in her gaze. If she only knew how frequently I think of her, how many things in my life remind me of her on a daily basis.

I clear my throat. "Your mom must be paying someone to keep the yard up. It still looks good."

"The yard, and quarterly cleaning," she says. "I guess she and Freemont come up every couple of months?"

"Yeah, I've seen them around. In the summer mostly. Probably escaping Florida heat."

"I can't think of any other reason she would have kept the house so long."

"Honestly, I was surprised she moved out of it in the first place. As much as your mom always chastised you for wanting to get out of town, she didn't waste much time before leaving herself."

"Tell me about it. I still don't understand. But that's nothing new. It's not like Mom and I have ever understood each other."

My heart stretches in her direction. I remember how annoyed she always was with her mom. Sometimes Kate would show up at the farm, not knowing or caring if I was home, because she needed somewhere to be that *wasn't* her own house. The last few years of high school, she probably spent more time in the goat barn with Mom than the rest of us did.

"It's nice that we're going to be neighbors," Kate says.

I nod. "Yeah. I'm glad you're back." I almost chuckle to myself. Glad is such a small word when my actual emotions feel too big for my chest. I *am* glad she's home, but I'm also terrified.

"It was time," she says simply. She shifts, her focus drifting before she takes a deep breath, like she's recentering herself in the moment. When she finally lifts her eyes, they are clear and full of conviction. "I recognize I need to be better at facing hard things head-on. I don't want to run away anymore."

There is a heavy awareness in her expression, almost like an apology. But she doesn't need to be sorry. Not to me.

Still, I smile, wanting her to know I understand. Whatever she's offering, I accept it. "Is that what's been happening all this time?" I joke. "And here I thought you were just traveling for work."

She laughs, tension draining out of her body. "You think I didn't pick this job on purpose? I knew what I was doing, Brody." She smiles, her voice lilting. "It makes an excellent cover story."

"You're awful good at it for it to only be a cover story."

"Meh. I do okay."

She's a lot better than okay, but I won't argue with her. "And now you're back."

She lifts her shoulders. Her gaze is serious, and I sense the strength of the commitment behind her words. "At least for a little while."

A little while.

It's a better timeline than usual, but still one with a deadline. She isn't here to stay. At some point, she's going to leave again. Just like she always does.

Kate gives her head a tiny shake, like she's ready to put the heaviness behind us, and rubs her hands together. "Can I quiz you? For old time's sake?"

It's a game I always got tired of playing with everyone else, but never with Kate. "All right. Shoot."

She grins and purses her lips like she's really thinking hard.

While I wait, I admire the slope of her bare shoulder, the long stretch of exposed neck next to her braid.

Just friends. Just friends. Just friends.

Kate sits up taller. "Okay. Four hundred, seventy-seven thousand, three hundred and thirty-three divided by eighty-one."

The waitress arrives with our churros before I can reply, but I won't forget the number. It's floating in my mind's eye, and it'll stay there until I say it out loud.

I take a huge bite of churro, the cinnamon and caramel flavors bursting on my tongue. Weird mariachi band and outlandish decorations aside, this place knows how to serve good food. "Five thousand, eight-hundred ninety-three," I say around my bite.

Kate lights up just like she did the first time she quizzed me on the school bus in the fourth grade. Like I'm the most interesting person she's ever met. She grins and takes a bite of her churro before giving me another problem.

"Five-hundred and six divided by thirteen."

Decimals. I wrinkle my brow. "Thirty-eight point . . . nine, two, three, zero, seven, six repeating."

She starts to laugh. "It never gets old."

She never gets old.

"Do you like teaching?" She sits up taller and runs a hand down her braid, just like she used to when we were kids. "I mean,

I'm not surprised you're teaching. You were always so good at it. But I'm surprised you aren't teaching math."

"You do a lot of math in chemistry." I have a sudden itch to reach over and tug the elastic that's holding her wild hair in place, see the dark waves cascading down her arms like river water rippling from a skipped stone.

"True. I bet your students love you," she says.

My lips twitch. They *do* love me. It helps that I'm young. I still recognize the music they listen to and remember enough about what it was like to be in high school that I know when to cut them slack and when they might be lying about how much homework they have in their other classes. I took all those other classes. I remember what it was like.

"I do love it," I say. "Almost as much as I love kayaking."

"It's amazing you've figured out a way to do both."

"Yeah, I'm lucky in that regard. Or I have been anyway. We'll see if I get to be after the meeting in a couple weeks."

"It'll work out," she says, and I want to believe her. She can't know that it will, but I appreciate her confidence in me anyway.

My eyes drift to the uneaten churro still sitting on Kate's plate. It's been a while since she's taken a bite.

Kate chuckles and shifts the plate to me with a knowing grin. "Go ahead," she says. "I think you need it more than I do."

I eat the churro in two bites.

"I'd love to see you kayaking." She reaches over and slides her finger across a drizzle of caramel on the plate. The gesture is innocent enough, but when she raises that finger to her mouth, my pulse immediately ticks up.

"Actually, can you teach *me* how to kayak?" she asks, a new hope blossoming in her eyes.

I shouldn't be surprised by the question. There is no adventure too grand, no challenge too difficult for Kate. Still, a little over a week ago, I thought I might never see her again. Then she texted and turned my world upside down. When she showed up on Siler earlier today, that upside-down world locked into place and started spinning the opposite direction.

And now she wants me to teach her to kayak?

On the upper Green, there's a three-mile section of river called the narrows. Tight turns, massive boulders, huge drops. Class IV and V rapids with names like *Go Left and Die, Thread the Needle,* and *Gorilla.*

Right now, I might as well be approaching the narrows without a paddle. I am powerless to resist this woman.

Even scarier? I know exactly how things are going to end, and I don't even care. I don't *want* to resist.

"You don't have to," Kate says quickly. "It was just a thought."

I must have been silent for too long. "No, that's not . . . I can teach you," I say. "Of course I can."

"Really?" She smiles wide, and my heart turns over.

Oh, no. Oh, no, no, no. There's no way I'm getting through this without falling even more in love with her. And not just the high school fantasy version, but the real her. The sitting-right-in-front-of-me her.

But then the summer will end, and she'll go, and I'll stay. Just like always. This is exactly what Perry warned me about.

"I was thinking I could write about it," she says like she still needs to convince me. "The Green River, it's a big kayaking location, right?"

I clear my throat and nod. "World-renowned. There's a race every November, the Green Race, and it's a pretty big deal. Actually, it's exactly the kind of thing you like to write about.

The whole culture that has grown up around the race."

She rubs her hands together. "I think I just found my next project," she says in a sing-song voice that makes me grin.

I shake my head, wondering again how I wound up here. Across the table from Kate. With plans to spend the rest of my summer teaching her how to kayak.

I don't know how any of this happened, but I know one thing.

It's going to take everything in me to keep my head above water and my heart intact.

Chapter Seven

Kate

I PULL THROUGH DOWNTOWN Silver Creek, hands gripping the steering wheel of my rented SUV, and stop at a red light beside the middle school.

It is . . . weird to be back. Uncomfortable, even. But I'm still breathing. Still moving forward. Still doing the hard thing I've been hiding from until now, no matter how vulnerable it makes me feel.

"It's a cute town," Kristyn says. Her body is turned so she's facing the window, her eyes scanning the landscape on her side of the car. The woods are thick and wild, a rocky creek bubbling with white frothy water barely visible through the trees.

My phone rings as I ease through the intersection, and Kristyn picks it up. "It's your mom. You want to answer it?"

"Yeah, go ahead. I'm sure she wants to know where I am and if I've made it to the house."

Kristyn puts the call on speaker and sets it on the center console between us.

"Are you there yet?" Mom asks after I say hello.

"Almost. We're pulling through downtown now."

"Oh. Then I'm glad I caught you."

My eyebrows go up. "Is everything okay?"

"Of course!" she says a little too enthusiastically. "Everything is fine. But there is one detail I forgot to mention when we first talked about the house."

My gaze darts to Kristyn who looks as concerned as I do.

"Is it a big deal? Because we're going to be there in less than five minutes, and we're planning on *staying* there."

"No, no, no. Nothing big. The house is livable. I even had the house cleaner drop by to make up fresh beds for you and adjust the thermostat, so it should be nice and comfortable."

"Oh. That was nice of you."

"Nonsense. It's what people do, Kate. You would know that if you ever came home. You'd *always* have a fresh bed ready for you."

I grit my teeth and force a breath in through my nose. "What's up with the house, Mom?"

"It's a small thing, really. It's just . . . well, your Grandma Nora's bedroom is a little more crowded than usual. It might take some extra time to go through her things."

"Crowded? Crowded with what?"

"Oh, you know. This and that."

"I don't know what that means."

I turn onto Millcreek Lane and slow down as I approach Grandma Nora's house, wondering which of the neighboring houses is Brody's. Though, neighboring is a relative term. The houses all sit on at least an acre, with huge yards and stretches of forest dividing them. A house that's three doors down might be a quarter mile away.

"She liked to hold onto things in the months right before she died," Mom says. "And she did all kinds of shopping. The home shopping channel, and online too. Honestly, I didn't even know she knew how to use the internet."

I pull the car into the circle drive in front of Grandma Nora's house. The yard is neatly trimmed, and there are fresh flowers in the pots on the front porch. It doesn't look like a house that's been sitting empty for four years.

"I don't think she always understood what she was buying," Mom continues. "But she got so upset when I tried to stop her. Anyway, I'm sure you'll see it all when you get there. It's mostly in the back bedroom and in the hall closet. I only mention it because I didn't want you to wonder where it all came from."

"Okay, well, thanks for the heads up." I cut the engine and look at Kristyn who has been working hard not to laugh as she listens to my mom's . . . warning? I don't know what else to call it.

I'm imagining a hoarding situation, piles of debris and garbage mixed with unopened Amazon boxes and storage bins full of broken lightbulbs, but I can't imagine Mom letting it get that bad. She's always been pretty fastidious. And Grandma Nora was too.

"We're here now, Mom, all right? I'll call you if I have any questions."

"There should be a lot that you can sell, Katherine. Things that are still in their original packaging, even."

A dull ache starts to pulse at the back of my head. Mom already made it clear she left most of Grandma Nora's things behind when she moved. Linens, housewares, décor. I was planning to keep what could be used to stage the house and donate the rest. Selling *anything,* original packaging or not, doesn't sound like much fun. "All right, well, I'll keep you posted."

I end the call, drop my phone into my lap and lean my head

against the seat, my eyes closed. "What have I gotten myself into?"

Kristyn unbuckles her seatbelt. "We might as well get inside and see."

I open my eyes and shoot her a look. "You seem way too excited about this."

She shrugs, but it doesn't do anything to diminish the literal glee dancing in her eyes. "I saw an episode of that hoarding show on Netflix that was all about a situation just like this. A grandma who had this crazy addiction to online shopping. She spent all her money on eBay though, on those mystery boxes people sell? Where you pay for the box having no idea what's inside it?"

"That's an actual thing?"

"Totally. And it's crazy what some of them sell for." She climbs out of the car, and I follow, moving to the hatch to retrieve our luggage.

"Anyway," she goes on, "they found the craziest stuff in her house. She had something like ten thousand spoons, none of them matching. What could someone possibly do with that many spoons?"

I half-wonder if Kristyn realizes the gift she's giving me with her random babbling. As long as she's talking, I'm not freaking out. And walking up the steps to my childhood home for the first time in half a decade—the first time since before Grandma Nora died—has significant freakout potential. "Only spoons?" I say as I retrieve the key from under the flowerpot next to the front door. It's right where Mom said she left it. "No forks and knives to match?"

"Only spoons. And no one in her family could figure out why."

I unlock the door and push it open, not letting myself hesitate.

I can handle this. I can do hard things. I can . . . stand right here on the porch without going inside.

It isn't that my childhood home was unhappy. I was safe and cared for. I had food to eat and clothes to wear. But my mother and me? We didn't get along. Still don't get along. We aren't . . . enemies, exactly. We just don't understand each other.

Even though I have no memory of life before my parents' divorce, and I only saw my dad a few times a year, I've always felt more connected to him, which has only ever made things worse with Mom. She resents him, even all these years later, and she resents me for *not* resenting him.

Still, she never stopped me from seeing him when I was growing up. Whenever it was possible, I spent holidays and summer vacations traveling with Dad, visiting all the far-off places his work took him. And I loved it. Lived for the weeks I was able to ditch small-town life *and* my mother's disappointment.

Because she was *always* disappointed. Disappointed when I never chose to spend holidays with her. Disappointed when I chose dinner at the Hawthornes over dinner with her and Grandma Nora. Disappointed when I told her I never wanted to live in Silver Creek.

Silver Creek was *her* town. Not mine.

But all that prickly, uncomfortable baggage still doesn't justify skipping out on Grandma Nora, and the guilt of that realization weighs heavier and heavier the longer I stand still.

Kristyn nudges me from behind. "You know, if my mother were here, she'd scold you for making her pay to air condition the outside."

I chuckle and finally push my way into the house. "Grandma

Nora always said the same thing."

Everything is exactly like I remember it. The smell, the furniture, even the crocheted afghan draped over the back of the sofa in the living room.

Tears prick my eyes as I push further into the room. Memories are flooding back, but I can't go down this road. I have a job to do. Standing around and blubbering won't bring Grandma Nora back, and it won't change the choices I made to keep me from being here when she needed me.

I take a deep breath. I'm okay. I've got this. I just have to keep breathing.

"Did your mom take *anything* with her when she moved?" Kristyn asks as she slowly moves around the room.

"It doesn't really seem like it, does it?" There are some empty shelves on the bookshelf and some pictures missing from the mantel above the fireplace, but those are the only signs anyone moved anywhere.

But that doesn't surprise me. Even though we lived here for almost eighteen years—longer than that for Mom—it always felt more like Grandma Nora's house than it did ours. My grandfather died when I was too little to remember, so it was just the three of us, and Grandma Nora was always the one in charge. She didn't treat us like guests, but she always made it clear it was her generosity that put a roof over our heads.

I *expected* Mom to gut the house and finally make it her own when her mother died. Instead, she moved to Florida with a man she met on the internet to live in a sand-colored condominium with shuffleboard courts and a community pool.

"Oh, hey. There's a note from your mom," Kristyn says, picking it up from the console table behind the sofa. She hands it to me.

"And some car keys, maybe?"

"Thought you might need the Subaru while you're in town. Freemont cleaned it and changed the oil for you, and we parked it in the garage," I read out loud. I look at Kristyn. "She left me her car?"

"Sounds like it."

"We also stocked the fridge and put some groceries in the pantry. Love you. Enjoy the house." I shake my head. "What on earth?"

Kristyn moves into the kitchen and opens the fridge. "Dang. She wasn't lying. There's a lot of food in here. Maybe she just really wants you to enjoy your stay?"

"This feels more pointed than that. Mom doesn't do stuff just for the sake of being nice. She has an agenda. She has to."

"Maybe her agenda *is* to be nice. You guys have both been through a lot the past few years. You're here, right? Because you feel like it's time to do better? Maybe she feels the same way."

"Yeah. Maybe," I say, but I'm still not convinced. I know Mom. And there is something else afoot.

We wander through the rest of the house and catalog what I'll have to do in each room to get it ready to sell. Mom's bedroom is already mostly empty, but she was right about Grandma Nora's room. It's chock full of boxes, some looking like they just arrived in the mail, not even opened. "Oh my word," Kristyn says from the doorway behind me. "Your mom wasn't lying." She steps up next to me. "Can we please open all these boxes before I go home?"

"It isn't going to feel like Christmas," I say. "You heard Mom earlier. She made it seem like Grandma Nora wasn't in her right mind. There could be dolls made out of discarded baby teeth and real human hair inside those boxes."

Kristyn reaches for the closest box with an overly exaggerated roll of her eyes. She rips it open, hiding the contents from me until she's had time to inspect her discovery. Finally, she grins. "Or there could just be ceramic salt and pepper shakers that look like praying kittens." She holds them up. "They're actually kind of cute."

I eye her. "Want to take them home with you? They're all yours."

She winces. "Not that cute." She drops the box back onto the stack nearest the door and rubs her hands together. "But seriously, what should we do first?" Kristyn asks. "You might have managed to procrastinate for half my trip, but you've still got me for three more days. We should tackle the hardest project first, while I'm still here to help."

We head back to the kitchen and I pull a bottled water out of the fridge, offering it to Kristyn before getting another for myself. "We should. Grandma Nora's bedroom is obviously going to be the hardest. But . . . let's go over to Stonebrook first."

She lifts her eyebrows. "Right now?"

"Why not? I want you to see it."

"Sounds more like you want to avoid working," she says with a smirk.

"One-hundred percent yes," I say, not missing a beat.

She laughs. "Fine. But you can't ignore this place forever. Promise me we'll start Grandma Nora's bedroom as soon as we get back?"

I heave a sigh. "You're going to be pushy about this, aren't you? You're going to make me do hard things."

"Only because of how much I love you."

I grab my purse from where I left it by the door and pull out the keys to the luxury SUV the rental place gave me when they didn't have the economy car I originally booked. Now that I have Mom's Subaru, I'll return the rental when I take Kristyn to the airport, but until then, we might as well drive around Silver Creek in style.

It's a short drive over to the farm, but not so short that I don't have time to worry about not calling ahead. Brody did say his mom would love to see me, but when we pull up the long, winding drive that cuts through the open pastures at the front of Stonebrook Farm's expansive property, I'm still nervous.

Goats are grazing in the distance, the rolling hills divided by white picket fencing. Massive maple trees line either side of the drive, their deep green leaves shading the pavement. We round a bend and can see the pavilion where the Hawthornes held a graduation party for each of their kids. The year Brody and I graduated, they made sure everyone knew the party was for both of us. The pavilion is bustling with activity, staff setting up for what looks like a wedding.

Kristyn gasps as she takes it all in. "Can people get married here? I thought it was just a farm."

"It is a farm. But they do all kinds of events, too. Weddings, reunions, corporate retreats." Another bend in the drive, and the farmhouse finally comes into view. Its white clapboard siding gleams in the sunlight, and the windows sparkle. Huge barrels overflowing with blooms line the front porch, and smaller versions adorn the steps. Half a dozen rocking chairs sit on either side of the enormous front door. At the end of the porch, a basset hound lazes against the sun-warm boards, angled so his body is entirely within the section of porch still touched by afternoon light.

"Wow," Kristyn says as I cut the engine and unbuckle my seatbelt. "This place is amazing."

We climb out, pausing at the base of the porch steps. "The Hawthornes used to live here"—I point up at the farmhouse—"but when Brody was in middle school, they converted it into offices and event space and built a family house on the back end of the property." I turn and point the opposite direction. "The strawberry fields are that way. And then over there, if we were to follow the road that cuts through those trees, we'd get to the barn and the livestock pens. Beyond that are the apple orchards and the main homestead."

Kristyn follows my gaze, her hands on her hips as she takes it all in. "I can't imagine getting to grow up at a place like this."

"It was magical even for me, and I was only here after school and on weekends." We slowly start climbing the steps, and I will my heart to slow down. "I was mostly with my dad when I wasn't in school, but Brody talked about their summers like they were the stuff dreams are made of. They worked a lot, but they also spent a lot of time sitting around the campfire, swimming in the creek, and playing with the baby goats."

"Stop it," Kristyn says. "Seriously. Every word you say brings me closer to leaving Jake and making a move on Brody just so I can call this place home."

An uncomfortable pressure expands in my chest. "There are *other* brothers. None of *them* are married either."

I sound defensive. Why am I defensive? I have nothing to be defensive about.

Kristyn stops and props her hands on her hips. "What's this, huh? Are you worried your very married cousin was going to make an actual move on your man?"

I scoff. "He's not my man."

"No, and *I* wasn't trying to get a rise out of you just then."

I purse my lips. "You aren't funny."

She makes a show of studying me closely, and I roll my eyes. If I didn't love her so much, I'd smack the smug expression right off her face. "It almost seems like you *care* about who Brody does or doesn't date."

I fold my arms. Two can play at this game, and she will not get me to cave. "I don't care. Who Brody dates in real or hypothetical situations is not my concern."

"Uh-huh," she says dryly. "Which is exactly why you got weird when I mentioned it."

"I didn't get weird. You're the one who said you would leave Jake like it was no big deal. You're the weird one."

She shakes her head and moves past me to the door, laughter still in her voice. "Whatever you say."

Once we're inside, a receptionist smiles warmly. She's young and pretty, and I suddenly wonder if Brody thinks she's pretty. He's so close to his family, he's probably on the farm all the time. Does he stop by when he's here so he can flirt with the pretty receptionist?

Kristyn nudges me, and I glance up, meeting the woman's expectant gaze. She said something, and I totally missed it.

"I'm sorry, what?"

"She said, 'Welcome to Stonebrook Farm,'" Kristyn says from just behind me.

"Are you interested in our event services?" the receptionist asks, her tone neutral.

Somewhere in the back of my mind, I recognize that I am thinking of Brody in ways I have never thought of him before. In less than three minutes, I've been jealous of two different women, first Kristyn and now a nameless receptionist, with zero grounds for justification. I don't know if it was triggered just by seeing him again, or if it was seeing him with muscle definition typically reserved for Greek Gods and Chris Hemsworth, but whatever the reason . . . I don't like it. It makes me itchy. Like I'm being reprogrammed to think and feel things I've never thought or felt before.

Focus, Fletcher. Focus on the here and now. "Actually, I'm an old family friend. Are there any Hawthornes around?" Based on Olivia's Instagram, which I may or may not have scoured last night looking for signs of Brody, she and Perry are handling day-to-day operations on the farm. Perry's obviously still with Brody on the trail, but if Olivia is here, she should be able to help us find her mom.

"Olivia is in today." The receptionist looks at her computer screen and purses her lips to the side. "She's in a meeting with a soon-to-be bride, but they've been in there for going on two hours now, so you shouldn't have to wait long."

I look at Kristyn. "Do you mind waiting a bit?"

She shrugs. "I'm down for whatever you want to do."

"There are warm cinnamon rolls and coffee just over there. You're welcome to help yourself."

"Yes, please," Kristyn says.

The cinnamon rolls *are* warm which feels like a fete of culinary engineering because they're just sitting on what looks like a very normal plate. They are also divine—so divine I can't keep myself from groaning out loud.

"Right?" the receptionist says from behind us. "Chef Hawthorne is trying out new dessert recipes for the restaurant and cinnamon roll bread pudding is on the menu. He sent those over this morning."

The way she says *Chef Hawthorne,* her voice all breathy and light, makes me think *she* might be the reason there are warm cinnamon rolls to go along with the coffee. Lennox always was a lady's man, and *Jenna,* I read off her nametag, looks perky and young enough to catch any man's eye.

Footsteps sound behind me, and I turn to see Olivia leading a pair of women down the hall. We make eye contact, and she smiles wide, her expression flashing with surprise. She holds up a finger, tilting her head toward the women behind her, and I nod my encouragement.

Once Jenna has scheduled a follow-up meeting with the bride and Olivia has said goodbye, she turns to me, practically squealing as she pulls me into a hug. "Kate Fletcher, I thought I might never see you again!" She hugs me tight, then pulls back, her hands still on my shoulders. "Good grief, could you be any more gorgeous? All that traveling—it looks good on you."

"Thanks. Marriage looks good on you."

Her hand flies to her stomach, curving around her baby bump. "Are you kidding? I spend at least half of every day puking my guts out. Mom keeps telling me it'll get better in the second trimester, but I am solidly in second-trimester territory, and so far? No such luck. Gah!" she says, pulling me in for another hug. "I can't believe you're really here! Oh my gosh. Mom is going to flip. And Brody!" She frowns. "Except Brody isn't here. He's backpacking. Please tell me you can stay around long enough for Brody to see you."

I start to laugh, warmed by Olivia's confident exuberance.

On the drive from Franklin down to Silver Creek, a part of me wondered if the Hawthornes would be angry I didn't do a better job staying in touch, but so far, we're three for three when it comes to Hawthorne warm welcomes. Well, lukewarm for Perry, but that counts as warm from him.

"I already saw Brody. I hiked in and surprised him. We did, actually." I pull Kristyn forward. "This is my cousin, Kristyn.

She's only in town for a couple of days, but I'll be here all summer."

Olivia freezes, and something I can't read flits across her expression. "Wow. All summer," she finally says. I half-wonder if she doesn't like that I'm planning to stick around, but she was clearly excited to see me fifteen seconds ago. Why would she feel differently now?

But then Olivia is smiling again, shaking Kristyn's hand and asking how I managed to find Brody in the middle of the Appalachian Mountains, and I let my suspicions go. I was probably seeing things.

"I love it," she says after I give her a SparkNotes version of the planning that led me to Brody's whereabouts. "I bet he flipped when he saw you. This is seriously the most Kate thing I could possibly imagine."

"You can say that again," Kristyn says. "You should have seen the way she researched and finagled her way into the information she needed to find him." I hadn't really thought about everything I did to find Brody as finagling, but I guess to someone else, it could totally seem that way.

"I'm not even a little surprised," Olivia says, clearly warming to the topic. "This woman has always had a way of making stuff work out. When I was in the seventh grade"—she looks at me—"I guess you and Brody were sophomores then? Do you remember convincing the entire boys' soccer team from that private school up in Hendersonville to drive down to Silver Creek and attend the homecoming dance?"

That private school up in Hendersonville was actually the very same school I attended from kindergarten through the third grade. My dad paid for me to attend, but then Mama got tired of driving me up the mountain every day and told me I'd have to "rough it" with the Silver Creek kids. In retrospect, I realize *she* was a Silver Creek kid and probably meant the remark as a jab against Dad, a native Chicagoan who is all big city and no small town. But I took her words literally and prepared myself for the worst.

Instead, I found Brody and the rest of the Hawthornes. It was the happiest surprise of my childhood.

I grin at the memory. "There was a notable lack of cute boys at Silver Creek High. I did what I had to do."

"How did you persuade them?" Kristyn asks around another bite of her cinnamon roll.

"I don't even remember. I just presented coming like it was an idea they should have thought of themselves."

My dad has always called my ability to make things happen my special brand of scrappiness. My finances are pretty solid now. I don't have a lot of excess, but I have enough to get around and sustain myself in between projects. Never longer than a month or two, but that's usually all I need before I'm on to the next thing. But for a while, I coasted on nothing but my own ingenuity. I once spent an entire week in a Zimbabwean village where I had to barter pieces of jewelry and clothing for my meals. That was after Preston, my boyfriend and fellow traveler for the first two years of my career, but before my first commissioned article. Back then, I had to fund everything, pay for all my own travel and research, then write a piece just hoping I'd be able to sell it. Now, it's easier to pitch ideas and get an advance on something I'm *going* to write.

Come to think of it, I'll have to reach out to my contacts and see if anyone bites on my Green River idea.

"Can you stay a while?" Olivia asks. She glances at her watch. "I've got a couple of hours free. Want to ride over and see Mom?

We can probably catch her in the barn."

"I would love that." I glance at Kristyn who just shrugs.

"I'm down," she says. "Can I have another cinnamon roll?"

Olivia smiles. "Have as many as you like."

She leads us through the farmhouse and to the back door. Outside, a couple of 4x4s, like golf carts except with much thicker tires, are parked in a row. She climbs into the one furthest from the house, likely because it has a row of extra seats in the back, and cranks the engine.

As she drives the familiar path through the main farm and toward the orchard, my mind drifts back to the countless times I ran through these fields, to the hours I spent with Brody sitting in the strawberry beds, eating fruit right off the vine until we both felt sick.

Brody might not be here in person, but he is in every memory, imprinted on my soul in a way that makes coming back feel like I'm coming home to *him.*

There's something comforting about that thought. About coming home to Brody. To Stonebrook Farm. If I focus on that feeling, the summer I have ahead of me actually feels *easy.*

But then I think about the way Brody looked at me across the table when we were eating dinner. The way my body reacted to seeing him again. Nothing about *that* seems easy.

Exciting, maybe. But not easy.

Chapter Eight

Kate

STONEBROOK IS A MUCH larger enterprise than it used to be. There are employees everywhere. There were at least two dozen in the pavilion when we drove in, and we've seen that many again on our way to the goat barn.

"Do all of these people work here full time?" I ask. Even just ten years ago, Stonebrook still felt like a family-run farm.

"Most of them are seasonal. We have summer staff who live onsite, either working the farm or events. Some stay through apple harvest in the fall, then things slow down again. It's the busiest you'll see it right now."

"I had no idea," I say, hardly able to take it all in. "It's really amazing how much it's grown."

She points down an eastern slope off to our left. "If you look down that way, you can see the expansion happening on the kitchen. It'll eventually be Lennox's restaurant."

"Right. I saw the press release you shared on Instagram." Lennox was making a pretty solid name for himself as a chef in downtown Charlotte before he moved home to open his own farm-to-table restaurant on Stonebrook's property.

"We're hoping it'll be ready to open about the time the baby's born, which, don't get me started on how complicated that's going to be, but we'll figure it out."

Kristyn leans up from the back seat. "Does everyone in the family work here?"

"Nearly," Olivia says. "Not Flint, obviously. Or Brody. But the rest of us are pretty much here all the time."

"That sounds amazing."

Kristyn *would* find it amazing. Her immediate family is the same way. All up in each other's business all the time.

We park in front of the enormous barn, and Olivia cuts the engine. A wave of homesickness washes over me. I spent hours and hours in this barn my senior year. It feels good to be back.

"Speaking of Brody," Olivia says, eyeing me mischievously as we approach the barn door. "He's had a little bit of a glow up the last few years, huh?"

Kristyn snorts, and I choke out a laugh. "Um. I don't—" I clear my throat. "How so?"

"Kate. Come on. I know you don't see him that way because you're *best friends*"—she says this last part with an added eye roll for emphasis—"but you can't tell me you didn't notice. He's been working out a lot."

"Really?" I say, shaking my head. I shrug my shoulders. "I um, I . . . nope. I didn't notice." My hands wave around in front of my body like they're connected to strings and a drunk puppeteer is controlling their movements. I stare at the offending appendages and tuck them into my armpits. "Muscles? I mean, maybe? He definitely looks . . . different, but not bad different. He's good. He looks good. Good different."

Those . . . were a lot of stupid words that just came out of my face.

"So convincing," Kristyn whispers behind me.

I try and stomp on her foot, but she darts out of the way at the last minute with a gleeful chuckle.

Olivia slides the barn door open with a heave, making it look easy despite her dress pants and heels. We step into the shadowy interior of the barn. "Hey Mom? You still here?"

Mrs. Hawthorne appears at the other end of the barn's center corridor. "I'm back here—" She freezes when she sees me, her hand flying to her chest, her smile stretching as wide as Olivia's did. I've only seen her a few times since graduation, and not since long before the last time I saw Brody, but she looks exactly the same anyway. A little more white in her hair, and a few more wrinkles, but she's just as beautiful as ever, and I find myself wishing I could figure out her secret. If I age half as well as Hannah Hawthorne has, I'll be content. "Well, look who the cat dragged in," she finally says.

"Hi, Mrs. Hawthorne."

She rushes forward and pulls me into a hug. "Look at you!" she says, giving my shoulders an extra squeeze. "Goodness, child. How are you? And call me Hannah. You're grown now. Enough with this Mrs. Hawthorne business."

I am . . . *overwhelmed.* And am I crying? I sniff as I pull back, not wanting to get mascara-tinted tears on Mrs. Hawthorne's—Hannah's—shirt. What is wrong with me? I don't mind hugs. I love hugs. But I'm not necessarily a person who *needs* them. A product of being an only child, maybe, and one practiced in traveling the world alone. But Hannah's hug . . . it's like it unlocks some dormant need buried in the hidden chambers of my heart.

I belong here.

The thought surprises me. I belong *here*? As in *here* here? I don't know who my subconscious thinks it is, but I don't need these unbidden smarty-pants revelations randomly popping into my head. I belong in Silver Creek about as much as I belong on the moon. And yet, that statement somehow doesn't feel as true as it might have two days ago.

"Oh, hey, it's all right," Hannah says.

I shake my head and start to laugh as I wipe my eyes. "I don't even know what's wrong with me."

She pats my back reassuringly. "You've got a lot of memories here. Coming back is bound to make you feel something." Her eyes dart to Olivia before landing back on me. "How long are you in town?"

"All summer," Olivia answers before I can, that same measure of something in her voice. She's worried about me being here. I can tell.

"Well, what a treat that's going to be." Hannah shoots Olivia a look that almost looks like a warning then tilts her head the opposite direction. "I've got a guy here fixing the milker. But there are plenty of new babies to see if you want to come visit for a bit."

Kristyn perks up. "Baby goats?"

I sniff and laugh. "My cousin, Kristyn," I say to Hannah.

Hannah smiles warmly. "Baby goats," she says, turning and heading down the corridor. "Come on, girls. I might even have some work you can help me do."

Thirty minutes later, Kristyn and I are gathering a dozen kids from the pen just behind the barn, ushering them inside for a vet visit scheduled to happen later this afternoon. We aren't very good at our job, mostly because we are way more interested in snuggling than in making the goats go anywhere.

"You're my favorite one," Kristyn whispers to the jet-black newborn she's cradling in her arms. "Don't tell the others."

Finally, I chase the last goat into the barn, and Kristyn follows. I close and latch the door behind us. It's been years since I've been here, but I still remember a lot of how things work. Hannah wouldn't have cared if I only ever wanted to hang out when I showed up with my high school angst and drama, but if I was willing, she always found something for me to do. I recognize now, all these years later, what a gift that was. Working on the farm kept my mind busy and drained the tension out of me in record time. Especially when I was spending time with the babies.

"I love it here," Kristyn whispers as we make our way back to Hannah and Olivia.

I smile. "It's great, right?"

"It's more than great. It's magical. It feels like a movie set. Like one of those places that makes you roll your eyes because no place is actually this idyllic unless it's fake."

Hannah is settling up with the repair guy when we approach. "All right," she says. "I'll call you if it gives me any more trouble, but Brody will be back next week. I'm sure he'll be able to handle things."

My heart trips when she mentions Brody, which is just ridiculous. *I* am ridiculous.

"How did it go?" Hannah asks, finally turning her attention to us.

"Thirteen goats collected and accounted for," I say.

"And thoroughly snuggled," Kristyn says.

Hannah grins. "Perfect. Let's go check on them and make sure they're settled, then what if we head over to the kitchen for some lunch?"

"We wouldn't want to trouble you. We didn't expect—"

"Nonsense," she says, cutting me off. "It's no trouble. Olivia is already on her way over to ask Lennox if he'll fix something up for us, and that boy hasn't figured out how to say no to his mama yet. I doubt he will today."

"That won't interfere with his work?" Kristyn asks as we walk toward the stall where we left the kids.

"Nah. There's another chef on staff that handles the catering—he's busy prepping for a wedding happening tomorrow night—but we'll stay out of his way."

Once Hannah has made sure the goats are settled to her liking, we wash up in the barn's utility room, then she drives us over to the kitchen to meet Olivia.

"Does Brody usually handle repairs and things around the farm?" I ask as we make our way across the farm.

"Not always. But whenever it's something technical, like the milker, his engineering brain can usually sort stuff out as well as any repairman can. You remember how he was. Problem-solving even when the rest of us didn't know there was a problem."

"Yeah, that sounds like him."

"I love that you're all so involved," Kristyn says. "That it's truly a family business."

Kristyn would love it. She's spent her entire twenty-seven years living in the same northern suburb of Chicago. She even lived at home during college, moving from her bedroom into the apartment above her parents' garage. All four of her siblings, all grown and married now, and most of her aunts and uncles, minus my dad, live within twelve blocks of each other, their lives so intertwined, it's hard to tell where one family stops and another starts. Home isn't just a place. A concrete thing with walls and a roof. It's a whole passel of people who love and visit and eat casseroles together every weekend.

Technically, Kristyn's family is my family too. But my dad didn't stay in Chicago. Except for the reunion he took me to every summer, I never really saw his family.

I'm not used to that kind of connectedness. I mean, yes. I knew the Hawthornes were close growing up, but seeing them *still* close, even though they're all adults and have their own lives? It's a lot. I'm not very good at needing people like they seem to need each other. I'm not very good at being *needed.*

Lennox greets his mother at the kitchen's back door, while Kristyn and I hang back. I still feel a weird about showing up and expecting him to feed us.

"Good grief," Kristyn says beside me. "You were not kidding about the blessed genetics thing. Every single person in this family is ridiculously beautiful. I mean, *look* at him."

"I know. *And* he cooks."

She grips my arm. "Listen. I know you were feeling a little iffy about the whole friends-to-lovers thing. And that's fine. But what if we try best friend's brother? It's an equally good trope, and—" She looks toward Lennox. "It's not like you'd be settling going for any of Brody's brothers."

"Ew. Gross, Kristyn. *No!* I could never."

She sighs like she can't believe my stubbornness. "I just feel like you really need to consider how much marrying into this family could benefit your children. They might be born with literal superpowers." Her eyes dart back to the restaurant, and she stiffens. "Oh my gosh. He's coming over here." She clears her throat. "He looks a lot like Flint, doesn't he? I feel like I'm meeting a celebrity. I'm sweating, Kate. I'm actually sweating right now."

I press my lips together to keep from laughing, but there isn't time to say anything before Lennox is standing in front of me. He's wearing a chef's coat, the sleeves rolled up to his elbow, which looks very professional, and a baseball hat flipped around backward, which looks very Lennox.

"Kate," he says easily, pulling me into a hug. "Good to see you."

"Hi, Lennox." I introduce him to Kristyn, and Lennox hugs her too.

"Oh my gosh," Kristyn says silently over his shoulder, her eyes wide.

"Mom says she worked you to death in the goat barn, and we owe you a meal to say thank you," Lennox says.

"That is not even close to the truth," I say. "But if you're offering . . ."

He motions toward the kitchen. "Come on in. It won't be fancy, but I'll come up with something."

Hannah has already disappeared inside, and I still haven't seen Olivia, but I can only assume they'll be eating too. "Olivia tells me you hiked in to surprise Brody on the trail?"

Ah. So when Olivia came ahead to see about lunch, she was also giving him the scoop.

That same discomfort from before niggles at my brain. "Yeah. We did."

Lennox grins as he holds the door open for us. "I wish I could have seen his face when he saw you."

"Trust me," Kristyn says. "It was pretty spectacular."

I wish Brody and his spectacular face were here right now. It's weird to be surrounded by so many of his family members without him.

"Mom and Olivia are just through there if you want to join them," Lennox says. "Food shouldn't take long."

The four of us settle at a long farm table in what I assume will be the main dining room of the restaurant. It doesn't quite look like it's still under construction, but it isn't finished yet either. Plastic sheeting is draped along one corner of the room, half-hiding a bar area, and there still isn't any décor. But I can see the bones of the place and can already tell it's going to be beautiful.

Without Brody around, it's Hannah who does the most to put me at ease, though it could be she's just trying to counter Olivia's pointed questions.

What are my plans after this summer?

Am I dating anyone?

Traveling anywhere exciting?

She could be very excited about my life and career.

Or she could be anxious to get me out of town and away from her big brother.

"Tell them about the couple in Italy," Kristyn prompts after Hannah asks me about my favorite places to visit.

The request doesn't surprise me. Kristyn always has been a romantic.

"I would love to go to Italy one day," Olivia says.

"You should go," I say. "But don't just go to the big cities. The Italian countryside is amazing. When I was working on this piece about the wineries in the Campania wine region, I stayed in a villa owned by this adorable couple. They were in their late eighties, both of them, but you'd never know it for how spry they were. They were retired by the time I was with them, obviously, but before retirement, they ran this tiny winery, using two particular varieties of grapes that only grow in Campania. They were very good at what they did, but no matter how many times they were approached about expanding their operations, they refused. They didn't want to sell wine all over the world. For them, they were content to make what they made, locally sell what they needed to meet their needs, and that was that."

"What happened when they retired?" Olivia asked. "Did they stop making wine?"

"They did. They have five hundred bottles stored in the wine cellar at their villa, and it's the last they ever made. When they die, it'll probably be worth a fortune because there are so few bottles. But they don't even care about that. Money? Fame? Who cares? For them, they were simply content to spend every day together, walking to this tiny marketplace just down the road and buying bread and cheese and fresh herbs for that day's meal. Cooking together. Singing together. They celebrated their sixtieth wedding anniversary while I was there. How crazy is that?"

"Sounds like a story Brody would love," Hannah says, her smile warm.

I scrunch my brow. "How so?"

Olivia is the one who answers. "Are you kidding me? Brody is a total romantic."

Hannah chuckles. "He's always going on about settling down and starting a family. Finding the kind of love you just described. He's a man who knows what he wants, I can say that much."

Olivia looks at me pointedly, almost like she's challenging me. "He'll be an excellent husband someday."

I smile, unsure if Olivia is trying to convince me or tell me to stay away. It doesn't help that suddenly my wandering, rootless soul keeps telling me I better settle in, because this place is *home*.

"If any of them manage it, it'll probably be Brody first," Hannah says. She glances toward the kitchen. "Then maybe he can rub off on his brothers."

Olivia's expression softens. "Lennox will be fine, Mama," she says, her tone gentle. Her eyes flick to me and then back again, but it happens so fast, I might have imagined it. "And the others too."

"Oh, I know," Hannah says. "I don't know why it's so much harder with these boys. I know they're grown men, and they have their own lives. And it's not like I want all the nitty-gritty details." She gives her head a good shake. "Let's just say they don't talk to their Mama like Liv over here does."

Olivia's hand moves to her baby bump. "I don't give you nitty-gritty details. Though, I can if you want me to."

"Oh, you hush," Hannah says with a scoff. "I want no such thing."

Olivia grins. "It was a hot and sultry night . . ."

"Don't you do it, Liv."

"Tyler was out of town all weekend, but then he came home looking scruffy and sexy and—"

"Oh, is that how you want to play it?" Hannah says, cutting Olivia off. She leans forward in her chair. "*Fine.* The first time me and your father—"

"No! Stop!" Olivia yells. "You win. No more details. I promise."

Hannah settles back into her chair with a smirk.

Kristyn grins wide, obviously enjoying the banter.

It's just like it always was. Brody's family knows how to have fun, to tease and pick on each other, but their dedication and love are evident even in the teasing. They're like a grove of trees. On the surface, it looks like they're all their own tree, but underneath the ground, their roots are entwined and connected, lending strength and support to whoever needs it most. I used to think it would be impossible to have a family like that. Maybe I still do.

"How did you know Tyler was the one?" I ask Olivia, suddenly curious. "I'm only asking because . . . I don't know. How is it anything but good luck? The couple in Italy married for sixty years, or your marriage," I say to Hannah. "How do you know when a relationship starts that it will endure instead of crashing and burning like my parents did?"

Olivia winces and I slap a hand to my mouth. "Sorry. I didn't mean—I'm sure your marriage with Tyler is great. I didn't mean to sound so doom and gloom."

"I get what you're saying." Olivia glances at her mom. "It was almost immediate for me. I mean, I didn't admit it for a long time. But I felt it right from the start. That bone-sizzling connection."

"Shoot, it wasn't like that for me," Kristyn says. "I wanted to strangle Jake for the first three months of knowing him. He drove me crazy."

Hannah chuckles. "I was somewhere in the middle. I'd known Ray all my life. I didn't love him all my life, but then one day I just looked at him and thought, well okay then. Here we are." She holds my gaze a long moment. "There are never any guarantees, Kate. Not in life, certainly not in love. But that doesn't mean you can't believe a love like that is possible, even hope for it. I'm willing to bet the people who do find it are the ones who always believed they would."

Lennox shows up with the food, interrupting our conversation, and I breathe out a silent sigh. Sitting with a group of women who are all happily in love is exhausting.

"Turkey paninis, homemade potato chips, fresh berries picked this morning," Lennox says, setting our plates down in front of us. He puts his hands on his mother's shoulders and leans down to kiss her cheek. "Now if you're done enlisting me as your private chef, I'm going to get back to work."

"I'm sorry, what was that? Something about the rent you aren't paying me and how kind I am to let you live here for free?"

He throws a grin over his shoulder as he heads back to the kitchen. "Love you, Mom."

"What about you?" Olivia says before I've even taken the first bite of my sandwich. She eyes me with blatant curiosity. "Do you think you'll ever settle down? Give up the traveling life and find your own happily-ever-after?"

I shrug. "I'm not sure it would have to be one or the other." Except, it would, wouldn't it? I'm never in the same place very long. I use my dad's place in Paris as a home base, but even my stays there only last six, maybe eight weeks before I'm up and traveling again.

"You were just saying the other day you'd never be able to have a family with the kind of traveling you do," Kristyn says. "You really think you'll be a nomad all your life? Never fall in love? Never have kids?"

"There's nothing wrong with that," I say. "A lot of people never have children, and they still have happy lives."

"Sure they do," Kristyn says. "But is that what *you* want?"

I squirm in my seat, suddenly uncomfortable. There's no denying that over the past couple of months, I've started to feel . . . impatient with my way of life. I've generally enjoyed settling into new locations and immersing myself in different cultures. I like to write while I'm still on-location rather than taking lots of notes, then returning home to hammer out a piece. It's an indulgence though. Most of the time, I don't *need* to stick around. I only do because it's fun. But lately, the "sticking around" hasn't been near as enjoyable. It's like I have this insatiable need for something more. The next thing. The next job. The next location. But then the next thing doesn't actually satisfy me.

Everyone's eyes are still on me, their expressions expectant. I finally shrug. "I don't know, really. I've been feeling like it might be time to make a change, but I've been doing this for so long, I don't even know what that would look like."

"Or who it might look like," Kristyn says pointedly.

I shoot her a look. "What's that supposed to mean?"

She grins. "It means I think you're lonely. What you're feeling is loneliness, and that has you all out of sorts because unless you're going to find a Kate groupie with no life who can just follow you everywhere work takes you, falling in love will mean making some sort of change."

"I'm not lonely," I say, a little too defensively.

Kristyn only raises her eyebrows.

"I'm a *little* lonely."

She crosses her arms.

"Fine! I'm lonely. I would love to fall in love. And yes, I'd love to have kids someday. Is that what you want me to admit?"

She smirks her satisfaction. "Only if it's true."

"You're young yet, child," Hannah says. "You've got time to decide. And in my experience, these things tend to have a way of working themselves out."

I want to believe her. I *do* believe her. But that doesn't mean I'm not terrified.

One of the things that makes me good at my job is my intuition. There are always the obvious stories. The ones that any journalist can spot the minute they land in a new location. But settling for the obvious story means writing a predictable piece—a take that's just like any other journalist's take. I've got a knack for sniffing out the stories that aren't obvious. Like the couple in Italy who made wine for no other reason than because they loved to make it.

Why does that matter now?

Because my intuition is telling me there's an untold story right here in Silver Creek.

And I'm pretty sure I'm the main character.

Chapter Nine

Brody

A HOT SHOWER AFTER seven days without one is a bliss not enough poets have used as inspiration. It is the only thing I'm thinking about when I pile my gear on my porch and push through my front door. I only pause long enough to pull my dirty laundry out of my bag, because it smells even worse than I do.

The house is a little musty—not surprising since it's been closed up for two weeks—so after starting a load of laundry, I quickly open some windows on either side of the house, hoping a cross breeze will pull in some fresh air.

I peel off my clothes while I wait for the shower to warm up. I smell so bad. Unbelievably bad.

Tyler stopped for us in Newfound Gap after picking up half a dozen pygmies from a breeder up in Virginia. With the way his face turned green when he gave Perry a hug, I nearly offered to ride in the trailer with the goats.

I let out a long sigh when I finally step into the shower.

The hike was good. *Mostly* good. Let's say it was long stretches of good punctuated by short stretches of Perry trying to get me to talk about Kate.

I don't want to talk about Kate.

That doesn't mean I'm not thinking about her.

I just don't know what Perry wants me to admit.

Was I excited to see her? Absolutely.

Am I glad she's home for the summer? Sure.

Did seeing her wake up all the feelings I've managed to suppress over the years? Maybe?

I felt something when I saw her standing at the top of Siler Bald, and I felt a whole lotta things sitting across from her eating churros. But in the days since then, I've worked hard to tap into the same logic that has kept me from obsessing over her Instagram feed or framing a hard copy of every article she's ever published. (It hasn't stopped me from *collecting* said hard copies, but we don't need to talk about that.)

I've been checking my feelings for Kate for years, keeping them so far in the periphery of my life they haven't interfered with me functioning like a normal adult. I've had a lot of practice, so there's no reason why I can't keep it up.

Granted, keeping my feelings in the periphery is going to be more difficult when she is real and in person, living three houses down the street. But there's nothing I can do about that but cross my fingers and soldier on.

After scrubbing myself near down to the bone, I turn to grab my razor only to realize it's still in my backpack. On the porch. *Outside.*

I groan in frustration. I don't have to shave.

I scratch my chin.

But I really want to. I could just wait and do it after, but I am a man who appreciates routine, and my routine has always been to shave *in* the shower.

I rinse the soap from my body then hop out and grab a towel to wrap around my waist. I don't even take time to cut the water or dry off. I'm only going to be out for a matter of seconds. I open the front door and push through the storm door, leaving it propped open with my foot while I lean forward to dig through my bag. I've got my razor in my hand when the cross breeze, strengthened by the open storm door, slams the wooden front door shut.

I freeze, knowing before I even check the handle that my front door is locked. The lock has been broken for weeks. If you've got your key in the actual door, you can unlock it, but as soon as you take out your key, the internal mechanism falls right back into a *locked* position.

I'd have fixed it by now, but most of the time, I park in the garage and go into the house that way. It usually doesn't matter if the front door stays locked.

I hitch my towel a little tighter around my waist, razor in hand, and try the knob anyway, leaning my forehead against the wood when I confirm that yes, yes, I am locked out of my own house.

In nothing but a towel.

"You need any help?" a voice calls from the road behind me.

But not just any voice.

Kate's voice.

I slowly turn around.

She's on a bike, stopped on the pavement in front of the house. She's wearing a pair of denim cutoffs, one toned leg leaning onto the ground while the other still sits on the pedal. Her hair is long and loose, hanging nearly to her elbows.

I swear under my breath. Keep Kate Fletcher in the periphery? Not a chance. She's a front and center kind of woman. She always has been.

"Hey," I say. "I uh, locked myself out."

She climbs off her bike and leans it on the ground before strolling forward, her hands pushed into her back pockets.

I tighten my hold on my towel. I glance down, noticing the way it hangs open at the bottom of one thigh. Seriously? Did I accidentally grab a hand towel on my way out of the bathroom?

"This is my house," I blurt out.

She smiles. "You don't say."

I close my eyes. "I just mean, it's this one. I'm assuming you didn't know. You wouldn't, right? Know. Which one it was. So I'm telling you."

"When I saw you standing here in a towel, I made the leap."

"I was in the shower."

"I gathered."

I don't miss the way her gaze rakes over my body, traveling down my arms and across my chest.

"I needed my razor, which was still in my bag, but then the door . . ."

She's biting her lip, an obvious effort to keep herself from laughing, but it's also drawing my attention, making me think of—*no*. I do *not* need to think about Kate's lips right now. Or kissing. Or Kate. Or anything even closely related to Kate. I close my eyes. *Think about baseball, Brody. Only baseball.*

"Can I do anything to help?" she asks. "Do you have a spare key anywhere?"

My mom has a spare key, but the idea of calling Mom so she can also see me in a towel, or worse, see me in a towel hanging out with Kate? No thank you. She's already going to have questions for me the next time we talk. I do not need this added layer of complication.

"Um, no key," I lie. "But the windows are open in the kitchen.

If I cut the screen, I can crawl through and unlock the door."

She props her hands on her hips, her eyes sparking with suppressed laughter. "You're going to crawl through your window? Naked?"

I scoff. "I'm not naked."

"No, but you're going to have to use your arms to pull yourself through a window, and I'm not sure that towel's gonna do you much good if you have to let it go."

I take a long slow breath, and Kate finally starts to laugh.

"This is not funny," I say, even as my own shoulders start to shake.

"Oh, it's definitely funny." She motions toward the side of the house with a tilt of her head. "Come on. Show me the window. I'll crawl through and open the door for you."

"I . . . can't ask you to do that."

She raises an eyebrow. "Do you have a better idea?"

I let my shoulders fall. I don't have a better idea, as much as it kills me to admit it. "Fine." I set my razor on the table next to the door and reach for the front pocket of my backpack, where there's a small pocketknife we can use to cut the screen. I pause when a breeze creeps up the back of my legs. I shoot into a standing position, one hand reaching back to make sure my towel is covering everything that needs to be covered. This towel is literally pint-sized. I am wearing a doll-sized towel.

Kate laughs again and reaches out, pressing a hand to my chest. "You and your tiny towel should stay completely upright. Tell me what you're reaching for, and I'll get it."

"There's a pocketknife in the front pocket," I say. "The small one at the top."

"This one right here?"

When I nod, she pulls out the knife. "Got it. Which window am

I looking for? Or . . ." She eyes my towel. "Do you want to show me?"

"I think I can stay upright while walking," I say with a grumble. "Come on. I'll show you."

I motion for her to go down the porch steps first mostly because I don't want her walking behind me watching my tiny towel sway in the breeze.

The back windows are higher off the ground than I thought, though they're closer to the ground than the windows out front, so they're our best bet for getting in. Kate can reach the screen easily enough and is able to use the pocketknife to slice it open, but she's too far below the windowsill to hoist herself up.

She looks around my backyard. "Is there anything I can stand on?"

Normally, there would be patio furniture on my back deck, but right now, it's all in my garage. Sometimes thunderstorms are bad enough to blow stuff around, and I didn't want to have to worry about anything happening while I was gone. "I put it all up before my trip."

She groans. "You are too responsible for your own good!"

"Here. What if you just . . ." I step forward, shifting one scantily towel-clad leg under the window. "Step on my knee and see if that will get you high enough."

"Are you sure? I won't hurt you?"

"Um, maybe take your shoes off so you don't rip all the hair out of my leg?"

She pauses. "The things you never thought you'd hear someone say."

She kicks her shoes off and lifts the ball of one foot onto my knee. "Ready?"

I brace myself. "Yep. Go for it."

She pushes off and grabs hold of the window frame. "I'm totally high enough," she says, but then she wobbles, her whole body swaying to the left. I grab her legs with both hands, stabilizing her . . . and completely losing my towel.

I close my eyes. This is not good. *Very not good.*

"Will you be able to get through?" I say, willing calm into my voice.

"Can you hoist me a tiny bit higher?" she asks.

Oh sure. No problem. No problem at all.

I glance at my towel. If I reach for it, I'll drop Kate. If I drop Kate, she'll see me reaching for the towel. The best shot I have of keeping her from seeing life, the universe, and *everything* is to get her *inside* my house, then grab the towel before she has the chance to turn around and look at me.

Assuming she doesn't look down before then. Or hasn't already.

At least we're on the side of my house that's facing the woods instead of the street.

I slide my hands a tiny bit further up Kate's legs, trying not to focus on her smooth, sun-warm skin, and lift her higher.

"How's that?" I ask, grunting from the strain.

"That's perfect. Are you sure you're—"

"Wait. Stop. Don't move." I can sense by the way she's shifting her weight that she's going to try and look at me. Make sure I'm okay with her own eyes.

She stills, more of her weight dropping back onto my leg. "Not moving," she says. "Are you okay?"

"Yep. I'm good. Just um, do me a favor and don't look down?"

Chapter Ten

Kate

Oh. That is a very fully naked Brody.

I gasp.

Brody swears.

We make eye contact. His jaw tightens. "I said *don't* look down."

I look away and scramble through his window so fast, I nearly face plant onto his kitchen floor. I hoist myself onto my feet, using his table for balance.

That was—

He was—

I don't even have words. To be fair, I couldn't actually see *all* of him. The way his arms were placed, holding up the backs of my legs, one of them obscured my view. This was not a full-frontal nudity situation. But I did see the entire length of his very muscular leg and the curve of his—oh, good grief. I saw *enough,* okay?

I turn back to the window and risk a peek, but Brody and his loin cloth, because let's be real, that towel is hardly big enough to be anything but, have disappeared.

Right. Because I'm supposed to be letting him in.

I scramble to the front door, trying hard not to think about how much Brody looks like his body was sculpted out of smooth marble.

A glow up? Was that the term Olivia used? It doesn't feel like enough. Not that I've ever seen Brody naked before. But even just his chest and shoulders, the way he's filled out . . . add in a week's worth of trail scruff? He has taken sexy to a whole new level.

I reach the front door and unlock it, but the knob won't turn. I jiggle it a little, pausing when Brody's voice sounds through the door.

"The lock is broken," he says, his voice muffled. "Twist the lock, then hold it in place as you turn the knob."

It works on the first try, and I swing open his front door to find him standing on his porch, towel securely in place.

He holds up his finger as he turns sideways to slip past me. "Don't say a word, Miss I Can't Listen to Basic Directions."

I stifle a laugh and press my lips together. "I just *did* listen to basic directions. I opened your door, didn't I?"

"Not those directions, the last directions," he calls as he hurries through his living room.

He's got me there. But the response was more reflex than anything. Had he said, "Kate, my towel fell off, so please don't look down," I might have paused before reacting long enough to control the impulse to, well, *look*.

"It was an accident!" I yell to his retreating form.

"Yeah, I bet." He disappears down the hall into what I can only assume is his bedroom. I have no idea if he wants me to stay or go. But I can't exactly blame him for not pausing long enough to issue a proper invitation. If I had been the one trapped outside in a towel, I'd want to be wearing pants before having a regular conversation too.

It feels weird to hang around, but it feels *more* weird to disappear. Because there is no way it won't look like he scared me off with his . . . I have to stop thinking about naked Brody.

But leaving *would* make things weird the next time we see each other. Better to just rip the band-aid off and talk about it.

Or in this case, are we putting the band-aid back on?

I wander around Brody's living room while I wait for him, pausing when I get to his bookshelf. The contents don't surprise me. Science books. Math books. Novels bigger than my head. All very Brody books. But then on the second shelf, I see several editions of *The Atlantic,* stacked with copies of *Southern Traditions and Travel, Explore Europe,* and half a dozen other magazines. It might seem random to anyone else, but this isn't random. These are all magazines that I'm published in.

He's collecting my bylines.

A door clicks open down the hall, and I spin around to see Brody entering the living room wearing jeans, a plain white T-shirt, and a sheepish expression that is maybe the cutest thing I've ever seen.

I've got to hand it to him. The man wears clothes as well as he . . . doesn't.

I swallow. "I saw you naked," I blurt. Why? Why did I blurt? It's like my mouth is working faster than my brain.

There are more words brewing. They're piling up on my tongue, and if Brody doesn't say something fast, I will start spewing them out like a word-slinging woodchipper.

When I'm nervous, words start flying with reckless abandon. I know this about myself.

Side note: I also hate this about myself.

Fortunately, there isn't much that makes me nervous these days.

I've been too many places and seen too many things to get riled up easily. But I'm nervous now.

Brody's cheeks flame red. "Geez, Kate. Way to state the obvious."

"I'm sorry! I didn't want it to be awkward."

"Good call. This isn't awkward at all."

I press my hands to my cheeks. "Brody, I didn't see anything."

He raises an eyebrow. "I don't know how that's possible."

"I mean, I saw things. But your arm was blocking my view. I didn't see . . . the *main* thing."

He barks out a laugh. "The main thing? This keeps getting better and better. Please, let's keep going."

Oh geez. I just called his *thing* a thing. I am twelve years old. Also, I'm going to die of embarrassment. Right now. Right here in Brody's living room. I drop onto the chair beside his bookshelf and press my hands over my face.

And then I start to laugh. Huge, body-heaving laughter. Tears streaming down my cheeks.

"You think this is funny?"

I peek my fingers open to see him standing across from me, his hands propped on his hips. His expression is stern, but his eyes are dancing. He's not truly angry. "Honestly, Brody, what else can I do but laugh?"

He moves to his couch and sinks into it. "You could have not looked, for starters," he says with a teasing grin. He props his feet up on his coffee table, and I'm momentarily distracted by his bare feet. I don't have a foot fetish. But the easy way he relaxes into his furniture, he just seems so . . . comfortable. Like he's really at home here. Which, duh. This is his house. He would be. But I've never seen him in it, which makes me realize how much I've missed.

"When I was little and couldn't sleep, I would call my dad and he would always say, 'Whatever you do, don't think about polar bears.' Of course, then all I could do was think about polar bears. When you said, 'don't look," I couldn't help it. It was like a reflex."

"I'm not actually sure we can still be friends, Kate. At least not friends who look each other in the eye."

"Oh, shut up. You have nothing to be embarrassed about. You know you look good."

"I . . . know no such thing."

"Whatever. Maybe you don't dwell on it like a lot of guys do, but you have eyeballs in your head. And I'm sure you notice women enjoying the view."

He smirks. "Did you?"

I roll my eyes. "Yeah, yeah. You 'glowed up,' and we're all proud of you for the time in the gym and the scruffy facial hair. It's all very manly and impressive."

I stand and move to the couch and drop onto the side opposite him.

"You've been talking to Olivia," he says as he shifts to face me. "That's her term."

"Yeah. I took Kristyn up to Stonebrook before she left town. We saw Olivia and your mom. And Lennox too, actually. He made us lunch."

He runs a hand across his almost beard, scratching at it before letting his hand drop back into his lap. "I bet Mom loved that."

I smile. "It was good to see her. And yes, Olivia *did* ask me what I thought of you. Of your transformation."

It's his turn to roll his eyes. "She's always calling it that. But I'm still me. I'm still the same guy."

His bare shoulder, the curve of his bicep, the slope of his

back, shadowed with muscle, as it angles down to his trim waist . . . the image flits through my brain.

He's maybe not *exactly* the same guy.

But I get what he's trying to say.

Even before he unlocked his superhero potential, he had a quiet, steady confidence, and he's always been comfortable in his own skin. Which is saying something, because the brothers on either side of him both had a physical presence that could have dwarfed Brody, had he let them. But he always held his own. He never cared that he was smaller. *Was* being the definitive term. He's definitely not smaller anymore.

"You are still the same guy," I say quietly. Brody has too much happening on the inside to want to be defined by what's on the outside. I hope he knows I know that. "And I'm glad."

He holds my gaze a long moment. "How are you? How's the house? Are you okay without Kristyn here?"

"I'm okay. She helped me get started, which was so nice. We were able to come up with a plan that makes the whole project feel more manageable."

We're leaning on the couch, our heads resting on the back cushion, our faces turned toward each other. We sat just like this countless times in the Hawthornes' living room, rehashing our days, talking about our dreams and hopes and plans.

It was sitting just like this that I told Brody at the end of our junior year that once I left, I'd never come back to Silver Creek again. I'd had a particularly bad fight with Mom and was ready to get out of town and never look back. I don't remember the exact subject of the argument, but I can guess. I was too much like my dad. Too unappreciative of all the sacrifices Mom made for me. I had no understanding of the *virtues* of small-town living. It was a tired argument—one I heard over and over again—and it never did any good. No matter how much Grandma Nora tried to coax us into getting along, Mom and I rarely managed it. The more she complained, the more she pushed me away.

Besides that, I loved being like my dad. Dad was adventure. Dad was possibility.

Brody listened—he always did—and simply said, "As long as you're happy, Kate. That's all I want for you."

A wave of nostalgia washes over me, even as a question pops into my head.

"Brody, are you happy?" I ask.

The question takes him by surprise. I can tell by the way his eyebrows shoot up. He doesn't break our gaze though. His eyes stay trained on me, like he's searching for something he isn't sure he's going to find.

"I am now," he finally says, and my heart swoops down into my belly. Now because I'm here? Do I want him to be talking about me?

"I wasn't completely sure I wanted to come back to Silver Creek after college," he says. "A part of me wanted to make my own way, you know? Not be so tied to my family. But I think I've found a way to do that with my kayaking and with the program at the academy."

"You would have missed your family," I say. "Had you gone somewhere else."

"Yeah, some. I like that we're close, though sometimes I wish I were a *little* farther away." He grins. "Don't tell Mom I said so."

"So I take it you're happy you aren't working on the farm with Olivia and Lennox."

"And Perry," he says. "Don't forget him. Though honestly, I'm there so often, sometimes it feels like I do work there."

"There was a repair guy fixing the milker while we were there. Your mom mentioned she'd normally have you do it."

He chuckles. "That stupid milker. I swear, it's the summer help that's always messing it up."

"Are you dating?" The question feels casual, like I'm asking because I'm his friend and not because I'm interested. I give myself a mental pat on the back, because on the inside, I feel anything but casual.

He takes a second to answer, and I barely keep myself from looking around his living room in search of evidence, like proof of a current girlfriend will jump up and start waving at me.

"Not dating," he says. "I went out with the drama teacher at the academy a few times, but it didn't go anywhere."

"And there's no one else you're interested in?"

"You know Silver Creek. Most of the women who live here I've known since we were kids and only two of them are still single. Actually, Monica—that's the theater teacher—graduated a couple of years after we did. You probably remember her."

"Are you counting her as one of the two single women? Who's the other one?" I don't know why I care. But some illogical—and jealous—part of my brain urges me forward. I am a dog with a bone, and I'm going to suck every last bit of marrow from this conversation.

"Heather Anderson," Brody says. "She graduated with us."

"Oh right. I remember her, too. But come on. Surely they aren't the *only* two single women in Silver Creek. The town isn't that small."

"It is that small, Miss World Traveler. You haven't lived here in a decade." He turns his head frontward, so it's tilted up toward the ceiling and closes his eyes. "Your memory is probably cloudy after so long away," he says, a teasing lilt to his words. "Just wait. Another few weeks of seeing the same twelve people every day, and you'll get what I mean."

"There are more than twelve people living in Silver Creek."

He opens one eye. "Fine. But they're all already married."

I chuckle. "Every single one, huh?"

"Lennox has been trying to get me up to Asheville with him, says dating is much more happening up there, but . . . I don't know. I just haven't been feeling it lately."

"Dating in general?"

"It's stupid, right?" He lifts his arms up and props them behind his head, giving me another welcome glimpse of his biceps. "I mean, I know what I want, and the only way I'm going to find it is by dating. But the whole scene makes me tired."

"If only a woman could fall out of the sky and land in your lap."

He grins. "That'd be perfect. You've been all over the world. I'm sure you have extensive resources. Think you could hook me up? Find a woman willing to settle for small-town life in Silver Creek?"

I don't know if he's intentionally sending me a message, but I'm hearing one loud and clear anyway. His life is here. And no matter how much attraction zings down my spine whenever I'm around him, unless I want to make my life here too, there isn't a future for me and Brody. Not as anything but friends. A twinge of sadness flits through me at the thought, but that's crazy. *So crazy*. I can't even begin to think about what a life in Silver Creek would look like for me.

I sigh, a little piece of me wishing I had the same dream. There's no doubt I want to be in love, but I've never imagined myself settling down. A house, two kids, a white picket fence, a dog. Brody had that growing up. Of course he believes he'll find it for himself.

But me?

I had parents who were divorced before I started preschool. A mom who resented me every day of my life and resented my father for taking me away every summer and every holiday. Family has never been a safe space for me.

"What about you?" Brody asks. "Are you happy?"

I'm not sure there's anyone else in the entire world who could ask me that question without making me feel like they'll judge my answer. But Brody has only ever wanted the truth from me. And he's always held whatever that truth is with the same quiet confidence he's done everything in life.

"No," I finally say. "I don't think I am."

He frowns, but I shake my head and reach out and touch his arm. "That sounded worse than it is. I've *been* happy. But I'm tired, you know? I keep feeling like there's something else out there, something I haven't found yet and . . . I don't know. I've been all over the world, Brody. What could I possibly still need to find?" I pull my knees up to my chest and wrap my arms around them. "Maybe that's why I was willing to come back to Silver Creek. It's what they say when you're lost out in the woods, right? You're easier to find if you're sitting still?"

He nods. "That's true."

"Maybe if I sit still for once, what I'm looking for will find me."

"Maybe you're looking for a *home,* Kate. A family."

I drop my head onto my knees. I want his words to be true, but all I do is shrug. "That's always been your dream, Brody, not mine."

Something in his eyes dims, but the warmth in his expression doesn't change.

"Hey." He reaches over and pats my knee. "You want to go with me to pick up my dog?" It's an abrupt subject change, but I'm happy for it.

"You have a dog?"

"A basset hound named Charlie. He stayed up at Stonebrook while I was gone."

"I saw him! He was sleeping on the porch when I went to visit."

Brody sits up. "He probably didn't even flinch when you walked by, did he?"

"He was laying in the sun. Kristyn wondered if he was dead."

Brody chuckles. "That sounds about right." He stands and holds out a hand. "Come on. There's a Gator out back. We can take the trail through the woods, just like old times."

I slip my hand into his, noting way too easily how warm and strong it feels against mine, and let him pull me to my feet. He holds my hand for a beat longer than I expect him to, giving it a little squeeze before he finally drops it.

Is he *trying* to unravel me? Because he is absolutely unraveling me.

"My shoes are still in your yard," I say. "Unless you happened to grab them on your way inside."

He grins. "Yeah. No. I was not in the frame of mind to stop and pick up *anything*."

We split up long enough for me to retrieve my shoes and pull my bike onto his porch. He's already got the Gator running when I find him out back. I climb in beside him, noting how familiar this all feels. The sun-warm vinyl against the backs of my legs. The way the setting sun slants through the treetops, bathing the world in evening light. The buzzing of the cicadas as their song moves like a rippling wave through the trees.

Maybe I don't need my own house to feel like I'm home. Maybe all I need is Brody.

Chapter Eleven

Brody

I DO NOT WANT to have a conversation about how right it feels to have Kate sitting next to me on the Gator, her shoulder pressed against mine.

I half-heartedly try to convince myself it's only because we did this so many times as kids, but my good sense—the good sense I swear I had locked and loaded before Kate showed up at my house—has abandoned me completely. Two hours in her company, and I'm already trying to think of ways I might convince her to stay.

I also don't want to talk about how very *naked* I was for part of that two hours. I don't even want to think about it, though hearing Kate say she enjoyed the view might have been worth the embarrassment.

I've never been so grateful for all the hours I've spent at the gym. And by gym, I mean my garage. Silver Creek is too small to have an actual gym, so I've slowly been adding equipment to my garage. Perry and now Lennox both work out with me and have contributed as well, adding extra weights and a second bench. It doesn't compare to something you'd find in a bigger city, but it's better than nothing.

When we pull up to the farmhouse at Stonebrook, Charlie is right where I expect him to be, lounging on the front porch. He lifts his head and woofs a greeting right as Olivia steps out the farmhouse door, with Monica, of all people, beside her.

Monica smiles when she sees me, but then her gaze shifts to Kate and her expression morphs into more of a grimace.

"Who's that?" Kate asks as I cut the ignition.

"That's Monica."

"The Monica you used to date? *Oh.* Right. I guess I recognize her. Is this going to be weird?"

I eye her carefully. "Is there a reason for it to be weird?"

Kate smirks. "Well, I *did* see you—"

"Ahhhp—" I cut her off. "Do not finish that sentence. We're not talking about that ever again."

She presses her lips together. "Understood."

Charlie reaches me before Olivia and Monica are down the stairs. I lean down and scratch his ears. "Hey, boy. Did you miss me? I hope you behaved."

"Are you kidding? I don't think he could misbehave if he tried," Olivia says from the bottom of the porch steps. "He hardly *moved.*"

"Congratulations, Charlie." I give him another good scratch. "You are officially the laziest basset hound in the history of all basset hounds."

Monica approaches the Gator and offers an awkward smile.

"Hey, Mon," I say casually.

"Hey. I was dropping some wedding cake samples off from the bakery. For mom. She was too busy to bring them over."

I nod. She doesn't really owe me an explanation. She and Olivia are friends. But with what's happened between us, I understand her wanting to give me one.

"When did you get back in town?" she asks, sending Kate a questioning glance.

"Earlier this afternoon." Kate is crouching down, petting Charlie, and Monica is obviously watching her. "You remember Kate," I say slowly. "She's back in town for the summer."

Monica smiles. "How could I forget?" She lifts her hands in mock celebration. "The dynamic duo back together again. Yaaay."

Her *yaaay* is so unenthusiastic, Olivia snorts with laughter.

To Monica's credit, her next words feel a lot more genuine. "Welcome home, Kate. I love your Instagram."

Her words surprise me. I had no idea Monica followed Kate's Instagram. Come to think of it, I don't think we ever even talked about Kate, which feels weird since Monica just called us the "dynamic duo."

Kate pushes her hands into her pockets. "Thanks. Brody says you teach theater at Green River Academy."

"Yeah. He was super helpful in showing me around the school." She shoots me a quick glance. "We've gotten to be really good friends."

Oh, geez. I don't like where this is going.

But Kate is unfazed, responding with a huge smile. "He is a really good friend. The best, actually. The kind who will help you break into your house when you get locked out. The kind that just—"

"Hey!" I say, stepping toward Kate and wrapping an arm around her shoulder. I give her an extra tight squeeze. "That's great. Good friends. We're good friends. We can drop the subject now."

She smirks, her expression teasing. "Are you concerned about how I'm going to finish my sentence, Brody? I'm talking about friendship. That kind of *naked* awareness you have with people you're really close to."

I press my lips together, my shoulders shaking with silent laughter. "You have got to stop."

Kate's laughing now too, and I don't even care that Olivia and Monica are looking at us like we're crazy.

Finally, Olivia clears her throat. "Okay. This is fun, but Monica was just saying she needed to head out." My sister shoots me a disapproving glare and I sober up quickly. I'm not trying to rub anything in Monica's face, but I can see how it might look like I am.

"Right. Sorry. It's good to see you, Monica."

She smiles, a sadness in her eyes that wasn't there before. "Walk me to my car?"

I glance at Olivia who gives me a tiny nod of encouragement. "Kate, want to walk over to the goat barn with me? Penelope is whelping for the first time right now. Tyler and Mom are with her, but I'd like to check on her too."

"Penelope from TikTok? Famous Penelope?"

Olivia nods. "That's her."

"Oh, yes. Definitely," Kate says. "Let's go see her."

Tyler is the one who made Penelope famous. His first summer working on the farm, before he and Olivia got married, he started posting videos of her following him around as a newborn, and her social media presence blew up almost overnight.

"I'll be that way in a sec," I say as they turn and head toward the barn.

I fall into step next to Monica. "Sorry about earlier," I say to her. "That thing with Kate. It was sort of an inside joke. I didn't mean to make you feel—"

"You don't have to explain," Monica says. "Honestly, it was probably good for me."

We reach her car, and she pulls out her keys.

"I'm not sure I follow."

She lets out a disheartened chuckle. "I guess I was still holding out hope. I thought if I was around enough, you might eventually change your mind about us. But seeing you with Kate?" She shakes her head. "Brody, it's so obvious. I can't compete with her."

"We're just friends," I say reflexively. "We've always just been friends."

Both statements are true no matter how much I dislike them.

Monica leans against her car. "Maybe, but don't pretend that's how you want things to be. It's almost as obvious now as it was back in high school."

I don't know about *now,* but there's no denying what Monica observed back in high school. "I was pretty obvious, wasn't I?"

She chuckles. "If she was the earth, you were her moon." She nudges my shoulder. "Did you ever tell her?"

"No," I say quickly. *And I never will.* "Some things aren't meant to be, Mon."

"Like you and me."

At least she's finally getting the picture. "I'm sorry."

She shrugs. "Nah, don't apologize. I meant what I said, Brody. I *do* consider you a good friend, which means I want you to be happy. I just saw what it looks like when you light up for another person. That makes it really easy to recognize you don't light up for me."

I want to laugh at the hopeless picture she's painting. "I don't know what this says about my future, but it can't be good."

"Why? If not her, then who?" It's a surprisingly simple

summary of my conflicted emotions.

"Exactly."

"And you're sure it *isn't* her?"

"No. But I'm pretty sure *she's* sure it isn't her."

Monica looks at me, a frown creasing her brow. "Well, she's an idiot then."

She opens the door to her car and tosses her bag into the seat. "You know, you could just tell her now," she says, like it's the easiest suggestion in the world. "She can't really make a choice if she doesn't know all her options, right?"

We say goodbye, and I head up the hill toward the barn, thinking on Monica's suggestion.

I could just tell Kate how I feel. How I felt? How I might feel again?

But Monica is proof enough that sometimes, the spark isn't there. What if that's the way Kate feels about me? I know she loves me. But if she doesn't feel the same spark I do, I can't make her feel it any more than Monica could make me feel it for her.

And honestly, after all these years, if she *did* feel a spark? Wouldn't we have figured it out by now? I want to believe that seeing her this time has felt different, like there's a new tension that's never been there before. But I don't trust myself not to be seeing it only because I'm hoping for it.

I find Kate and Olivia with Mom, all three of them leaning against the half-wall that separates the corridor from Penelope's stall. Tyler is in the stall with Penelope who is still up and moving around, if a little awkwardly.

Mom pulls me into a hug, giving my shoulders an extra squeeze. "Welcome home. How was the trip? How was it spending all that time with Perry?"

I swallow the half-dozen sarcastic answers that push into my brain—Mom is not the right audience for those—and offer her a genuine smile. "It was great. I'm glad I went with him."

"Oh, I'm so glad. Olivia told me about the school board meeting. Do you feel ready?"

I lift my shoulders in a shrug. "As ready as I can be, I think."

She cups her hand around my cheek. "You just speak your truth, Brody. They'll see it. They'll recognize the good you're doing."

"Thanks, Mom." I lean against the wall next to Kate and look in on Penelope. "How's she doing?"

"So far so good," Tyler says. "The vet was just here, and she said everything is progressing like it should."

"You called the vet already?" I ask. Mom has helped countless goats with their first whelping. Normally she only calls the vet if she senses trouble.

Mom looks at me over Olivia's head. "New parents," she whispers.

"I heard that," Tyler says, and Mom grins.

"I think he's more worried about Penelope's baby than he is our own," Olivia says.

Tyler jumps up and moves over to Olivia, leaning forward and giving her a kiss that lasts long enough for me to feel like I ought to look away. "That isn't even a little bit true," he says.

Beside me, Kate breathes out a sigh.

"Hey, help me with something really quick?" Olivia asks.

I eye my sister, wondering what she could possibly need, but when she takes off down the corridor, I follow.

She stops at the stairs that lead up to the hay loft. "I just wanted to check on you," she says. "How is it having her home again?"

"It's only been four hours. Ask me again next week, and I might have an answer for you."

She rolls her eyes. "You've known about her being in town longer than that though. And she showed up on the trail? Were you totally stunned?"

I run a hand through my hair. "Yeah. I was—it's still weird, honestly. Like any minute she might disappear, and I'll realize it's all a dream."

Her expression shifts, her eyes filling with worry. "Brody, I know you. If you spend time with her, you're going to start to hope. You know you will."

My jaw tightens. "I'm fine, Liv. I've got things under control."

She lifts an accusatory eyebrow. "That display I saw earlier with you two laughing like a bunch of teenagers didn't look like it."

"It was an inside joke."

"Oh, right. That makes it totally innocent." She props her hands on her hips, obviously warming to the subject. "You should have seen her when I asked her about your glow up. She was all flustered and talking over herself in this weird squeaky voice. I think she might be attracted to you."

"I thought you were telling me *not* to get my hopes up."

"That's just it. When I thought Kate was never going to love you back—"

I grab her arm and tug her further down the corridor. "You want to talk a little louder, Liv?" I whisper yell. I glance down the corridor, but all of Kate's attention is still on Penelope.

"When I thought Kate wasn't going to love you back," she repeats, her voice softer but no less stern, "I worried about you because unrequited love really sucks. But you know what sucks more? Experiencing love, and then having it ripped away."

"What are you trying to say?"

"I'm saying if Kate is actually into you, and you go for it, and it's the most amazing summer of your life, blah, blah, blah? Do you honestly think she'll stay? I've never known anyone so bent on getting out of town, Brody. Even if she does feel something, I don't see her changing. I don't see her *staying*."

"I appreciate the concern. I do. But I'm fine, Liv. You have to trust me on this. I'm fine."

She looks about as convinced as I feel, but what would she have me do? I'm not going to *not* spend time with Kate.

"Listen to me. I want you to have what I have. And I know you want that too." She grips my arms, just above the elbow, giving them a quick squeeze. "But I don't think Kate is that person for you. You are worth staying for. You deserve someone who sees that."

"Hey, Liv!" Tyler calls from Penelope's stall. "Can you come film this? Stuff is starting to happen."

Olivia takes a deep breath, her gaze lifting to the ceiling. "I can't believe I'm saying this, but I have to go livestream the birth of my husband's grand-goat for his millions of TikTok followers."

I smile. "And I'm the one you're worried about?"

"Just be careful, all right? And think about what I said."

I nod, but she's already stalking down the corridor, pulling out her phone.

I know there's validity to Olivia's point. And I can't fault my family for worrying. But as Kate and I take Charlie and drive back home, it isn't Olivia's warning that I'm thinking about. It's Monica's encouragement and Olivia saying Kate was flustered when they talked about me.

I'm doing the exact thing my family doesn't want me to do. I'm

starting to hope.
Maybe things can be different.
Maybe she'll change her mind.
Maybe this time . . . she'll stay.

Chapter Twelve

Kate

I'M SITTING IN THE middle of my grandmother's bedroom.

Boxes are everywhere. *Stuff* is everywhere. When I say stuff, I really mean *stuff.* Like the most random stuff you could possibly imagine. Mom did try to warn me, but I had no idea what I was in for. She probably breathed the biggest sigh of relief when I agreed to come.

As if she can sense me thinking about her, my phone rings and my screen lights up with my mother's picture.

I brace myself like I always do for our chats and answer the call. "Hi, Mom," I say, infusing my voice with false cheer.

"How's it going?" she asks. "Have you met with the realtor yet?"

"Nice to talk to you too," I say. "How's Florida?"

She sighs. "Hot, like always. Sorry. I didn't mean to be short. How are things going?"

"They're . . . going," I say. "I just found a new-in-the-box wooden moose that poops M&Ms when you lift his tail."

"I wish I could tell you that's going to be the weirdest thing you'll find."

"It's almost as weird as the breast pillow," I say. "Listen to this."

I reach across the couch and pick up the box, reading from the side. "Are you a side sleeper? Does the weight of one breast falling onto the other get you down? Then this pillow is for you."

"Well that doesn't make sense. Your grandmother's boobs looked like tube socks with pennies at the bottom."

"Mom, gross. I do not need that visual."

"So I take it you're not in the talking with the realtor stage yet?"

"Not even close," I say. "Mom, there's stuff here that was ordered years ago. Decades, even. How did I not realize all of this was happening?"

"She always loved the Home Shopping Network. You remember all her jewelry, and that rhinestone tracksuit she used to wear everywhere. She ordered that off the television. Maybe you were too busy with your friends to notice."

I take a deep breath, slow and easy.

"It didn't get really bad until after you left home," Mom adds as if to soften her earlier comment. This is the way she tends to roll. It feels like our relationship is a constant push and pull of her luring me closer only to knock me upside the head with one of her snide remarks, then soothe the wound with more kindness. It feels like whiplash.

"Mom, I know you said I should sell some of this stuff, but I don't even know where I'd start. I'm just going to donate it. Is that okay? Selling it feels like a lot of work. This isn't pawn shop kind of stuff."

"How about the internet? One man's trash is another man's treasure. Isn't that what they say? You do owe me this, Katherine."

I pinch the bridge of my nose and silently count to five. "Okay,

Mom. I'll do the best I can."

"Good. But save the moose. Freemont might like it."

I still haven't met mom's new husband in person. I've heard him in the background of our phone conversations a few times and seen the pictures that Mom has put on Facebook. I know he's a retired commercial real estate agent, he has three grown children who live in Florida but has no grandchildren, he has a bad—and I mean *bad*—combover, and he drives a bright red Miata that, at least in pictures, looks much too small for his lanky frame. And apparently, he likes moose. Or candy? Maybe both?

I give my head a little shake. I'm giving this way too much thought.

"I'll save the moose for Freemont," I say. "Mom, can I ask you a question?"

I give myself a mental pat on the back. I'm being direct. I'm asking questions. I'm engaging in conversation instead of making assumptions.

"All right," Mom says.

"Why did you leave Silver Creek? I thought you loved it here."

She immediately scoffs. "Well, that's a funny question coming from you, Miss I-don't-need-this-town-and-I-don't-need-you. *You* left everything behind. Why shouldn't I?"

I shake my head. "Mom, that's not—" I take another deep breath. "You know what? Never mind. Forget I asked."

It doesn't matter that I said those words when I was sixteen and spitting mad over Mama grounding me instead of letting me go up to Stonebrook to stargaze with the Hawthornes. She reminds me every time we talk how much I don't need her.

It only ever makes me want to prove her right.

"I gotta go, okay?" I say.

"Wait, Kate. That was . . . I'm sorry. Let me try again."

I pause. An apology is new. We've had this conversation what feels like a thousand times. But she's never apologized. "Okay."

"I did love Silver Creek. I *do* love it. But I also love Freemont."

But you didn't love Dad? The question sits on the tip of my tongue, but I can't bring myself to ask it. It's why they divorced, after all. Dad wanted a life that was bigger than Silver Creek, and Mom refused to leave.

"I'll keep you posted on my progress with the house, okay?"

"All right, dear. But don't rush on my account. Enjoy yourself. Enjoy Silver Creek."

"I thought you called to see if I'd met with the realtor yet. Aren't you anxious for me to finish?"

"Me? No! The opposite, actually. Freemont even thinks we could wait until fall to sell. Benefit from all the leaf-lookers that come through town. How's the Subaru driving?"

I . . . am so confused. Mom called me home to get the house ready to sell, but now she wants me to take my time and enjoy Silver Creek? I would understand her wanting me home if she was also here, but she hasn't even mentioned coming up from Florida.

"Katherine?" she says. "Did I lose you?"

"No, I'm here. The car is fine. It's driving great."

"All right, well, carry on. I'll call you next week."

I hang up the phone and look around the cluttered room, feeling slightly derailed from my conversation with Mom.

A few things in the house still feel familiar. The 1992 edition of Encyclopedia Britannica that lines the bottom of the bookshelf in the corner. The plastic tablecloth on the kitchen table. And of course, my childhood bedroom is exactly like I left it. But everything I've pulled out of Grandma Nora's closets? Digging through her dresser drawers? It feels like I'm rooting through someone else's belongings.

It makes me feel detached. Somehow separated from my own life. This was my *home* for almost eighteen years, but it doesn't feel like it. My eyes catch on the crocheted afghan that's draped over the back of the sofa. Okay. *Some* things feel like home.

I brush at my nose, the dusty air finally getting to me, then sneeze three times in quick succession. A sense of déjà vu washes over me. My grandmother never sneezed just once. It was always three times. A feeling steals over me, like a whispered exhale, a feather touch, and I sense my grandmother near. The sensation is gone as quickly as it came. So quickly, I might have imagined it.

Either way, I feel a renewed sense of purpose. I might not have much motivation to make my mother happy. But I can do this for my grandmother.

A knock sounds on the front door before Brody's deep voice calls out. "Kate? Are you home?"

"In here," I call. I wipe away the tears pooling in my eyes—when did I become a person who cries without warning?—and stand up, glancing down at my clothes to make sure I'm presentable.

Brody appears in the bedroom doorway with a bag of something that smells so delicious, my stomach immediately rumbles loud enough for him to hear it all the way across the room.

He grins. "Hungry, Kate?"

"Always." I inhale deeply, picking up notes of . . . cilantro? Cheese? "Especially for . . . tacos?"

He holds up the bag. "It's your lucky day."

"Oh, bless you," I say, stepping around the bed.

His gaze tracks around the room. "You've been busy."

"I feel like I've barely made a dent. You wouldn't believe some of the stuff I've found."

He tilts his head toward the kitchen. "Come eat and tell me about it."

I follow him gladly, uncertain if I'm lured more by the delicious smell of tacos or by the look of him in his shorts and polo shirt. Sunglasses are hooked over the collar of his shirt in a way that makes him look effortlessly cool.

"When did you stop wearing glasses?" I ask as I slip into one of the metal chairs that surround the kitchen table.

He slides a white Styrofoam container toward me. "I still wear them sometimes. For close work. When I'm at school, mostly. But I don't need them for everything like I used to."

"Oh, that's right. The Captain America super serum would have fixed your eyesight."

He drops into the chair across from me. "Very funny."

I smirk. It will never not be fun to tease Brody about his new physique. Especially now that I've seen so much of it. Not that I'm spending any time at all remembering Brody's physique.

And by any time at all what I really mean is always. *All* the time.

Except, that's not entirely true. I'm not only thinking about his body, beautiful though it is. I'm also thinking about how good it feels to be around him. How much I look forward to seeing him when we aren't together. I haven't even been back in Silver Creek three weeks, and he's almost always on my mind.

I knew I'd want to see him.

I didn't expect to want to see him *all the time.* In the six days I waited for him to get off the trail, I must have walked up and down the road twenty times wondering which house was his, anticipating the moment I would see him again.

It was just dumb luck that when I did happen to see him again, all he was wearing was a towel.

I lift the lid of my to-go container to reveal the most beautiful tacos I have ever seen. I breathe out a sigh. "I love tacos so much."

"I know you do. You've never had these though. There's a stand next to the river school—I swear in the summer I eat there at least three times a week—and they're better than anything I've had anywhere else." He pauses, his hands hovering over his tacos. "Try one. I want to know what you think."

It only takes one bite to decide these are the best tacos I've ever had. And I have eaten a lot of tacos in a lot of different countries.

"Oh my word," I say in between bites. "How do they make these? What do they do differently?"

Brody grins. "I've been trying to figure out the same thing. I think it has something to do with how they season the meat, but they won't tell me. I've even taken Lennox, hoping he could figure it out, but he's stumped too."

"They're really similar to tacos I had in Mexico City." I take another huge bite. "Seriously. These are fantastic."

"And you can get them right here in Silver Creek."

I look up to see Brody's gaze fixed on me.

"Small towns aren't all bad, right?" he says as he lifts up his taco as if offering a toast. "Sometimes they have tacos."

His comment is so pointed, I have to wonder if he means anything by it. Is he trying to sell me on small towns? I take another bite. It's working. Few things woo me quite as well as an exceptional taco.

"Tell me what you've found," he says. "Unearthed any family secrets?"

"My mother was right about my grandmother's addiction to the home shopping network. Are you interested in an eighteen-inch dancing Santa Claus? He sings *Rockin' Around the Christmas Tree* and everything."

"Man. My Santa collection is already full. But thanks for thinking of me."

I grin and put down my taco so I can reach for my laptop. "Actually, there's something else I want to ask you." I open the laptop and navigate to the YouTube channel I had playing the entire time I was eating breakfast this morning. I press play—I've already got the video cued up to a certain spot—and turn the laptop around so Brody can see. "Is this you?"

He leans forward and slowly starts to nod. "That's last year's race."

The video is twenty minutes of racing kayakers making their way through Gorilla—a section of Class V rapids in a part of the Green River known as the narrows. The river drops one hundred and seventy-six feet per mile through the narrows, eighteen of which happen in Gorilla. The channels of frothing whitewater, steep descents, and massive boulders look like an actual death wish to me, but what do I know?

That I won't ever kayak the narrows. That's what I know. With utter and absolute certainty.

I've been watching videos about the race all morning, my shock that this is something Brody participates in growing by the second.

In the video, most of the racers are upside down in their boats by the time they reach the bottom of Gorilla. Even though I've watched it more than once, and I know they always roll back up, I still hold my breath when Brody's boat tips downward and the whitewater swallows him up. But then he emerges, paddle propelling him out of the swirling water at the base of the falls.

"That was an intense ride," Brody says as I pause the video.

"Intense? I consider myself pretty adventurous, and you couldn't pay me to get anywhere near that water."

"To be fair, you're watching the carnage reel," Brody says. "It's all the shots of people getting thrashed."

"You didn't get thrashed."

"But I rolled for a second."

I click over to a different window. "Have you seen what it says on the race registration page?"

I shift the screen closer and point to the bolded message at the top of the section titled *racer information.* "We do not recommend participating in this event," I read out loud. "Then further down the page, it says, 'Seriously, racing is not a good idea.' Why does anyone sign up for this thing?"

He cracks a smile. 'That's to keep the casual kayakers from signing up. You have to know what you're doing to race the narrows."

"And you know what you're doing," I say, a statement, not a question.

"I mean, I'm not winning. But I've raced twice, and I finished both times without swimming."

"What does that mean?"

He grins. "It means I stayed in my boat."

"Oh, right. So that's mostly what was happening in the carnage reel."

"It's common. The narrows are brutal. It's easy to flip, and when the water's churning, sometimes the only way to get out of the rapid is to wet-exit."

Wet-exit. It's the second time I've heard him use the term. "Right. Which is what the problem kid *didn't* know how to do when he flipped upside down?"

"Exactly."

This makes twice now that I have listened to Brody talk about kayaking while eating delicious Mexican food. I am not complaining. It's the best kind of research. In fact, I'd like *all* new information to be delivered in this manner from now on. Delicious tacos? *Check.* Sexy teacher? *Check.*

There is no topic I will not find interesting in this setting.

"So you've raced the Green twice? Have you ever competed anywhere else?" It was only after I started watching the video coverage of last year's race that I wondered about Brody racing. I checked the race results for his name, gasped out loud because *oh my word he could die doing this thing*, noted his bib number, then studied the video until I found him. The bib number is the only way to identify any of the racers, unless you know what color boat they're in because they're all wearing helmets and gear that covers every inch of their skin. The race happens in November, which means *it's cold.*

"A few times," Brody says. "But nothing has quite the same vibe as the Green Race."

"The crowd in the video. Is it always that crazy? Cowbells, horns, and everyone is holding a beer."

"Like I said, the race has a pretty unique vibe." He holds my gaze. "You should come if you're going to write about it. Or come just to experience it. I think you'd dig it."

"It's in November?" Something stirs in my gut. Do I want a reason to stay in Silver Creek longer?

He nods. "On the fifth."

"Are you racing again?"

"Most likely."

A tiny thrill at the thought of seeing Brody race in person snakes through me, even as I shake my head. I still can't believe the Brody sitting across from me, the cool and confident daredevil kayaker Brody, is the same Brody who was my best friend.

"Four thousand sixty-seven divided by three hundred eighty-one," I say.

He stills, his eyes darting around like they always do when he's calculating.

"Ten point six seven four five four zero . . ." He pauses. "Do you want me to keep going?"

I laugh and shake my head.

He eyes me, his expression curious. "Where did that come from?"

I press my hands to my cheeks. "I don't even know. I guess I'm trying to make sure it's still you."

He closes up his to-go container and carries it to the kitchen trashcan. "I'm not following."

"I don't want to seem like I'm beating a dead horse here, I'm still having a hard time imagining high school Brody doing something like whitewater kayaking the Green River narrows."

He leans against the counter and crosses his arms. "What *can* you imagine high school Brody doing?"

"Calculus," I say without missing a beat. "Maybe some chemistry? And of course, all the work on the farm. But even then, you were always trying to *science* the work, looking for ways to make things more efficient." I stand up and throw away my lunch trash. The kitchen isn't very wide, so when I lean on the counter across from him, our feet are almost touching.

"That's all true. But then you left." He reaches out and nudges my foot with the toe of his shoe, his hands pushed into his pockets. There's a vulnerability to the way he's holding himself, his eyes focused on our feet. Finally, he looks up. "Funny thing. You leaving is actually what made me decide I wanted to run the narrows in the first place."

A new tightness squeezes around my heart. "Why?"

He shrugs. "You were so brave, Kate. Eighteen years old, and you packed your bags and took off like you owned the world. You weren't afraid of anything. I was hiking along the river with Flint one afternoon a couple weeks after you left, not far from Gorilla, actually. Five or six kayakers came through while we watched, and I thought to myself, *I want to do that.* I wanted to do something different, something scary. And whitewater kayaking looked scary."

I shake my head. "So then you just . . . did it?"

He chuckles. "Not exactly. I told Flint what I was thinking, and he told me I was crazy and would probably get myself killed. But something happened out on that hike, and I couldn't forget it. So I called Triple Mountain and signed up for a beginner course."

"And now you work for them?"

He nods. "I didn't do anything but Class I or II rapids that first summer, but that was all it took to get me hooked. Every summer since, and whenever else I can swing it, I've been on the water."

"All because of me?" I tease. I nudge his toe back. "I always worried you didn't think about me at all when I was gone." I wrap my arms around my middle, willing myself to push through the vulnerability and be honest. "Then after that last time, after I ignored you for so long, I hoped you didn't. I didn't think I deserved it."

He holds my gaze a long moment, then extends his hand, palm up. Without even thinking, I slip my hand into his and let him tug me across the kitchen and into his arms. His hug is warm and strong, and I melt against his chest as his arms wrap fully around my lower back.

It could be a hug between friends.

It *is* a hug between friends. But my senses are on high alert anyway, cataloging every single detail. All the places our bodies touch, the way they're sparking with heat.

(Is he also sparking? Is the sparkiness only happening inside of me?)

Then there's how good he smells. How *strong* he feels. I have never enjoyed a hug like I am enjoying this hug.

"I thought about you every day, Kate," he says softly into my hair. "I never stopped thinking about you."

Oh. Oh, that confession is doing strange things to my heart. I close my eyes and bite my lip, imagining for the tiniest moment what it would be like to look up, catch Brody's gaze, and press my lips against his.

But then he shifts, standing fully upright, his hands on my arms as he bodily moves me back across the kitchen. He clears his throat and looks away, taking a giant step away from me. He's further away now than he was *before* the hug.

That was . . . I only just stop myself from leaning down and sniffing my armpits. Maybe I smell bad? I've been digging around in closets all morning. I could absolutely smell like mothballs and old people. Or maybe he felt me sparking and realized he was giving me the wrong impression? But then, he did say he never stopped thinking about me.

I am . . . so confused. "Urrb." And tongue-tied, apparently.

"I should go," Brody says at the exact moment I say, "Thanks for bringing me lunch."

"No problem," he says while I say, "Right. Of course."

We both laugh, and it dispels a tiny bit of the tension hovering between us. Except, why is there tension between us? There has *never* been tension between us.

"I found a KitchenAid hand mixer," I blurt out. "Still in the box. It's never been used."

Oh no. It's happening. My woodchipper word-slinging. I'm nervous again, and Brody isn't even naked this time.

Brody gives me a funny look. "What?"

I nod. "It's baby poop yellow."

That at least makes him crack a smile. *I'm funny when I'm nervous! Hooray!* "Kate, what are you talking about?"

I feel like I'm hovering above this entire interaction, watching me make a fool of myself, but I'm too far in to turn back now. I sneak past him and lead him into the living room where I go to the pile of kitchen supplies amassing by the fireplace. "I checked online, and this thing hasn't been sold since 1987. It was a QVC exclusive." I heft the box and carry it to Brody. "See? Isn't that color the worst?"

"It's very 1987," he says. "I bet you could sell it. I'm sure there are people who love stuff like this."

"Yeah, maybe. Mom wants me to sell as much as I can. But I'm more likely to take it all to Goodwill and donate it. Maybe it'll make someone's day to find vintage KitchenAid. The hard part is that I keep uncovering things I've never seen before. Mom said most of the weird shopping happened after I left home, but some of this stuff has obviously been here longer than that." I hold up the baby poop yellow mixer like I'm submitting evidence in a courtroom. My words are tumbling now, like water gushing down a mountain creek after a thunderstorm.

"How did I live here and not know about all this stuff? It's weird. And stressful. And I feel . . . guilty?" I drop the mixer onto the couch with a thud and rub my hands across my stomach. "I'm all smarmy inside. Like I'm the one at fault for not knowing about all this stuff. Then I talk to my mom, and she reminds me that I *should* feel guilty and I just . . . what if she's right? I think I was a terrible daughter, Brody. Or a terrible granddaughter. Or both."

"Hey." He sets his hands on my shoulders, and they have an immediate grounding effect. Somehow in the last ten seconds, my nerves-induced word-slinging turned a ridiculous narrative about outdated kitchen appliances into a therapy session. "You aren't a terrible daughter," he says. "Or a terrible granddaughter. It's just stuff. So you didn't know what your grandmother stored in her closets. That doesn't have to mean anything."

"But I feel like it does. I loved her. But I'm not sure I *saw* her. Not like I should have."

"You're not remembering clearly, Kate. You were always sweet to Grandma Nora. She loved you. I know she loved you."

"Then why does my mother use my *lack* of relationship as ammunition every time we talk?"

"Because your mother is insecure and making other people feel small is how she makes herself feel better."

My eyes go wide, and Brody winces. "Sorry. That was probably too honest."

"No, no you're right. I've just never heard anyone say it so concisely." I shake my head. "I just feel like I'm remembering all the times Mom tried, and I pushed her away. I was never here, and when I was here, I lived in my room. I thought I was so much better than her, that she was . . . I don't know. I just know

I said some really awful things."

"You were a kid. We all say stupid stuff when we're teenagers. But she said some stupid stuff too."

My earlier conversation with Mom is evidence enough of that, but it still helps to know that Brody remembers Mom's negativity too.

I almost hug him, but I'm still buzzing from the last time his arms were around me. I might short a circuit somewhere if I try again so soon. "This is hard, Brody," I say softly. "Makes me understand why I ran away for so long."

His grip tightens, squeezing my shoulders with gentle strength. "Nah. No more running. You can do hard things. We'll do it together."

I smile. "You're good to me."

"Tomorrow after your kayaking lesson, I'll bring my truck over and we can haul a load of stuff over to Goodwill. Maybe getting rid of some literal junk will make the figurative feel lighter."

I had momentarily forgotten that my first kayaking lesson is in the morning—amazing for how much time I've spent thinking about Brody.

Brody hiking.

Brody kayaking.

Brody lounging on an innertube tanned and shirtless.

Fine. I made that last one up, but after I broke into his house the other day, I have *all* the visuals I need to imagine him just about anywhere.

But tomorrow we will not be lounging. And I won't just be observing. A pulse of anticipation fills me, radiating all the way out to my fingertips. I have never shirked a challenge, but whitewater kayaking might be the thing that breaks that record.

"You aren't going to make me kayak the narrows, are you?"

Brody chuckles. "Not if you paid me."

I look up sharply. "But I *am* paying you. These are lessons through the school. I have to pay you."

He scrunches his brow as if considering. "Mmm, technically through the school? Okay. But I've talked to my boss, and Griffin is fine with me teaching you on the side. Either way," he says, dropping his hands from my arms, "we won't be anywhere near the narrows."

I lift my hands to my arms, missing the warmth of his palms. "And you won't mind coming over to help me haul stuff even after we spend the morning together? You'll be with me all day."

He grins. "Just like old times." He glances at his watch. "I really do have to go now though. I've got a class at two."

I nod and follow behind him as he moves to the front door. He pauses on the porch and slips on his sunglasses. He looks back at me and smiles. His truck is behind him, a bright red kayak lashed to the back, and his smile is wide and warm. "Tomorrow?"

"I don't deserve you," I say with a little head shake. I always felt that way growing up. Brody was always the one taking care of me. Talking me down after fights with my mom. Helping me study my way through difficult classes.

And here we are again. I blustered my way back into town and picked up right where we left off. Needing him. Making demands of him.

He says I inspired him to do something scary, something brave. But I don't feel very brave right now. I feel like walking out the front door and catching the next flight to New Zealand. I bet there's something I could write about in New Zealand. The Māori culture is beautiful, and the food—I could absolutely write about the food.

But Brody isn't in New Zealand.

The thought gives me pause.

For years I've lived without him. Traveled without him. Ten years we've been living separate lives.

Why does it matter now?

I don't know the answer. I only know that it does.

Chapter Thirteen

Brody

It has been a very long time since I've been nervous about teaching anyone how to kayak. I've worked with beginners. With pros who are only looking to improve their technique. With teenagers who think they're too good to listen and kids who ask questions faster than I can answer them. Whenever he can swing it, Griffin gives me the clients he suspects are going to be more difficult because he says I keep my cool better than any of the other instructors.

All that experience, that evidence, means I shouldn't be nervous. I should be chill. Cool as a cucumber. Easy, breezy. I've got this. If I can talk down a ten-year-old who is terrified of getting water up his nose and teach him how to successfully wet exit out of a rolled kayak, I can handle today.

I can handle—

Kate climbs out of her mom's Subaru wearing a black bikini top and a pair of gym shorts slung low on her hips. A gauzy white button-down hangs loose on her shoulders, unbuttoned, making it easy for me to notice every inch of her curves. She is toned and tan and I . . . cannot handle today.

Griffin steps up beside me holding the waiver Kate will need to sign before I can take her out on the water. He isn't making me charge her, but he's smart not to turn his back on this part.

"How's the flow?" I ask, my eyes still on Kate.

"River's at ten inches," he answers. "2000 CFS, medium flow—"

I can tell the moment Griffin's eyes have shifted to Kate. His words stall in his throat, and he slams the waiver into my chest. "Whoa," he says under his breath as Kate nears.

My thoughts exactly.

"You'll introduce me, right?"

My jaw clenches, and my hand curls into a fist before I realize what's happening and snap myself out of it. I intentionally shake out my shoulders. I do not have the right to react like some jealous animal. *Me Tarzan. Kate my woman. You jump off cliff.* Maybe I ought to start pounding my chest. Throw in a grunt or two for good measure.

"Ohhh," Griffin says. "Got it. When you said she was your best friend, what you really meant was she's your best friend . . . who you're in love with."

"I'm not," I say almost reflexively. How many times have I given the same answer? Claiming I'm *not* in love with Kate is second nature at this point.

"Right. That's exactly why you tensed up like you were ready to punch me for expressing interest."

"I'm not," I say again. "I'll introduce you." I swallow. "You can—"

Griffin holds up his hands, stopping me. "I really can't, man. I respect you too much. Whatever is happening right now, you don't need me getting in the middle of it."

Kate finally makes her way into the shop, an oversized bag slung over her shoulder.

"Hey," I say when she's finally within earshot.

She smiles wide. "Hey." She looks around appreciatively. "This place is great."

There isn't much to Triple Mountain. The main building is simple. Metal walls on a concrete slab, with enormous doors that, when they're open—and they almost always are—make the place feel more like a picnic pavilion than an actual building. In the winter when it's cold, Griffin pulls the doors closed, but in the summer months, it's easy to leave them open. This close to the water, and with the shade of the tree cover overhead, we don't have to worry about it getting too hot.

"Griffin gets the credit for that," I say, tilting my head toward the counter behind me. "Come on. I'll introduce you." I hold up the paperwork. "And there's some stuff for you to sign before we get you geared up."

Griffin is polite but distant as he explains what Kate is signing. "I know the drill," she says casually as she scribbles her signature across the bottom of the form. "Basically, if I manage to drown, it isn't your fault." She eyes me. "Or Brody's."

Griffin smiles. "You'd have to work pretty hard to drown on Brody's watch. I'd trust him to take my grandma down the rapids, and she can't swim."

"I guess I'm in good hands then."

Oh, I want her to be in my hands, all right. Every inch of her. In my hands. In my arms. In my living room sprawled on my couch while we watch movies and talk about nothing. In my bed when I wake up in the morning. In my kitchen when I fix my morning coffee. I want all of it. All of *her.*

I was a fool to ever think I could survive having her around all summer and come out on the other side unscathed. Kate Fletcher is my kryptonite. I was done for the minute she sent that first text before my hike. Before she ever set foot back in Silver Creek. "Come on. I've got all our gear ready to go."

She waves goodbye to Griffin, and after storing her stuff in one of the lockers that line the back wall, she follows me outside. "Is there not anyone else in the class?" she asks as she looks around. I intentionally picked a time for Kate's lesson when the school wasn't busy, so there isn't anyone else around.

I lift an eyebrow. "Were you expecting there to be?"

She shrugs. "I guess I was. I just assumed there would be a bunch of us learning at once."

"Even when we have a group, we never have more than three kayakers to one instructor. But today, you get me all to yourself."

She shoots a saucy grin over her shoulder. "Do you talk this way to all the girls?" She bats her eyelashes playfully.

I run a hand across my face. If she even had half a clue what she's doing to me . . .

I gather up our gear, handing her a couple of paddles to carry, then lead her down to the river where I've already left our kayaks.

"Am I going to be cold?" Kate asks, looking down at her exposed torso. "I know you said to bring layers just in case. I have a base layer I can put on if you think I'll need it."

I glance toward the sky, but where we're standing, it's a futile gesture. I can only see tiny slivers of blue through all the trees. But I double and triple-checked the forecast. There's no threat of rain, and where we'll be on the river, there will be enough sun to keep us comfortable. "You'll be fine without it."

"What about my shoes?" She holds up one foot, her well-worn Chaco sandal on display. I can only imagine the places she's been in those shoes. "I don't have any water shoes, but I figured since these strap on, they would probably work?"

"They'll work great." I pick up her PFD. "Here. Let's do this first. Before we get in the kayaks, I want you to swim around for a minute and make sure you're comfortable in your PFD."

"Is that the same thing as a life jacket?" She takes it and slips it on, and I step closer so I can adjust the fit.

"Not quite. Well, more like yes and no. All life jackets are personal flotation devices—PFDs—but not all PFDs are life jackets." My fingers graze along her abdomen as I check her straps and make sure she's in securely, and a trail of goose flesh erupts across her skin. My fingers still for the briefest moment—it's *my* touch she's reacting to—and I clear my throat. "A PFD allows for more mobility, which is necessary when you're kayaking. It *will* keep you afloat, but it won't necessarily save your life. It's just meant to assist you when you need it, so don't get cocky."

"Got it. No cockiness allowed," she says. "But I promise the last thing I'm feeling is overconfident."

I pause. "Is the great adventurer Kate Fletcher feeling nervous about getting in a kayak? Honestly, I'm surprised you've never done this before. It feels like you've done everything."

"Not everything. I did go on a three-day kayak trip through the Southern French Alps, but the water was calm the whole way. There were no spray skirts or helmets involved."

"Actually, that experience should help you a lot. Kayaks can be pretty tippy. If you're used to feeling the way your body movements can rock them, you're better off than a lot of beginners."

After a few more minutes in the water, making sure all of her gear fits comfortably, I walk Kate through the steps necessary for a wet exit, should she find herself upside down once she's inside her kayak. She's a quick study, so within a few more minutes, we're in the water, Kate in her kayak, me standing in the water beside her.

"How are you feeling?" I ask.

She nods. "So far so good. But I have a feeling you're getting ready to flip me upside down."

I grin. "I'll be right here the whole time. This first time, I don't want you to worry about trying to exit. Just hold your breath and try to relax. Count while you're underwater and if you can swing it, go all the way to ten, even twenty seconds. When you want to come back up, or when you get to twenty, whichever comes first, reach up and tap the bottom of your boat, and I'll flip you back up."

She looks at me, her blue eyes open wide, and takes a slow breath. "So I'll be hanging upside down in the water."

I nod. "But I'll be right here beside you the whole time."

"Okay. Let's do it."

She makes it about fifteen seconds before her hand lifts out of the water and taps the boat. I flip her back up and she takes an enormous breath, but she's smiling, and my shoulders relax the tiniest bit. A lot of students panic at this point. It *is* a weird sensation to be suspended underwater upside down. When people can't get the hang of it or relax enough to even *try* to get the hang of it, I usually end up taking them downriver without a spray skirt so if they flip, they just fall out of their boat. It works fine for Class I, maybe even Class II rapids, which is all we ever do with beginners anyway.

But I'm glad Kate is doing so well. I imagine taking her with me to run more serious rapids, sharing this part of my life with her, and a pulse of longing fills my gut. I don't *need* her—or any woman I date—to love whitewater kayaking like I do. That doesn't mean it wouldn't be fun if she did.

"What's next?" Kate asks, her eyes bright. "An actual wet exit?"

"Yep. This time, you'll flip, and then go through the steps to get yourself out of the boat and swim."

"Right. I can totally do it."

"Walk me through the steps one more time." I rest one hand on her kayak, holding her steady.

She scrunches her nose as she thinks. "First, I lean forward."

"Right."

"Then I grab the 'oh crap' strap and pull." Her hands move to the strap that will release her spray skirt. "Then I relax my knees, pull them into the middle of the boat, and push myself out."

"You got it."

She rolls her eyes. "Saying it while sitting here perfectly comfortable and doing it while underwater are entirely different things."

"You're going to do great. Remember, you only need four seconds. And you just hung upside down for fifteen without freaking out. You have plenty of time. Just relax, think through the steps, and do what you've got to do."

She takes another steadying breath. "You're a good teacher, Brody."

I smile. "You're a good student. You ready?"

She manages the wet exit on her first try, popping up out of the water a few feet away from her kayak, a jubilant expression on her face. "I did it!"

"And on your first try."

She swims forward and stands up beside me. "Can we go down the river now?"

"Easy, turbo. We've got to do a little paddle work first. Let's make sure you can steer your way through currents. *Then* we'll go down the river."

Kate is a natural. Her previous kayaking experience and her natural athleticism make the next part of our lesson easy, and soon we're heading downriver together. She could be pretending just for me, but it seems like she's having a really good time. I don't miss how much I want her to be having a good time.

She doesn't swim until the final—and the largest—rapid. When her kayak flips at the top of the rapid, I hold my breath and wait for her to appear. When she doesn't surface after five or six seconds, I start paddling toward her boat, panic rising in my chest. But then her helmet breaks the surface, followed by her toes. She's doing exactly what she should be, nose up, toes up as she swims the rapid.

Once she reaches the bottom and I know she's safe, I paddle over to retrieve her boat and hoist it up to drain the water it collected when she flipped. With most of the water drained, I maneuver the boat around to a shallower part of the river where it will be easier for her to get back in.

Kate watches, an expression on her face I can't quite interpret. "You okay?" I say when I'm close enough for her to hear me.

"Did you seriously just lift a kayak full of water over your head? While sitting in your own kayak?"

"You can't get back in a boat full of water."

"But how did you even . . . do your *muscles* have muscles? That was crazy."

A pulse of pride fills my chest, but I'm too worried about her to dwell on it. "How are you? You had me a little nervous when you flipped."

She lifts her arm and cranes her neck like she's trying to see the back of it. "I'm okay. I scraped my shoulder when I pushed out of the boat, but I don't think it did any real damage. There's no blood anyway."

Her toughness, her resilience, stirs something deep in my gut. No, that's not really accurate. My gut is already a churning mess of attraction and desire and a billion other feelings. But seeing Kate face something she's never done before head-on, to see her flip and stumble and still want to get back in the boat? It makes all those churning feelings crystallize into something specific. Something tangible.

Once we're out of the water, we lounge on the banks of the river eating lunch. Griffin will be down with the truck to haul us and our kayaks back up to Triple Mountain within the hour.

"So what did you think?" I almost don't need to ask her. I've been doing this long enough, I've learned to recognize the excitement that buzzes in people who really loved the experience.

Kate's still humming, energy pulsing right under her skin. She smiles wide at my question. "I want to do it again. And can we do bigger rapids? I mean, not *big* big rapids. Nothing like what I watched in the videos of the Green Race. But something bigger than what we did today. Will you take me?"

Yep. I'm totally done for. This woman has me.

"I would love to take you." *And give you anything else you want.*

"It was seriously such a rush. I felt so fast. And in control. It's easy for me to understand why you love it so much. And also why your program is so successful. You're a really good teacher."

"Better stop. Anymore, and my ego will be too big to fit in my boat."

She collapses back onto the grass and lifts an arm up to shield her eyes. "Nope. If your ridiculous muscles haven't done that yet, my compliments definitely won't."

I relax back beside her, propped up on my elbows. I tilt my face up and close my eyes, enjoying the warm sun on my water-chilled skin.

"Do you ever wish you could stay somewhere forever?" Kate asks softly.

My mind immediately goes to her staying in Silver Creek forever. "What, like . . . in a certain place?"

She turns her face to look at me. "More like, in a moment. Like this one."

"Yeah?"

She smiles. "I just did something really fun. And now my belly is full. The sun is warm." She pauses. "The company is good."

There is so much I could say. So much I want to say. But nothing I say is going to change the fact that Kate is only in town for a couple of months. When her grandmother's house is ready to sell, she'll be off on her next adventure. Her next assignment. The very nature of her career depends on her always leaving places. I swallow the words clogging up my throat. "It's nice to have you back, Kate."

Back in the parking lot of Triple Mountain, I walk Kate to her car. She retrieves her cell phone from her bag and holds it up. "Can we take a selfie next to the kayaks?"

"Of course," I say. "But I also took a few photos of you while we were on the river. I'll text those over later."

"What? When did you do that?"

"It's just part of the whole experience."

She rolls her eyes. "I forget the rapids we did are like splashing in a kiddie pool for you. Of course you had time to take pictures.

Did you file your taxes too? Do your grocery shopping?"

"Just stop it and get in here for a picture," I say, pulling her close to me. My hand wraps around her waist, heat searing my fingertips when they press against her bare skin. She lifts the phone and tries to capture us both in the frame, but it's obvious after a couple of attempts that with my longer arms, I should be the one holding the camera. I take it from her with my free hand, and she snuggles even closer into my side, one hand pressed against my chest.

I take a half-dozen different pictures—having a sister has taught me that one single photo is never enough—and hand the phone back to her. It buzzes as it passes from my hand to hers and I watch as Kate reads the notification. She pauses, her face shifting from shock to surprise to something that looks like excitement? But then she looks toward me and it's like a mask slips into place, her face shifting into an easy neutral.

"Everything okay?" I ask.

"Yeah. Sure. That was just . . . a work thing."

My heart drops to my toes. "Your next assignment?"

"Um, sort of? Not exactly." She looks over my shoulder. "It's hard to explain. Hey, you should probably help Griffin unload those kayaks."

I follow her gaze to where Griffin is lifting the boats off his truck to store them on the rack behind the gear shed. He doesn't really need my help. There are only two boats, but I'm smart enough to recognize this as the dismissal it's meant to be. "Okay," I say evenly. "You still want some help hauling some stuff to Goodwill this afternoon?"

"Yes!" she says a little too eagerly. "Absolutely. I would love the help."

She gives me a quick hug and then she's in her car and gone.

I move wordlessly to Griffin's truck and grab the last of the gear out of the back. He slides the paddles into a giant storage barrel while I hang the PFD Kate wore over a line to dry.

"For what it's worth, man, it definitely looks like there's something going on between you two."

"There's not," I say. I slide the helmets onto a shelf. "I told you we're just friends." A wave of weariness washes over me. I am so tired of telling this story.

Griffin eyes me warily, like I'm a tiger about to pounce. I *feel* like a tiger about to pounce. Like I'm full of energy—*emotion*—I can't channel into anything useful. It's maddening.

I turn to leave, then pause. "Hey, thanks for today," I say to Griffin. "I appreciate it."

He nods. "Anytime, man."

I head toward my truck, pausing when Griffin calls my name. "Brody."

I turn around.

"You okay?"

I nod and lift my hand in acknowledgment. It's not like I haven't played this game before.

Spend time with Kate. Fall more in love with Kate. Remember that Kate isn't mine to love. And repeat it all again the next day.

Still, the way she looked at me today, the way she—

I stop the thought and shake my head. Even if the email she isn't telling me about isn't one that will send her off again, some other email or phone call or shiny new idea eventually will.

Just like it always does. Like it always has before. Like it always will.

Chapter Fourteen

Kate

OHMYLANTA SEEING BRODY LIFT a kayak over his head was something.

Let's just state the obvious right up front. Seeing a man combine talent with hard-earned skill then top it all off with a blatant display of raw masculinity? Good grief. I was tempted to flip out of my kayak a dozen more times just to watch him do it again.

I would have had fun kayaking today with anyone as my guide. Once I got over the fear of flipping upside down, the thrill of moving through the rapids so quickly was intoxicating. It made me feel powerful. Capable.

At the same time, I was constantly aware of the water's dominance, how much it would control me if I stopped paying attention even for a second. The excitement of that contrast? I could get used to that.

But there's no denying it was *more* fun because Brody was the one teaching me how to do it. I loved watching him love what he was doing.

He was perfect. Patient. Attentive. Steady. Strong. He was everywhere I needed him to be at the precise moment I needed him to be there. It's his job, I know. But it felt like more than that.

Then we got back to my car and my phone . . . and I got an email.

An unbelievable email.

A wholly unexpected email.

Here's the thing. I am not the world's greatest travel writer. I am scrappy and resilient and very good at getting myself into places where unusual stories are found. That's the only thing that makes me great at my job. I don't have an English degree. I never attended college at all. The only thing that qualifies me to keep doing my job is the fact that I've been doing it for so long. I have earned my place at the freelance table.

But I'm not qualified for real jobs.

Real jobs are given to people with letters after their name. MFAs and PhDs. Even a BA is better than what I've got. Because what I've got is nothing. And, newsflash, when you're dealing with a pool of applicants, nothing is the very easiest qualification to beat.

Imagine my surprise when the above-mentioned email tells me *Expedition*, travel magazine based out of London, wants to bring me on as an associate editor. They trust my eye, they say, and think I'll have valuable input regarding the reach and scope of the entire magazine. The email ends with an invitation to visit London the first week in July, complete with a tentative itinerary they'll formalize as soon as I agree.

It's been hours since the email arrived, and despite my best efforts to keep myself busy, I haven't been able to focus on anything else. Well, aside from Brody bench pressing a water-logged kayak like it was built out of feathers and air.

I'm in the shower now, expecting Brody any minute to help haul off a load of my grandmother's belongings. My thoughts are so disjointed, bouncing like a ping pong ball between Brody and London and fancy job offers, I can't even remember if I washed my hair before applying conditioner. Or maybe I conditioned twice? I sigh and reach for my shampoo. I have got to get a hold of myself.

Pros and cons, Fletcher. Let's break this down like a normal, logical person.

The email came from a senior editor named Marge whom I've worked with before. The magazine has purchased a few of my articles, and they've always been great. That goes in the pro column. Working with good people is important.

But I can't even imagine what being on staff full time would look like.

Having a consistent salary would be amazing. And insurance. And benefits! I've never had benefits. That's three more for the pro list.

But the email made it clear this was not a position I could handle remotely. They want me on location, in the office with everyone else, collaborating, contributing.

I suppose I should feel flattered. I am flattered.

But London?

I've been there, of course, but I've never considered living there full time. To be fair, I've never really considered living *anywhere* full time.

But I have been feeling like I'm ready for the next thing in my life. I told Brody if I sit still long enough, maybe that thing will find me. Could this be it? A tiny sliver of hesitation wiggles into my brain. Do I want this to be it?

I cut off the shower and reach for a towel, pausing when I

hear footsteps downstairs. My heart trips, then steadies when I recognize the cadence of Brody's walk.

I wrap a second towel around my hair and step into the hallway long enough to shout down the stairs. "Hey! I'll be down in a sec," I call.

"No rush," he calls from . . . the kitchen? He sounds like he's in the kitchen. "Can I eat whatever this is on the counter?"

I grin. As soon as I got home from kayaking, I dealt with my buzzing energy by making a batch of homemade granola bars. "Go ahead!" I yell. I hurry to my room and throw on a pair of leggings and a sports bra, then layer on an oversized sweatshirt. I toss my hair into a messy bun, pausing long enough to consider whether I want to put on mascara. Highschool Kate would not have felt like she needed makeup around Brody.

I pick up my mascara, then drop it back on the bathroom counter.

Things aren't different now, are they?

I pick it back up.

Can things be different if you're moving to London?

"Gah!" I say out loud, tossing the mascara down one more time. "Get a hold of yourself, Kate."

I flip off the light with a huff and turn to head downstairs, my face bare.

Brody is leaning against the kitchen counter, his mouth full of granola.

"These are amazing," he says through a large bite.

"I'm glad you like them. I got the recipe from Preston's little sister."

Brody frowns and grumbles. "I don't like them as much anymore."

I roll my eyes. "Oh, come on. Preston wasn't that bad."

"I'm sure he wasn't."

I grab a granola bar off the cooling rack where I left them and break it in half. "Like it or not, he was a big part of me getting my start."

My long-distance high school boyfriend Preston, who I met while visiting my dad in New York, was a trust fund kid with endless resources. After graduation, when I was finally ready to see the world, he would have paid my way to anywhere I wanted to go, then tag along just for the fun of it. My pride wouldn't let me freeload so blatantly, so I always insisted on paying my own way. But it was hard to refuse when we traveled to places where his family owned property. His father is some sort of real estate mogul and has villas and beachside condominiums all over the world.

For a while, Preston thought himself a photographer, and so we worked together. He took the pictures, while I wrote the articles. But then my stuff started selling, and his didn't. That was the beginning of the end of our relationship.

"How did you guys break up?" Brody asks, his face so neutral, it can only be intentional.

I frown and take a bite of my granola bar. My relationship with Preston was going nowhere long before he called things off. We got comfortable with each other, interacting more like friends than two people who were actually in love.

"He called things off," I finally say. "But the fact that I didn't really care probably tells you everything you need to know about our relationship. The hardest thing was that he was basically my only traveling companion, and then, all of a sudden, I was alone. For pretty much the first time." I jump up and sit on the counter so my legs are dangling. "What about you? Any serious girlfriends?"

He gives his head an easy shake. "Not really. Well, one, sort of. Jill. We dated in college. It lasted a year, and then we broke up."

"Wow," I say, my tone thick with sarcasm. "Sounds like you really liked her."

He grins. "What do you want me to say? There just . . . wasn't anything there."

It shouldn't make me happy to hear him say it. I have no claim, no right to concern myself with his dating life, past, present, or future.

"I get it. That's how it felt with Preston too. Our relationship always felt like it had an expiration date. Still, I learned a lot. I think I have a better idea now of what I really want in a boyfriend."

Brody's body is very still, only his jaw moving as he chews the last of his granola bar. "Or a husband? Do you think you'll ever want one of those?"

An image of me walking down Piccadilly in London, arm in arm with a dapper British man wearing shiny dress shoes and a Burberry wool fedora dances through my mind. It's so ridiculous and wrong, I almost burst out laughing. I think I *do* want a husband at some point, but I don't think I'll find him in London. At least not one who looks like that.

"I hope so," I say.

Brody lifts his eyes to meet mine. He holds my gaze for one beat, then two. "I just hope when you do, you find someone who really sees you, Kate. I'm not sure Preston ever did that."

He's not wrong about Preston. I was always more of a convenience to him than someone he truly wanted to know. But nobody has ever seen me like Brody does. He's setting the bar pretty high. "Like you do?"

He shrugs. "You like to sell yourself short, but you deserve to be with someone who recognizes how great you are."

My heart squeezes uncomfortably. "More like how *needy* I am," I say with an eye roll. I clear my throat. "Speaking of, care to haul a bunch of enormous boxes out to your truck?"

I give myself an internal salute for steering the conversation away from the vulnerability Brody is so casually demanding. *Excellent deflection, soldier. Well done.*

Yes, I told him I'm working on being more vulnerable, and I am. But I'm *here.* Talking to Mom. Cleaning out Grandma Nora's house. My bandwidth is a little thin at the moment. I don't have it in me to tackle something as deep as "the happiness I deserve." Mostly because I don't know how to separate it from the happiness I *want.* Assuming I can even figure out what that happiness is. Or answer the question of whether those two things can even be the same thing.

"Just tell me what to carry," Brody says, pushing himself away from the counter.

I lead him into the living room where several boxes sit near the front door. I was up late last night after Brody left, packing up everything in the living room and hall closets, minus the wooden moose for Freemont, and a stack of things I begrudgingly decided I can try and sell on eBay.

I also created a pile of things I think Mom will want to keep. Or I will if she doesn't. There's an entire shoebox full of photos from when I was a baby, and a box twice that size of photos of my parents, pre-divorce. I barely scratched the surface of that box, even after spending a solid hour sitting in the middle of the floor, pictures spread out around me.

I reach for a specific picture I left on top of the box. "Actually, I wanted to show you this first." I hand Brody the photo and watch as he studies the images of me, a year old or so, holding onto my mother's fingers and taking what looks like my first step. I'm smiling a toothy grin at whoever is holding the camera. Grandma Nora, probably. But there's something else I noticed about the photo, and I'm wondering if Brody is going to notice the same thing.

His face shifts, his brow furrowing. He *does* notice. He looks up. "This looks like my front porch." He points at the fuzzy tree line in the background. "See the trees? The way they're spaced? I mean, they're smaller. Obviously. But . . . that's weird." He hands the photo back.

"I thought the same thing. I'll have to ask my mom who lived there. Maybe they were friends?"

"Yeah, maybe. All the houses on this street are at least fifty years old, mine included. Someone had to live there."

I put the pictures back, making a mental note to call Mom and ask about the house in the photo as soon as I have the fortitude to do it. Which, let's be real. After our last conversation, it may be a while.

I point out which boxes need to go in the truck, and Brody grabs the first one. I follow behind him, then climb into the truck bed to shuttle the boxes into the back. None of them are particularly heavy, save the one holding the encyclopedias, so it's easy enough to shift them around and fill the bed.

"That's the last one," Brody says five minutes later, lifting the last box onto the tailgate.

I slide it forward, situating it next to the others, then move to hop down from the truck. "Looks like we had just enough room."

Brody lifts his hands up to help me down, and I lean onto his shoulders, letting him guide my jump with his hands on my waist. Only, when I hit the ground, he doesn't let go.

And I don't let go.

We just stand there, arms around each other, staring into each other's eyes.

The afternoon sun is slanting low in the sky, hiding behind the trees. Birds are chirping overhead, cicadas are humming, a lawnmower is running somewhere in the distance. All of it fades to a distant hum, faint compared to the sound of my heart pounding in my ears.

Brody was always the one who could read my mood just by looking at me, detect how I was feeling faster than anyone else. But right now, he's the one with his emotions crawling all over his face. He's just as conflicted as I am. Because let me tell you, I am *conflicted* with a capital C.

There is something deliciously right about being in Brody's arms. Here, I am safe. Comfortable. Completely at home.

But I also feel *charged.* Like all my nerve endings are on fire, except the heat is exhilarating instead of painful. I am aware of every inch of him, every place that he is pressed against me. I feel the touch of each individual finger, the gentle strength of his grip on my waist branding me, claiming me.

I *want* that. To belong to him.

But I also can't shake the feeling that I am not who Brody needs or deserves. Brody needs someone in Silver Creek. He needs someone reliable. Someone who isn't a flight risk. I've never stayed in one place long enough to know if I'm even capable of being reliable. I've come close a time or two. Stayed somewhere long enough for people to start needing me around. And that's generally my cue to start looking for my next adventure. Leaving is easier than being needed. It's easier than *needing.*

Kristyn is always telling me that my parents' failed relationship doesn't have to dictate my own ability to have a successful one. But that's easier said than done. And Brody is too important to me to risk what we have because I *might* be capable.

But you want this man.

And you can see it in his eyes. He wants you too.

For a split second, I see myself in London, not with a Burberry-wearing Brit on my arm, but with Brody beside me. The image morphs, and I see us in Silver Creek. *Together* in Silver Creek.

Maybe. Maybe it could work?

Brody's expression shifts, a question clear in his gaze, and I breathe out a sigh. I close my eyes and lean my forehead against his chest. If I'm reading Brody right, and he's feeling as much attraction as I am, I can't give him false hope. I've made a lot of progress in the past year. I'm *here.* I'm *trying* to stop fleeing whenever things get hard. But I didn't anticipate what's happening with Brody right now, and I'm not prepared for the onslaught of emotion he brings. Even though I know it's a cliched line that people use too often, I really do feel like Brody is too good for me. He deserves *more* than me.

What we have—this friendship—is good and true and pure. Reliable in exactly the way it has always been. That's all I can trust right now. Anything else might risk hurting Brody, and that's the last thing I want to do. But I also can't pretend like this isn't different. We hugged all the time growing up. But we didn't stand like this. We didn't *hold* each other.

"Kate?" Brody's voice sounds close to my ear. He doesn't have to speak the question for me to hear it. He's wondering, questioning the meaning behind my sigh.

I step out of his arms. "We should get this stuff hauled away. Goodwill is going to close soon."

He stands perfectly still for a long moment, his arms hanging loosely by his sides. He turns away from me and runs a hand through his hair before clearing his throat. "Right. You're right. Do you want me to just drive it over?" He pulls out his keys. "I don't mind."

"No, I'll go with you. I can't ask you to haul it all by yourself." I don't want us to part ways like this. With this weird tension between us. An idea pops into my head. "What if I buy you dinner as a thank you? Burgers and fries out on the ledge?" It was our favorite way to celebrate random accomplishments back in high school. Perfect scores on calculus tests for Brody. *Passing* scores on calculus tests for me. Brody's swim team wins. My promotion to editor-in-chief of the high school newspaper. Our college acceptance letters, even though I turned down all of mine.

Brody smiles, but it doesn't quite reach his eyes. "I would love that, but I have to meet with the school board tomorrow night. I need to get home so I can figure out what I'm going to say."

"Oh. Oh, that's so much more important."

His jaw visibly tenses, but he doesn't say anything in response.

"Come on. Let's just go then. We can have dinner another time."

We don't talk as we drive over to Goodwill, but at least the silence isn't uncomfortable. It never has been between us, but after our *prolonged* hug, I'm surprised it isn't. I'm also surprised Brody can't hear my thoughts for how loud they are inside my head. We're talking full-on bellowing. Punctuated with ringing cowbells and the off-rhythm snare drum that used to mess up every marching band performance at the high school.

My brain is replaying the hug on a repeated loop. The sound of his voice as he whispered my name. The way his hands held me snug against him.

A part of me wants to talk about it. Be the one brave enough to acknowledge that our relationship feels different than it ever has before. But then, what would be the point? Talking about it won't change anything. Brody's life is here. And my life is . . . well, it's nowhere right now.

I'm a boat without an anchor. I used to love that sense of freedom, the ability to go wherever I please, but suddenly it feels like I'm missing my compass, too.

If there's nothing to hold me steady, and nothing to show me where I need to go, how am I supposed to feel anything but lost?

When Brody eases back into my driveway, he leaves the engine running and makes no move to get out of the car. I don't know what I expected, but I'm still sad the night is ending this way. I reach for the door handle but pause when Brody says my name.

"Kate," he says gently, tenderness in his voice.

I turn to face him.

"Sunday. Do you want to have breakfast with my family? We normally have dinner on Sundays, but Olivia has a thing Sunday night, so this week, it's breakfast instead."

Something in my heart flickers back to life. "I'd like that."

"And I was thinking we could go on a hike after? The Pulliam Creek Trail will take us down to the Green River, and from there we can hike the narrows."

I nod my agreement. I would stroll the grocery store aisles with Brody if he asked me to, but I would love to see the narrows, so this is an easy yes. In fact, I'd go just about anywhere he asked me to go. For the first time, I realize that if he asked, I might even be tempted to stay.

Chapter Fifteen

Brody

There are more parents than I expect at the school board meeting. More parents than I've ever seen at *any* school board meeting. The Carsons must have gone all out in rallying their troops. There are a few people I recognize as former students or parents of former students who are there in support of me, and my parents and Olivia and Perry are sitting near the door, but other than that, the room is mostly full of people who are looking at me like I make a regular habit of throwing puppies into raging waterfalls.

Dad called an hour ago while I was on my way over and reminded me that no matter what the other side claims, I have truth on my side. I want to believe it's enough, but these people look like they're out for blood.

Principal Talbot approaches me, a grim look on his face. He motions me over to the edge of the room and places a steadying hand on my shoulder. "All right. Here's what I know. Two school board members have kids in their extended families who have been a part of the kayaking program in the last five years and are behind it one hundred percent. Two more are neutral. But one—Nancy Shelbourne—she's going to be the one to cause the most trouble. She's got a list of questions a mile long, and every single one of them is going to try and discredit you."

"Why do I feel like I just stepped into the pages of a John Grisham novel?"

John smiles. "Look. You know no matter what happens to the kayaking program, you're still a part of the Green River Academy family. Your job isn't on the line here. You understand that, right?"

I nod along, though the idea of my job without the kayaking program isn't near as fun.

"We'll get through this. Just speak the truth. The Carsons talk a big game, but they live with their kid every day. They know how much of an idiot he is." John winks and moves back to his seat just as the meeting is called to order. I move toward my own chair on the front row, but not before a flash of dark hair coming through the back door catches my eye.

Kate is here.

We make eye contact, and she smiles, warming me from the inside out. No matter the uncertainty of our current relationship, there's no denying how much better I feel now that she's here.

My phone vibrates as I sit down, and I pull it out of my pocket to see a text message from Kate.

Kate: You're going to be great. I believe in you like I believe in Cherry Coke and buttered popcorn.

I chuckle as I slip my phone back into my pocket. Whenever I would help Kate cram for tests, Cherry Coke and buttered popcorn were our preferred study snacks. Right before her tests, I would always text her the exact message she just sent me.

I love that she remembers.

I love that she's here.

But how much longer will she be around?

The first half of the meeting is routine stuff. A reading of the minutes from the last meeting, suggested changes to the annual budget for the upcoming school year, an update on the new science curriculum adopted by the state of North Carolina, and now, finally, the concern of a number of local parents regarding the safety of the whitewater kayaking program at Green River Academy.

Diane Carson is given the floor first.

It takes all my focus to keep my breathing steady as she lists grievance after grievance regarding her son's "experience" in my program. His questions were ignored. He was constantly overlooked. He was belittled and made fun of by other students. And then his "very life was compromised when he was allowed in the water without supervision or instruction, in a boat that held him captive and inhibited his ability to free himself."

The board president thanks Mrs. Carson, then turns the time over to me. "Perhaps, Mr. Hawthorne, you could give us a rundown of what happened from your perspective?"

I stand and nod, then move to the podium Mrs. Carson just vacated. I clear my throat. "Thank you for the opportunity to be here. If I could, before getting into the events of the afternoon in question, I'd like to provide a brief summary of the safety measures in place within Green River Academy's whitewater kayaking program, as well as my qualifications as an instructor. I believe it's important context."

The board president nods. "Very well."

I grip the edges of the podium and launch into a recitation of everything that qualifies me to be on the water as an instructor. CPR certification. Level five senior instructor certification from the ACA. Certification in swift water rescue. Ten years' experience as a kayaker and five years' experience as an instructor. "It's also worth noting," I add, "that per industry recommendations, we maintain a three-to-one instructor-to-student ratio at all times. I take the kids out in groups of six, with one additional instructor present."

A woman sitting near the end of the table at the head of the room raises her hand. Her nameplate reads Nancy Shelbourne. "I'm sorry, there are *two* instructors? Does that mean the district is paying for an additional instructor to make this program functional?"

"The other instructor is a volunteer," I say. "He is fully credentialed and certified, but he's just a volunteer."

She scoffs. "Seems like a big commitment for someone unassociated with the school. Could it be he isn't as invested as he should be? Maybe he doesn't always pay full attention?"

I clench my jaw. The only way out of this is to admit something I haven't even admitted to Principal Talbot. It's above board. On paper, anyway. I double and triple-checked to make sure. But he still isn't going to like it. "The volunteer who works with me is Griffin Hughes. He's the owner of Triple Mountain Paddling School, where I am employed during the summer months as a kayak instructor. During the two eight-week seasons when the academy program is active, I volunteer to cover one of Griffin's weekend classes at Triple Mountain so he has the time to volunteer for me."

Nancy Shelbourne purses her lips and huffs, but the board president holds up a hand, stopping her. "Let me get this straight," the president says. "You teach for free at a business here in Silver Creek just so you can have an additional instructor present within your school kayaking program?"

"That's correct."

"Can I ask why? Is it required by law that your teacher-to-student ratio remain three to one?"

"Not required, but it is *my* rule. And Triple Mountain's rule. In my experience, in order to keep everyone safe, one instructor shouldn't be in charge of more than three kayakers at a time."

"And you never approached the school about paying Mr. Hughes for his time?"

"With all due respect, ma'am, I'm not aware of any public education programs that are rolling around in extra funding. It already took a herculean effort to acquire the gear required to get the program launched through donations and other education grants. This seemed like a small thing I could manage on my own."

She nods. "The point is, you sacrificed your personal time and energy *just* to keep the kids *more* safe?"

I almost downplay her claim, minimize what I'm doing, because, in my mind, it isn't really a big deal. But that doesn't mean it shouldn't look like a big deal to everyone else. It can only help. "Yes," I say simply. Might as well own it.

She smiles. "That's what I thought."

I spend the next ten minutes walking everyone through what happened the afternoon Dillon Carson *claims* he almost drowned. "There is inherent risk in any sport," I say, my heart rate finally slowing down. "A football player understands when he puts on his pads and hits the field that he might get injured. But he also knows he'll have a better shot if he listens to his coach instead of running at the biggest guy on the opposing team just because he thinks he can take him on his own. My kayakers understand that when they're in the water, they might get hurt. And they're more likely to get hurt if they get cocky or behave stupidly. But if they listen, if they pay attention, I will do everything in my power to keep them safe."

At this point, I'm a little sad I'm *not* in a John Grisham novel. I'm ready to throw in a *Ladies and Gentleman of the jury* in my best Matthew McConaughey voice, slam my fist against the podium and declare my innocence. *Innocent, your honor! I am innocent!*

But nothing's being declared tonight. They won't hold a vote until later in the summer after they've had time to fully "deliberate and evaluate" the particulars of the situation. After Nancy Shelbourne launches half a dozen questions at me, everything from where I earned my teaching degree to whether I see myself as a lifetime citizen of Silver Creek—I still have no idea what that question is about—the meeting ends and that is that.

John Talbot gave me two thumbs up from across the room before offering a quick salute and disappearing out the door. He's got kids at home, and the meeting ran long, so I don't fault him for taking off. We'll be in touch about everything soon enough.

My family surrounds me next, offering me hugs all around before Mom pulls me off to the side. "You did good, Brody," she says gently.

"Thanks, Mom."

"I'm surprised that Nancy Shelbourne nutso didn't ask for your ACT scores, though I kind of wish she would have." She grins. "That would have shown her, wouldn't it?"

I glance over Mom's shoulder to where Kate is standing at the back of the room, waiting for me.

Mom follows my gaze. "Oh, I see how it is."

I shake my head. "Sorry, I—"

"Oh, hush, child. I know I can't compete. But I do wonder . . ."

Her words trail off, and she tilts her head toward Kate. "How are things? How are *you*?"

She's asking me a thousand questions with those three words. I try and infuse as much confidence as I can into my response. She'll worry about me anyway, but I still give it my best shot. "We're friends, Mom."

She narrows her gaze. "I feel like there's something you aren't telling me."

There's a ton I'm not telling her. I tested the waters last night, gave Kate an opening, and she shut me down. I'm pretty sure she was feeling something, so I'm not ready to give up completely, but I'm also not ready to share what's happening with my family. "There's nothing to tell. I promise."

She breathes out a sigh. "Oh, honey. I don't believe you in the slightest."

I lean forward and kiss her on the cheek. "Thanks for caring. And thanks for being here. It means a lot."

By the time my family leaves, Kate and I are the last two people left in the room. I stop right in front of her. "Hey." I slip my hands into the pockets of my khakis. "Thanks for coming."

She nods and smiles. "I wouldn't have missed it. You did great, Brody. Truly an A-plus performance."

I grin. "I'll take it."

She loops her arm through mine, and we walk out to the parking lot and head toward her mom's Subaru. "You look nice all dressed up," she says. "I like your tie. And it's nice to see your glasses again."

"I thought they would make me look more like a teacher." I take them off and slip them into the pocket of my dress shirt. "Did it work?"

She smiles. "Definitely. But for real, you were so good. So

professional. I love that you didn't back down when it came to calling Dillon out for his bad behavior."

She's still holding on to my arm when we reach her car, and I let her tug me over so we're both leaning against the driver-side door.

"I only hope it'll make a difference."

"What will you do if it doesn't?" she asks. "I mean, I think it will. I don't think you're going to get shut down. But . . . what if you do?"

"I'll keep teaching, I guess. Griffin asked me a few months ago if I wanted to come on as a full-time instructor at Triple Mountain. It's tempting, but . . . I don't know. I feel like what I do at the school really matters. It would be hard to give that up."

She leans her head against my shoulder, her hands tucked around my bicep. "You always shine brightest when you have the chance to really connect with people. It's easy to imagine you building that connection in a classroom."

Kate is close to me, as close as she was last night, but right now, the closeness only feels companionable. There's no denying the chemistry that's been crackling between us since she came back to town, but I also appreciate that she knows me well enough to support me like this, too. I want physical chemistry. But I also want friendship.

My heart stretches and aches. *I want her.*

"How did today go? Did you make any progress on the house?"

"A little," she answers through a yawn. "I spent half the morning looking through pictures of my parents before I was born."

"You haven't seen them before?"

"Never. I honestly thought Mom threw away everything that reminded her of Dad. I mean, I've seen the photos that have me in them. She saved those. But these, the two of them are so young. And they look really happy, which . . . I don't know. It wasn't what I expected."

"They did get married, Kate. They had to have loved each other at some point."

"Logically, I know that. It's just hard for me to imagine. I don't have a single memory of them married, Brody. They've always been divorced. And Mom has *always* been angry about it."

It's not a wonder Kate has a hard time imagining her own happily ever after. "Marriage doesn't always end like that," I say.

She nods without picking her head up, and I feel it shifting against my shoulder. "I know." She gives my arm a squeeze. "It won't end that way for you."

"What makes you so sure?"

She lifts her head and looks at me. "Because you believe it won't." She smiles. "It was your mom who told me that, and I think she's right. Believing that love can last has to be half the battle."

That sounds like something my mother would say. And she's right. I do believe marriage can last. When I think about my future, it is always in the long term, from the here and now all the way to grand kids and great-grandkids, all with the woman I love beside me.

I'm not naïve enough to believe it *always* works out that way. Life happens. People die. We screw up. People betray us, lie to us, leave us, break our hearts. But call me an optimist, I'd rather believe the good can still happen. That the right love can endure any hardship.

"What about you?" I ask. "Do you believe love can last?"

She stares at her hands for a long moment. "I'm trying to," she finally says. Then, with a little more conviction, "I want to." She lifts her shoulder in a playful shrug and smiles. "If only all this baggage I'm lugging around wasn't so heavy."

"I think you've done a pretty good job carrying everything."

"That's just it. I *don't* carry it. I walled it up in Silver Creek and left it all behind. I already told you. When it comes to relationships, all I'm really good at is running."

She's saying the words like she's playing around, but I hear the truth in them. "Nah. I don't believe it. You don't have to run. And you *do* deserve to be happy. I'm going to keep telling you that until you believe it."

I only hope she eventually will.

Chapter Sixteen

Kate

I AM NERVOUS ABOUT having breakfast with Brody's family.

I shouldn't be nervous. I love the Hawthornes, and I know they love me. But with my feelings for Brody changing by the minute, I worry his mother will see my confusion written all over my face. Hypothetically, if I did have feelings for Brody, would his family approve? They know pretty much everything there is to know about me. But loving me despite my flaws and wanting their son to be saddled with those flaws for the rest of his life are two different things.

I spend way too much time trying to decide what to wear. Picking an outfit that will both tell the Hawthornes I care about their invitation and want to look nice and also be comfortable enough to hike in is basically impossible. In the end, I settle for a pair of shorts and a lightweight denim button-down, cinched at the waist, and my Birkenstocks. I toss my sneakers into a bag. After breakfast, I can lose the button-down and hike in the tank I'm wearing underneath and change my shoes in the car on the way to the trail.

I stand in the empty living room while I wait for Brody. I've made two more trips to Goodwill since Brody helped me haul off the first load, and the same number of trips to the post office to ship the items I've sold on eBay. Someone even bought the boob pillow and paid thirty bucks for it. The room is entirely empty now except for the furniture, and that's going to be hauled off first thing on Monday morning.

I'll move onto the kitchen next, then tackle the bedrooms upstairs.

What I didn't expect coming into this is that the more I haul away, the more I'm starting to recognize the house's potential. It has good bones. Mom didn't necessarily ask me to do any actual remodeling, but with just a little bit of updating, the house would probably sell for a lot more. The question is whether Mom will want to spend the money to do it.

I pull out my phone and send her a quick text, asking her what she thinks about a kitchen update before we list the house. Her response comes in faster than I expect.

Mom: I think it's a great idea. But I'm surprised you're the one suggesting it. I was expecting you to do bare minimum and then get out of there as quickly as possible.

I force myself to breathe before responding. She's not wrong. When I first agreed to come, that's exactly what I thought I would do. But sticking around, at least for a few extra weeks, doesn't feel so bad anymore.

Kate: It hasn't been so bad. I'm happy to stay and take care of it. Want to give me a budget?

We text back and forth about appliance prices and what a basic kitchen update will cost. I don't have the first clue about this sort of thing, but Freemont's real estate experience gives him a pretty good idea, so it doesn't take long for Mom to text over a few guidelines and suggestions about what and how to update. By the time the conversation is over, I'm pretty sure we've set a new record for number of consecutive texts sent without any bickering. But then Mom's last text gives me pause.

Mom: Be sure to pick out things you really like. Don't just be economical. Make it beautiful, too. How you would want it if you were going to live there.

It almost feels like mom *wants* me to live here. I think about the note she left. The way she prepared the house. Stocked it with groceries. For all her nitpicking, she paved the way for me to have a good experience. But why? Why would she want me in Silver Creek when she has no plans to be here herself?

I spend the last fifteen minutes before Brody picks me up sitting on the front porch, scrolling through Pinterest pins and looking for kitchen ideas.

I'm weirdly *excited* about a kitchen remodel, and I don't know how to feel about that. Yes, it sounds more fun than cleaning out closets and selling things on eBay. But it will also prolong my time in Silver Creek. By a month, maybe even two months. By then the summer will basically be over and November—and the Green Race—will be right around the corner.

Taking the job in London would of course be a factor. But *Expedition* has already told me the end of the summer won't be a problem. When I mentioned my time constraints, they encouraged me to come out in July to get a feel for the place, then once we're all sure we want to move forward, we can talk about an official start day. If I even want an official start day. The longer I'm in Silver Creek, the less sure I feel.

I turn off my phone and lean my head back against the rocking chair. For a brief moment, I close my eyes and think about what it would feel like to stay in Silver Creek indefinitely instead. A pulse of anxiety skitters through me, but I push it aside. For once, I try and pretend what it would feel like if I *wasn't* a complete mess full of doubts and hang-ups and fear. What would it feel like if I didn't have a job that required so much travel? What would it feel like if London wasn't even on the table? What would it feel like to just . . . *stay*?

A dream unfolds in my mind, slowly at first, but then with startling clarity. Hiking in the mountains. Picking apples in the Stonebrook orchards. Taking long walks on Sunday afternoons. Eating tacos from the stand next to Triple Mountain.

I can see it. I can almost taste it. At least the taco part of the dream.

But I won't let myself dwell on it.

It isn't practical.

It isn't even logical.

I don't realize until I'm climbing into Brody's truck that he was a part of every dreamed scenario.

"Morning," he says as I buckle my seatbelt.

"Morning," I say brightly. I haven't seen him since the school board meeting on Thursday night, and it feels good to be with him again.

"I hope you're hungry. Lennox is the one feeding us this morning."

"Does he ever get tired of cooking?" My stomach grumbles, making Brody grin, and I press a hand against my midsection.

"Not that I've ever seen," he says. "We're test subjects this morning. He and Olivia have decided to offer Sunday brunch at the restaurant, so he's been focusing on breakfast foods lately."

The conversation flows as we drive the short distance over to his parents' house. We don't talk about anything important. Not really. I tell him about my plans to update the kitchen. He tells me about a couple he had a kayaking lesson with yesterday, and an email he got from one of his former AP Chemistry students. It's all completely inconsequential. Just normal, everyday stuff. But I want to know it all anyway. I tell myself it's not all that different from how our friendship has always been. I've always cared about things going on in Brody's life. But now it *feels* different.

Even if it shouldn't, it does.

We don't use the main entrance to the farm but cut up a back road that leads right to the family homestead without meandering through the event and farm space. If the number of cars in the driveway is any indication, everyone else is already here.

"Do you guys really do this every Sunday?" I ask as I follow Brody to the front door.

"There's always a meal," Brody says. "But not everyone comes every week. Perry always comes. And I usually do. Tyler and Olivia go down to Charleston a lot to see his family, so they're here maybe half the time. Lennox was never here until he moved back, so it's been nice having him come."

"And Flint?"

"Once or twice a year, maybe? He does the best he can. I'm honestly surprised he's able to make it as often as he does."

As soon as Brody pushes through the front door, I am quickly enveloped by the familiar bustle of a Hawthorne family gathering. Hannah hugs me first, then Lennox gives me a quick hug before darting back into the kitchen.

Olivia is standing off to the side with her husband Tyler, who walks forward long enough to shake my hand, but Olivia only waves, her smile tight and her expression wary. Perry is sitting in the corner of the living room reading a book.

"Come and see Ray," Hannah says, ushering me away from

my worries about Olivia and toward Mr. Hawthorne, who is already seated at the head of the enormous farm table in the dining room. "He's been so excited to see you."

Ray Hawthorne greets me with kind eyes and invites me to sit beside him and tell him about my latest adventure.

The first thing that pops into my head is kayaking the Lower Green with Brody, but I know that isn't what Mr. Hawthorne means. Instead, I tell him about the time I spent in Ireland just before coming home.

Olivia soon joins us, sliding into the chair across from me, one hand resting on her baby bump. "You must be itching to get back on the road, Kate," she says a little too sweetly. "You've been back in Silver Creek, what, a month? That's long enough for a lot of people."

There's something about her assumption that rubs me the wrong way. The same uneasiness I felt when I first visited with Olivia and her mom wiggles its way into my mind. It almost feels like she *wants* me to leave. "No, I'm enjoying myself. There's still a lot of work to do to get the house ready to sell. That's enough to keep my mind busy."

She asks a few more questions about the house, and we chat back and forth, but as soon as the conversation shifts to something farm related, I get up to find Brody. He's in the kitchen with Lennox, leaning against the counter while his brother pulls something that smells delicious out of the oven.

"Hey," Brody says as he sees me approach. "You okay?"

I nod, but gesture for him to follow me into the hallway.

"What's going on?" he asks once we're alone.

"I don't know exactly. But . . . I think Olivia doesn't want me here."

His eyebrows go up. "What? Like, here at breakfast?"

I shake my head. "No. Here in Silver Creek. I can't explain why. She hasn't said anything specific. I just get the sense that . . . I don't know. That she's worried, maybe?"

A flash of understanding crosses Brody's face, but then he just smiles and squeezes my shoulder. "I'm sure it's nothing, Kate. Olivia loves you."

A knot forms in the pit of my stomach. There's something he isn't telling me. Still, it isn't a conversation I want to have with half a dozen Hawthornes standing around, so I return his smile and nod. "I'm sure you're right."

"Foods up!" Lennox calls from around the corner.

"Come on," Brody says. "Let's eat, and then we can get out of here."

The food is amazing. A frittata with fresh tomato, arugula, and crumbled goat cheese. Thick slices of French toast with sliced strawberries and some sort of maple bourbon drizzle that makes me moan out loud. A tossed salad with baby greens, thinly sliced pears, candied walnuts, and a lemon vinaigrette that is somehow sweet and spicy at the same time.

By the time I'm finished with my meal, I've made a million mental notes for the article pitch I'm going to write about Lennox's new restaurant. Come to think of it, I could probably get two or three articles out of Stonebrook. The commercial side of the farm, the event side, and now the restaurant.

The thought starts a cascade of thoughts, likely prompted by my morning foray into considering a more permanent life in Silver Creek.

It only takes a moment for my brain to catalog half a dozen destinations I could write about in Western North Carolina. The food scene in Asheville is big, and the brewery scene is even bigger. Plus, there are multiple national forests, the Great

Smoky Mountains National Park, the Biltmore House. There are endless hiking trails and waterfalls. There's whitewater rafting and kayaking, and of course, the Green River Green Race.

I wouldn't find the same sponsored trips that have been the bread and butter for my mostly European-based career, and it would probably narrow my audience. The pay per article probably wouldn't be as good, but if I'm not living abroad, maybe making less wouldn't be such a big deal.

It's a risky thought. More of a career pivot than a subtle shift. But no less so than hanging up my suitcase altogether and moving to London to be an editor.

I carry a stack of plates into the kitchen, hesitating when I find Brody and Olivia standing next to the refrigerator talking. Or maybe arguing? Olivia's arms are folded, her expression stern, and Brody has his hands perched on his hips.

"I'm not the only one who is worried," Olivia says. Her words cut off when Brody's eyes cut to me.

She turns her back, and Brody immediately rushes over to take the dishes out of my hands.

"Come on," he says after setting them in the sink. "You ready to go?"

My eyes flit to Olivia, but she's turned away from us, rummaging through the cabinet above the stove.

"I was going to help your mom do the dishes."

"Don't worry about it. Perry will do them. Let's hit the trail before it gets too hot."

I offer the rest of his family a too-quick goodbye, then follow Brody to his truck. There *is* something he isn't telling me, and he's going to tell me what it is right now.

"What's going on, Brody?" I ask as soon as he cranks the engine.

"Why are we leaving so fast? And what aren't you telling me about Olivia? She *doesn't* want me in Silver Creek, does she?"

He blows out a sigh. "It isn't that."

"Then what is it?"

"They're just worried about . . . me, I guess."

"Because of me?"

"Because of our friendship."

"I'm still not following."

He turns the truck onto Big Hungry Road. "Kate, it really doesn't matter. You don't need to worry about it. Olivia is being unreasonable about this."

"About what? Please just tell me. I promise I can handle it."

He huffs out a heavy sigh. "She's worried that as long as you're home, I won't date." He lifts his shoulders in a loose shrug. "Because I'll spend all my free time with you."

I sink back into my seat. Honestly, I can't fault her the worry. It makes sense. "Oh."

"It's not a big—"

"No," I say, cutting him off. "I get it. I guess I have been monopolizing your time."

"It doesn't feel that way. *I'm* not complaining, all right? I like spending time with you. I don't mind not dating for a couple of months. It's nice to have a break if I'm being honest."

I don't know why his comment stings, but it does. Maybe because he's labeling the time he spends with me as *not dating.* Even though it isn't. There was the holding that happened the other night before we took things to Goodwill, and when we hugged in my grandmother's kitchen, I felt like my entire body was wrapped in a live wire.

But I could be making all of that up.

Oh no. What if I *am* making it all up?

What if this is all one-sided, and Brody isn't feeling any of the same sparks I am? He can handle not dating for a couple of months. Which is about how long I first told him I was going to be here.

I gave him a time limit. A deadline. And he isn't looking for anything beyond that.

"You can still date while I'm around, Brody. You don't have to spend all your time with me."

He smiles. "I know. But I want to."

My mind is a jumbled mess. Every time I think I'm starting to figure out what I want, something happens to shake me back up again. The idea of London sounds appealing because I really *would* love to have a job with more stability than what I have now. But I'm not sure I want to live in London. I've lived my entire life believing I'd never want to live in Silver Creek, but then I spent half my morning imagining what it would be like if I did, making mental lists of articles I could pitch that would keep me here.

But I can't stay in Silver Creek if I'm going to interfere with Brody finding the happily-ever-after I know he wants. Unless that happily-ever-after is with *me*. A tiny thrill shoots through me at the thought. Could he want that too? The more I think about it, the more I *don't* think I made up the attraction in his eyes when he helped me down from his truck. But physical attraction isn't all that matters.

The scariest thought of all pops into my head next. What if he does want it, we try, and I fail? What if my efforts to keep a career going locally aren't enough, and I only make it a year before I have to start traveling again? What if I'm not really built for a slower, stabler life and pretending like I am winds up breaking us both? Maybe it wouldn't happen, but maybe it would. Am I truly willing to risk our friendship on a maybe?

"You okay over there?" Brody asks. "I can almost hear you thinking."

"Sure. Just enjoying the view."

The view really *is* amazing. Lush green trees and loamy earth and dense thickets of rhododendron line either side of the road. I roll my window down and breath in, the familiar smell of the forest tickling my nose.

I don't know what I'm supposed to do. But the longer we drive, the longer I breathe in the clean mountain air, the more certain I am about one thing.

I've missed this.

I never thought I would say it, and it only complicates things that I'm saying it now.

But I've missed . . . *home.*

Chapter Seventeen

Kate

The Pulliam Creek Trail is a pretty easy hike, but when we leave the main path and head down to the narrows, I understand why Brody double and triple checked that I had good shoes to wear. The descent is steep—so steep there are ropes tied in between the trees for us to hold onto. At one point, it's easier to turn around and lower myself down the trail backward. Which of course makes me super excited about the return trip, when we'll be climbing up instead of down.

"The craziest thing is that during the Green Race," Brody says, "spectators have to make this hike down to Gorilla if they want to watch. So just imagine this trail with two hundred people hiking down at once."

"Um, that feels terrifying," I say, though as soon as we reach the water, it makes sense why people are willing to do it. The river is gorgeous.

We follow the trail as it snakes along the edge of the water, the gorge cutting up steeply on either side. The river is full of massive boulders, some large enough for a dozen people or more to stand on at once, creating narrow channels of water and steep drops. I recognize what I'm seeing from the videos of the Green Race I watched online but seeing it in person is an entirely different experience. And thinking about Brody paddling through these rapids in a kayak? It leaves me speechless.

"Oh hey, there's Griffin," Brody says, pointing off the trail to where Griffin and several other kayakers are maneuvering their boats out of the water.

"What are they doing?"

Brody tilts his head toward the river. "They're portaging around Gorilla," he says. "Walking their boats around the rapid instead of running it."

"Do people do that a lot?"

"With Gorilla? All the time. It's brutal to run. Unless you have people setting safety at the bottom, which can be an ordeal, it's risky. Too risky for most kayakers."

We say hello to Griffin, and Brody introduces me to everyone else, all friends of his, then we follow them down trail so we can watch them get back in the water. We can't see much from our vantage point, but I still hold my breath when I see them disappear over a rapid. This kind of kayaking is very different than the baby rapids I ran on the Lower Green.

"This is crazy," I say to Brody as we walk back toward Gorilla.

He only grins. "It can be."

A huge rock overlooks the rapid, and we stretch out, the sun warming my bare arms and legs. The water is loud—I understand now why spectators at the Green Race ring cowbells—but it's soothing too. I lean back on my hands and close my eyes. There are so many decisions in my future. But I don't have to make any of them right *now.*

"Hey, I've got a favor to ask," Brody says, breaking the silence.

"Okay."

"I debated whether to ask you because I don't want you to feel like you have to say yes. It's not a big deal if you can't do it."

"Just ask. I can almost promise I'm going to want to say yes."

He grins. "Don't speak too soon."

"Brody."

"Okay, okay. So, the Fourth of July is next Saturday," he says, "and I've got this kayaking trip planned with Griffin and a couple other guys. Actually, you just met one of them. Ryan. Anyway, we're hoping to head up to Robbinsville to hit the Cheoah River, and we need a shuttle bunny."

My brain temporarily hitches on the date. I'm supposed to fly to London late afternoon on the fifth—a trip Brody still doesn't know about. But we can circle back to that. If it's just a day trip, it shouldn't interfere anyway. I raise my eyebrows. "A shuttle what?"

He grins. "A shuttle bunny. Someone who can drop us off at the put-in, then drive downriver to meet us at the take-out when we finish." He runs a hand across his face, like he's nervous I won't want to do it. "It would pretty much be the entire day, so if you feel like you've got too much to do . . ."

"No, I'd love to do it," I say. "Especially if there are places where I can watch." A thrill shoots through me at the idea of watching Brody kayak.

"There are a few places. Are you sure you wouldn't mind? It would eat up any chance of you having any kind of Fourth of July celebration, and it would just be you and . . . four guys."

"You're the only person in town I would spend the Fourth of July with anyway. I promise I don't mind. And I can handle four guys. I promise I've handled worse."

"Great. That's awesome." His obvious enthusiasm sends a little beat of joy to my heart. "We're wanting to leave Triple

Mountain around seven a.m. Can I pick you up a little before?"

"Sounds perfect. I'll be . . ." My words trail off when Brody tenses beside me, his eyes focused upriver.

"What is it?" I ask.

"Kayakers."

"Are they doing the portage thing like Griffin did?"

He stands up and offers me his hand so I can do the same. "It looks like they're going to run it. At least one of them is."

"Do you know who they are?"

Brody hasn't taken his eyes off the river. "I can't tell from here."

A couple of guys come running down the trail, stopping just past us, and turn to face the rapid. One of them is holding what looks like a rope tucked inside a bag.

"Did someone fall in?" I ask.

"Not yet." Brody's entire body is tense. "But if someone does, his buddy better not throw the rope from there."

The kayaker crests the rapid, and I hold my breath. He disappears into the whitewater, but then his boat pops up, upside down. The water churns around the kayak, knocking it against a boulder. For all I know, the kayaker is still suspended beneath it, but then Brody swears and takes off running down the trail. "He's swimming," he calls to the guy with the rope. "Give me the rope, give me the rope!"

The guy must trust that Brody knows what he's doing because he hands it over without question. Rope in hand, Brody keeps running. I follow as far as I can, but then he's off the trail and cutting across the water, shimmying and leaping over rocks like a gazelle, and I don't trust myself to go any further. Not without compromising my own safety, which would only complicate things for Brody.

Because he is obviously on a rescue mission.

A little further down the trail, the path turns, and I suddenly have a vantage point of Brody, crouched low and braced against a boulder, tugging the kayaker, who is holding onto the rope, toward the shore. The two other kayakers, who followed the same path I did, stop beside me. "That was wicked," one of them mutters.

"Dude. I told him he shouldn't run it," the other guy says.

I can hardly focus on their conversation because I am too hung up on the fact that Brody just turned into a freaking superhero.

Listen. It's sexy for a guy to be really good at something. It's even sexier when being good at something gives said guy the kind of muscle definition that Brody has. But take that sexiness and then have that guy *save someone's life* in a perfect display of strength, knowledge, and masculinity?

I have never witnessed this level of sexiness before. Brody was magnificent. He *is* magnificent.

I stand off to the side while Brody gently chastises the kayakers for doing something as stupid as running Gorilla without proper precautions. He explains something about why the original guy with the rope shouldn't have thrown the rope bag from where he was standing, encourages all of them to take a swift water rescue class before *ever* kayaking the narrows again, then sends them on their merry way.

Or not-so-merry way based on their expressions. They seem to realize how lucky they were that Brody just happened to be nearby.

"You okay?" Brody asks me once we're alone again.

I am not okay. I am . . . overwhelmed. Buzzed on adrenaline and, let's be totally honest here, *desire.*

It's the only explanation for what I do next.

I lunge across the trail, curl my hand around his neck, and kiss Brody Hawthorne right on the mouth.

I'm not talking a *hooray, you saved someone* kiss. I'm talking a *kiss* kiss. My hands on either side of his face, my lips pressed against his.

At first, he doesn't react—maybe he's too stunned—but then he wakes up, his lips moving against mine as he wraps his arms around me. I might have started the kiss, but I feel the moment he takes control of the situation. He keeps one hand pressed to the small of my back while he lifts the other to my face. His fingers stroke my cheek as he deepens the kiss, tasting me, tilting me toward him. My hands slide over his shoulders, then down to his biceps. When I slip my hands under the sleeves of his t-shirt, he lets out a low groan and pulls me even closer.

That noise—it sends a bolt of fear crashing right through me. There is a fervency to his response, a depth I didn't anticipate—

What am I doing?

I break the kiss and step back. "Oh my gosh," I whisper. "Oh my gosh, oh my gosh, oh my gosh." My hand flies to my mouth, and I shake my head.

I take one giant breath and look up to meet Brody's gaze. His eyes are wide, his chest heaving.

"Brody, I shouldn't have done that."

Chapter Eighteen

Brody

In all the times I have imagined my first kiss with Kate, I have never come close to imagining what actually happened.

First of all, Kate kissed *me*. Surprised me.

Maybe because I've been the one in love with her for so long, I always thought it would be the other way around. I would kiss her, wake up her feelings, show her what she's been missing all these years.

Instead, she's the one who woke me up. In the brief moments when her lips were on mine, my world switched from monochrome to full, blinding technicolor.

She's shaking her head and backing away, but I don't know how I'm supposed to go back after this. It was too fast. I didn't have time to truly process . . . and now it might not ever happen again.

"I just . . . you were so amazing with the rope and the guy," Kate says, "and I . . . I don't know what I was thinking. I got caught up in the moment."

"Kate," I say softly, reaching for her.

"I'm sorry." She takes another step back. "I'm really, really—"

"Kate."

"Sorry," she finishes, her voice a whisper.

"Please stop apologizing."

"But I shouldn't have done it. I mean, I wanted to do it. But I shouldn't have wanted to do it. It isn't fair. Especially not to you."

I pause at this. *Especially* not to me? "Why isn't it fair?" I ask. "If I told you I'm glad you kissed me, will that change what you're saying right now?"

She closes her eyes, her lips pressed together, her breathing ragged.

"Kate, just talk to me."

When she opens her eyes, there's a storm raging behind them. "I've been offered a job," she says simply. "That was the email I got right after we finished kayaking. It was a job offer. And it's in London."

All the air whooshes out of my lungs. Even knowing it would come to this—to her leaving—it's still a gut punch to hear her say it. It's too early for us to already be having this conversation. "A job?"

She nods and eases away, and for once, I'm grateful for the distance. I need space. Air. Clarity.

"A real one," she says. "Not freelance work. Salary, benefits, all of it."

I channel my inner calm. The deepest part of my love for Kate wants only what is best for Kate. Even if it sucks for me. "That's . . . wow. That's great."

"I didn't even apply for it. Didn't expect it. It's with this travel magazine called *Expedition*. They're flying me out next week for a meeting."

"Next week?"

"Just for a few days. I leave on the fifth."

As my heart rate slows, my grip on reality returns, and I remember the things a friend would say in this situation.

True, *friends* wouldn't have been kissing two minutes ago, but Kate already labeled the kiss a mistake. I don't have any choice but to get on board. "That's really amazing," I say. I clear my throat and swallow. "Really."

She bites her lip. "Even though it's in London?"

There is uncertainty in her eyes. Does she want me to care? Does she want me to tell her to stay instead? Or is she simply worried about hurting me when she leaves again?

I . . . do not have the bandwidth to figure this out. My brain is too full of her, my body too charged from the kiss.

I turn from Kate and walk a few steps away, my hands resting on top of my head. I shouldn't feel so stunned. Except, Kate leaving to settle down somewhere else feels different than Kate just *leaving*. If she's willing to put down roots, why not put them down here? This doesn't feel like incompatible lifestyles, this feels like rejection.

"I still don't know if I'm going to take it," she says from behind me. "I'm not sure about living in London, but I do love the idea of something more stable. I never even thought that was an option for me, so I feel like I have to at least consider it."

I should turn around. Say something. Be the best friend she needs me to be. I would love for her to have something stable. To have the opportunity to truly settle down if that's what she wants.

A sharp pain snakes across my chest. Even if it isn't with me.

"I shouldn't have kissed you, Brody. Not when I don't know what I'm doing, when we don't know—"

Her words crack and tremble.

I have to dig deep to find what little composure I have left, but

I slip it into place and turn around, moving back to where she's standing. I reach for her hand and pull her toward me, wrapping her into a hug that I hope feels brotherly. "You're right," I say into her hair. "It isn't fair. But you have to live your life, Kate. If this is something you want, you have to go for it."

She tilts her head up, her arms still wrapped around me. "But what if I don't know what I want? What if all I feel is confusion?"

"You've always figured things out before, right?" I drop my arms and step away from her. I can't keep touching her. Not if I'm going to get out of the gorge and back to the truck without completely losing it. I move toward the trail, and Kate follows. "Do you like London?"

She shrugs. "I guess so. I don't love the cold. Or the rain. But I like the people. And I really like the editor who offered the position."

I cock my head. "I'm not sure London is the place for you if you don't like the cold. I was cold the last time I was there, and it was July."

Her eyebrows jump. "You've been to London?"

"Twice. I did a semester abroad in school. England, France, and Italy."

"Oh, that's right. I'd forgotten about that."

"Then I went back with Griffin and a couple other guys last summer to do some kayaking. We were mostly in Wales, but we flew into London."

She studies me, her eyebrows knit together, her expression saying the idea of me traveling outside of Silver Creek is a foreign concept. "Have you traveled anywhere else?" she asks, confirming my suspicion.

"That's it outside the US. But I've been all over the states."

"To kayak?"

I nod. "Oh, and Costa Rica, too. Last spring break."

"But you . . ." Her words trail off, and she shakes her head.

"But I what?"

"Nothing. It's nothing. I'm just glad you've gotten to travel some."

I shoot her a knowing look. "It's pretty tough seeing as how I have to use horse and wagon to go places, living in this here small town. We don't have things like cars. Or airports."

She rolls her eyes. "Shut up. That's not what I meant."

"Yes it is," I say. "You look at me and think small town, small life."

"I do not."

I raise my eyebrows.

"At least, I don't *now,*" she says. "There's nothing about your life that's small."

We turn and move up the trail, both of us grabbing hold of the rope that will make it easier to haul ourselves up the mountain. Kate is walking in front of me, so I can't see her face when I ask, "But it's still too small for you?"

We climb in silence for a few minutes, and I wonder if Kate will simply let the question go. But as soon as we reach a level spot, she turns to me. "I never imagined a life for myself in Silver Creek, Brody. You know it's never been a part of the plan."

"Why?" It's the first time I've ever challenged her on it. "Because you don't want to be near your mom? That doesn't work anymore, Kate. She left."

She shakes her head, emotion filling her eyes. "Because I don't want to *be* my mom. She wasn't willing to leave, and it ended her marriage." She turns and pushes her way up the trail, the muscles in her arms and shoulders flexing as she grips the rope and tugs herself up. I am momentarily distracted by the grace and athleticism that infuse her movements. She makes everything look natural, even hoisting herself up the side of a mountain.

I climb after her, quickly catching up. "Kate, you aren't your mother. You're never going to be your mother."

She whirls around. "It's more complicated than that. It will always be more complicated for me, because I'm the one with the screwed up family. I recognize it isn't healthy that my feelings about Silver Creek and my feelings about my mom are so tangled. I do. Just . . ." She breathes out a weary sigh. "Just know I'm trying, okay? I'm trying to make sense of things, but most of the time, I can't tell the difference between what I want, and what I *think* I should want, and what I think I can't want because it's what my mother wants."

I almost ask her what category I'm in, but I'm afraid her answer will be none of them. And after that kiss, I don't know that I could handle the blatant rejection.

We hike the rest of the trail in silence. Her brain is probably whirring just as fast as mine is, but what is there to say? Even with all the chemistry sparking between us the past few weeks, I've been afraid to truly let myself hope, convinced she'd never feel the same way.

Now, it's possible she does feel the same way—she at least owned that she wanted to kiss me—and I still can't do anything about it. I'm not sure if this is better or worse.

When we get back to the truck, I unlock her door first and open it for her.

She hesitates, one foot propped on the running board, and looks back. "I don't have to go with you to Robbinsville on Saturday."

Fear tightens my gut. I don't want our relationship to end over this. "Do you still *want* to go?"

"I'd like to. But I don't want to make it hard for you."

It's too late for that, but right now, the only thing that feels harder than spending time with Kate is spending time without her. "Kate, we're still friends. This doesn't have to change that."

"So I can come on Saturday as your friend?"

"I invited you to come as my friend." We've used that word so much lately, I'd like to retire it altogether. *Please* no more friend talk. I smile, sensing that levity might be the only thing that pulls us out of whatever tailspin her kiss started. "You're the one who kissed me and made things weird."

She scoffs as she climbs all the way into the truck. "So that's how you're going to play it?"

I smirk and move around the truck bed to climb in. Once I crank the engine, I look at Kate and slip on my sunglasses. "I hope that kiss was worth it because I plan to get mileage out of this thing for *days*."

Kate smiles and shakes her head, huffing out a laugh, and suddenly we're back on solid ground.

At least for now.

At least until I can drop her off.

I can pretend that long. I can joke and tease. Act like one, amazing, life-changing kiss wasn't enough to rip my heart out and place it directly in her hands.

But the reality is, with that kiss, Kate changed me. Claimed me.

I'll never be the same again.

My only hope now is that somehow, she'll reach the same conclusion. One kiss will never be enough.

Chapter Nineteen

Kate

KRISTYN HAS CALLED ME four times in the past three days.

And I have been "too busy to talk" all four times because Kristyn will want to ask me about what's happening with Brody.

I am not ready to talk about what's happening with Brody. Or tell her I'm technically supposed to fly to London tomorrow, though honestly, the thought of bailing has been jumping into my brain with surprising frequency lately.

In between my trips to Hendersonville to visit appliance stores and pick out tile and countertops for the kitchen, I have seen Brody twice since our hike along the narrows. Once when he took me kayaking, and once when he brought by a basket of goat's milk soap his mom put together for me. Both times, we did not talk about the kiss, and we did not talk about London, but Brody did give me long, lingering hugs that made me question everything I know about life. I don't know what those hugs mean, especially after how we left things last weekend. But I know how they make me feel, and I do not want them to stop.

When Kristyn texted last night, she threatened to call Brody herself if I didn't respond with an update.

I still haven't responded, but she wouldn't *actually* call.

Okay, fine. She totally would. But how would I even begin to share everything that has happened?

I sigh and tap my phone against my knee. If I respond right now, she probably won't get my text until I'm on my way to Robbinsville with Brody. I for sure won't be able to have a conversation *about* Brody while he's close enough to listen, which means I'll be able to delay the conversation at least another twenty-four hours.

I key out my message.

Kate: Hey! Sorry to have missed you so many times. Ha. She'll see right through that one. *I've been really busy. I'll give you an update soon!*

There. Vague but cheerful. I hit send and move to drop my phone into my backpack, but it immediately starts to ring, Kristyn's face lighting up the screen.

I swear under my breath, then answer the call. "Are you serious? What are you even doing up right now?"

"I'm a teacher," Kristyn responds. "My internal clock wakes me up whether I'm working or not. What are *you* doing up?"

"I'm waiting for Brody to pick me up."

"What? This early? Why?"

I lean back into the front-porch rocking chair and pull my knees up to my chest. "He's kayaking with his friends today, and I'm their shuttle bunny."

"Ummm, what?"

"A shuttle bunny. It means I'm driving with them over to Robbinsville so I can drop them off at the top of the rapids, then drive down and meet them at the bottom."

"Aww, how cute. And sexist."

"How is it sexist?"

"Do you think they'd call their shuttle driver a 'bunny' if you were a six-foot-four biker covered in tats?"

"Please don't ever call them *tats* again."

"I'm just saying. You're a bunny because you're a cute little girlfriend driving the big strong men to do their big strong activity."

I huff and shift the phone from one ear to the other. "You literally just sucked all the fun out of my day. And I'm not anyone's girlfriend."

She finally laughs. "Then ignore me. But the urban dictionary says to be the best kind of shuttle bunny, you should have beer on hand when you pick them up at the end of the day."

"Did you seriously just consult the urban dictionary?"

"I teach seventh graders," she says. "If I didn't consult the urban dictionary on a regular basis, I'd never survive. So are you going to give me an update or what?"

"I have no idea what update to give you. I'm making progress on the house. Most of the junk is cleared out except for what I'm saving for Mom and keeping for myself. I just ordered new appliances and countertops for the kitchen—it was desperately in need of an update—and most of the old furniture I can't use for staging the house has been picked up and hauled away."

"Wow. But how do you know anything about staging a house?"

"I don't. But Freemont does. And so does the internet. Me and YouTube have been best friends the past few days."

Kristyn sighs like I'm trying her patience. "I'm glad things are coming along, but you know that's not really the update I want, right?"

"We're friends, Kristyn."

"Have you kissed him yet?"

"*Friends*," I repeat.

"Have you *wanted* to kiss him yet?"

There is no way I'm telling her about our kiss. Kisses fueled by witnessing acts of heroism do not count. Especially when those kisses come very close to ruining a friendship nineteen years in the making. "Uggh, do you even realize what you're asking? Do you know what it would do to our friendship?" I ask, making at least half my point.

"Absolutely. It would make it *so. much. hotter.*" She has no idea how right she is about this one.

Headlights flash at the end of the road, and I breathe a sigh of relief.

"Hey, Brody is here. I gotta go."

"No!" she says. "You still haven't told me anything good!"

"That's because there's nothing to tell. I promise as soon as there is, you'll be the first person I call."

I hang up and move to the steps as Brody pulls into the circle drive in front of the house. I climb into his truck, where I am assaulted in the best way possible with the same clean manly smell I encountered when I found Brody fresh out of the shower, locked out of his house. Brody's hair is still damp, his t-shirt dotted with water like he tossed it on before he was fully dry.

"Hi," I say on an exhale as I settle back into my seat.

"Hey," he says. "Thanks again for doing this."

I smile. "Of course. I'm excited." Our interactions since last weekend have been brief, so I anticipate some sort of weirdness between us, but as Brody gives me a rundown of how the day is going to go, I start to relax. This doesn't feel weird at all. It feels like us.

My responsibilities aren't very complicated. For most of the day, I'll just be tagging along. The only time I really have to do anything is when they're on the water, and that can take as little or as long as I want as long as I'm at the take-out when they finish.

"Got it," I say after his explanation. "So, will I drive the whole way? Or . . ."

"Nah. Not unless you just want to. Griffin will drive on the way there, and you can ride in the back with me. Then you'll hop in and drive once we're on the water. I'm gonna warn you though. Griffin's Suburban smells like a locker room. There's wet gear going in and out all the time, and it can get a little musty."

"I can handle musty." And will do so gladly if it means two hours in the backseat with Brody, even though that's *not* something I should be excited about. At least we won't be alone. The car will be full of other men.

Turns out, we *are* kind of alone. Squeezed into the third row of Griffin's Suburban because Ryan brought a friend at the last minute.

A *woman* friend, Aislynn, who is perfectly comfortable putting her hands *all. over. Ryan* despite the full car. The way she's dressed, it looks like she'll be kayaking too. Which, more power to her. If I had the experience and skill, I'd want to be joining in as well. But all the *touching*. We haven't even been driving ten minutes, and she's kissed him half a dozen times already. When I shoot Brody a questioning look, he pulls out his cell phone.

Brody: I can't be mad at the guy. He doesn't date much, so this is a pretty big deal for him.

Kate: Check his body language though. I'm not so sure he's down with all the PDA.

His eyes dart to the seat in front of us, and I follow his gaze, watching as Ryan extricates himself from one of Aislynn's side-arm hugs. Brody stifles a laugh, but he doesn't do a very good job, the noise coming out of his nose in an awkward snort. He presses his lips together and looks back at his phone, but not before Aislynn shoots a look over the back seat. Except, her look isn't directed at Brody, it's directed at me, and she is clearly saying *this man belongs to me.*

My eyes widen. She thinks I might go after *Ryan*? The thought is only made more ridiculous by Brody sitting next to me. If there is any man in this car I'm going after, it's him.

My phone buzzes with another text.

Brody: She's staking her claim, temptress. You better not glance Ryan's way today.

Kate: Temptress?! I am nothing of the sort.

Brody: I hate to break it to you, but you only have to stand there to be tempting. You could have the whole car completely at your mercy if you wished it. Minus AJ, of course.

AJ, the fourth kayaker in the group, has a wife and twin daughters at home.

I type out my next message, emboldened by Brody's flirting.

Maybe this part of today *does* feel different. We've always been close. He's always been attentive. But Brody has never flirted like this.

I know. *I know*. This is exactly the opposite of what I'm supposed to be doing. But he started it. And have I mentioned how good he smells? Or how good he looks today? I'm beginning to feel like resistance is futile.

Kate: The whole car? Even you?

Brody looks up from his phone and levels me with a look that can only be called a smolder.

Like, an actual, straight out of the urban dictionary *smolder*.

Brody: I might be the last to fall. But only because I have years of experience resisting.

Resisting. Resisting me? And for years?

I don't look up from my phone for a long moment. Is he trying to tell me something? Has he . . . for me . . . for years?

There were a few times growing up when I suspected Brody might have real feelings for me. More than friendship feelings. But there were so many opportunities for him to tell me, and he never did. Brody was always so good at talking about things, the fact that he didn't convinced me I'd made everything up.

Griffin calls something over his shoulder, and Brody leans forward, slipping his phone into his pocket and joining the conversation about the best rapids this side of the Mississippi. Or something like that. I don't know enough to truly follow along, and I'm too distracted anyway.

I lean my head against the back of the seat and close my eyes, thoughts running through my head a million miles a minute. Brody could have been teasing. Joking about how long we've known each other. Playing into Aislynn's erroneous assumption that I'm some sort of temptress trying to get her man.

Keeping my eyes closed, I do a breathing exercise to try and slow my thoughts. Stressing about the unknown isn't going to help me figure things out. Whatever happens next, it will be easier to sort through with a clear head.

After a few minutes of intentional breathing, the ridiculous hour I went to bed last night catches up with me, and I start to doze. I'm jolted awake when the Suburban hits a bump in the highway, only to feel Brody's arms around me, guiding me toward him. He's angled sideways, his back against the window, and . . . now I'm lying on his chest, my arms wrapped around his torso because there is nowhere else for them to go. His arms close around my back, one hand rubbing up and down over my shoulder blades as if to soothe me back to sleep.

Despite the heat coursing through me at his touch, it actually starts to work, and I sink into him.

Take that, Aislynn, I think, hovering on the edge of consciousness. *I have my own man.*

The thing is, I *don't* have years of experience resisting Brody. I feel almost powerless against whatever this is, this force that is drawing me to him. And the longer I'm around him, the more I'm realizing, I don't really *want* to resist. I *should* want to. There's so much at stake. So much to lose if things go badly. Even if I wanted to stay in Silver Creek, I don't know that I could. That I could find work enough to sustain me. But right here, right now, his arms around me, the sound of his steady heartbeat thumping under my ear, I can't bring myself to care about any of that. I want to stay here forever. *I want . . .*

"Hey," Brody whispers. "Wake up. We're here."

I shift, untangling my arms from around him, and sit up. Everyone else has already gotten out of the Suburban. I yawn and stretch my arms over my head. "Wow. I didn't realize I was so tired." I glance at his t-shirt, hoping I didn't drool on him while I slept.

He grins and leans forward, folding up the seat in front of him so we can reach the door. "I promise I didn't mind."

He didn't mind . . . holding me in his arms? I'm suddenly *very* awake. And a little turned on.

"So what happens now?" I ask as I climb out after him.

"We gear up and hit the water."

The rest of the guys are already unloading kayaks and paddles off the trailer. Brody moves to the back of the Suburban and opens the hatch where spray skirts, helmets, PFDs, and other gear has been stashed. Leaving the hatch open, he grabs his bag, then steps off to the side where he drops his stuff and pulls his t-shirt over his head.

He should have warned me. Held up a big sign that says *KATE: BRACE YOURSELF FOR THE VIEW.* Because *good grief* the view is spectacular. I mean, *yes,* I've seen all this before. And a warning would have helped then, too.

Brody is not muscled like someone who spends hours and hours working the same muscle groups in the gym. He is not the kind of guy who can't rest his arms against his sides for how enormous his biceps are. He's muscled like an athlete—like someone who uses his muscles outside the gym. He is lean and lithe, with the perfect amount of definition in all the right places. I particularly appreciate the line of his shoulder curving into his bicep—

Oh my word now his shorts are coming off. He's got compression shorts on underneath, but *still.* He quickly pulls on a pair of board shorts and a long-sleeved rash guard, then slips on a pair of bootie-looking things that must be specific for kayaking because all the guys are wearing them. Aislynn steps out from behind the Suburban wearing a dry suit, her spray skirt already hanging from her waist.

She looks very serious about her sport. She holds her paddle in one hand and taps it against the ground. "Let's do this, men," she says as she walks toward the kayaks. "Ryan, you're with me."

I look at Brody, my lips pressed together to keep from laughing.

His eyes are dancing as he mouths the word, "*temptress.*"

I bark out a laugh, my hand flying up to cover my mouth.

Griffin walks over to give me the keys. "So, if you take this road downriver about five miles, you'll see the take-out just past Tapoco Lodge. The river is pretty much roadside the whole way, so if you want to watch, you can drive ahead and watch us coming. There are multiple places you can stop the whole way down."

"Got it."

I take the keys and make my way over to Brody who is securing his PFD. His helmet is at his feet, and I pick it up, holding it until he's ready to pull it on. "Have fun out there," I say. "But be careful too, yeah?" A surge of anxiety pulses through me. The feeling is foreign and a little overwhelming. I really don't want Brody to get hurt.

He reaches for his helmet, his gaze searing into me like it always does. "I'll be careful," he says, his tone serious enough that I know he isn't mocking my concern. He gently tugs his helmet out of my hands. "I promise."

I take a step back and push my hands into the back pockets of my shorts. "Okay. I'll be watching as much as I can."

He pulls his helmet on. "You be careful too, all right?"

I watch from the shore as the group moves downriver, my eyes on Brody the entire time.

Be careful? My heart tugs and pulls. We blew past careful the first time we kissed. I can only hope we aren't heading for a crash.

Chapter Twenty

Kate

JUST AS GRIFFIN TOLD me, there are multiple places along the road where I'm able to pull over and watch the kayakers move downriver.

The feeling of watching Brody paddle through rapids that look like they could swallow him whole is difficult to describe. It's thrilling to see a display of his talent and skill, but it's also terrifying. I am an adventurer at heart and have a long list of risky activities filling my resume. Sky diving, cave diving, ice climbing. I even ran with the bulls in Pamplona. I shouldn't be worried about something I know Brody is qualified to do.

But I can't stop running scenarios through my head of things that might go wrong. I feel like I've only just gotten Brody back. What if I were to lose him again?

It isn't a rational thought. Not even a little bit rational.

I still can't chase it out of my brain. It's not that I don't *want* him to do it. But I am hyper-focused on his safety. I don't think I'll actually take a full breath until he's out of the water again.

The last stretch of rapids runs right behind a lodge where a dining area and patio sit at the water's edge. I contemplate getting a table, but I'm too anxious to eat, and the place looks busy. I don't want to waste a table while others are waiting. Instead, I find a blanket in the back of the Suburban and spread it out on the grass where I'll have a good view of the kayakers as they approach.

Based on what Griffin projected before they left, I have another half hour before they make it downriver, so I kill time by reading through articles and online information about the Green Race. The editor I emailed at *Southern Traditions and Travel* expressed mild interest in a piece and asked me to send it over after I've attended and have something written up. But they weren't interested enough to offer me an advance. I still haven't found an angle, but that probably won't come until I've been to the race myself. I keep hoping something in my research will jump out at me. But so far, I haven't felt that tingle up my spine that tells me I'm on to the right story.

As I scroll through my Google search, my eyes catch on Brody's name, published in the newspaper one town over from Silver Creek. The town is still in the same school district, so I shouldn't be surprised to open the link and find a letter to the editor from yesterday's newspaper talking about last week's school board meeting.

The more I read, the angrier I get. This person's summary of Brody's remarks is so heavily biased, it almost feels like slander. I'm surprised the paper even ran it. Words have so much power, and whoever wrote this letter is doing their level best to use that power to shut Brody's program down.

I pause.

That's it.

Words *do* have power. And words are one thing I know I do well.

There's the spine tingle I've been missing. I've been looking for a story, and I've had one in front of me this whole time. I don't need to write about the Green Race. At least not yet. I need to write about Brody's whitewater kayaking program at Green River Academy.

It'll be a slightly harder sell getting a national publication interested in something that's so local. But if I broaden the scope a little bit, pull in the inherent risk involved in *all* school sports, maybe mention other outdoor experiential learning-based schools . . .

But that won't feel like travel writing. It will feel more like investigative journalism.

I bite my lip. I'm not sure I have the chops for it.

But I have to do something. Worst case scenario, I take whatever I write to the newspapers in Silver Creek, Saluda, Hendersonville, maybe even Asheville, and ask them to run it for free. I would love to do more, to generate some national attention on how beneficial programs like Brody's can be. A huge flux of positive national press attention would stomp out measly letters to the editor like this one in a second.

My mind starts racing with everything I'll need to do. I'll need to talk to some students who are in the whitewater kayaking program now. Or at least *were* at the end of the school year. Some students who have already graduated and moved on would also be great. Brody's principal—I think I saw him at the school board meeting. Griffin. Brody himself, obviously, but a part of me wants to do this without him knowing. I don't want to give him false hope. And it might be fun to make it a surprise.

A flash of red in the distance immediately ends my planning.

Brody's in a red kayak.

I stand up, hands on my hips as I watch the kayaker approach. It *is* Brody. I recognize the shirt he put on before he left. I take a few steps closer to the water, my heart racing as he nears the final rapid. I've seen a few other kayakers navigate this particular stretch, but it didn't feel like this.

My heart jumps into my throat when, at the base of the rapid, Brody's kayak spins and flips. But then seconds later he rolls back to the surface—I cannot imagine the hip action that made that happen—and he's cruising again, his paddling slowing as he approaches the calm section of river where he'll get out of the river.

By the time I reach him, Brody is already out of his kayak, pulling it onto the shore. I move forward, driven by some inexplicable need to have my hands on him, to feel him solid and warm and breathing under my touch. He's barely out of his PFD when I plow into him, my arms wrapping around his waist. I don't even care that he's wet.

"Whoa, hey." He drops the paddle he still has in one hand so he can hug me back. Awkwardly, since he's still wearing his spray skirt. "You okay?"

"Yes. Sorry. I just . . . I don't know. You just ran some crazy rapids."

"And I'm okay," he says on a chuckle. "Great, actually."

I take another deep breath and take a step back. Whatever she-bear reaction I'm having to the idea of Brody getting hurt needs to chill. He's fine. I'm fine. Everything is totally *fine.* "Did you have a good time?"

The man is actually glowing, his skin flushed, his eyes bright.

"It was awesome," he says. "A little frustrating at first. A couple of beaters put in right before us and slowed us up, but once we got past them, everything was pretty smooth."

"Beaters?"

"Kayakers who don't have the skill to paddle the river they're on. They spend most of their time either swimming or getting beat up."

I wonder if I will ever pick up on all the lingo. "How did Aislynn do?"

Brody's face morphs into something like awe. "Dude. She can paddle. She totally killed it out there."

Despite Kristyn's teasing, I am plenty happy to be filling the role of shuttle bunny if only to see Brody doing something he really loves. But I'm glad Aislynn is here to represent women doing something other than spectating.

The rest of the group is showing up now, laughing and clapping each other on the back, buzzing with the same energy I see in Brody. Even Aislynn offers me a smile. Maybe seeing me cuddle with Brody the whole drive down convinced her I have no intentions of making any sort of move on Ryan.

Once everyone is changed and gear is loaded up, we grab a late lunch at the lodge.

I really like Brody's friends. I like Brody *with* his friends. Griffin is technically boss to two of the guys who are here—Ryan is also an instructor—but it still feels like Brody is the one who sets the tone and steers the conversations. He's the peacekeeper here just like he is in his family. I'm willing to bet he's the same way at his school, too.

"Okay, Kate," Griffin says, leaning toward me. We've all finished eating at this point, but we're sitting on the patio next to the river, and no one seems in much of a hurry to leave. "You know Brody better than all of us. Tell us something we don't know about him."

I study Brody, my lips pursed playfully. There are a million different stories I could tell, but the one with adorable video evidence seems like the obvious place to start. "Has he ever told you he was on the Ellen Degeneres show when he was a kid?" Brody groans.

"What?" Griffin says. "You met Ellen Degeneres? Why?"

"He was on one of her segments highlighting little genius whiz kids or whatever. He was her human calculator."

"Dude, you are good at math," Griffin says. "But you can like, calculate stuff in your head?"

Brody shoots me a look, shaking his head.

I only grin. "Dance, monkey, dance," I say, and he rolls his eyes.

"Give me a math problem," Brody says to Griffin.

"Any math problem?" AJ asks.

"I mean, not *any* math problem," Brody answers. "I can't do calculus in my head. But your basic calculator stuff. Big numbers, small numbers, whatever."

"Seven thousand, six hundred twenty-two divided by sixteen," Ryan says, jumping into the conversation.

"Four . . . hundred seventy-six point three seven five?" Brody says. He made his answer a question, but he's playing it down. He knows he got it right. I've never seen him get one wrong.

"You just made that number up," Griffin says.

Brody chuckles. "Go ahead and use a calculator and check my math."

Aislynn holds up her phone. "He's right. I already checked."

"No way," Griffin says. "And you did this on the Ellen show?"

"And he was adorable doing it," I say, handing over my phone. I already have the video cued up.

Brody shakes his head. "Oh, you're going to pay for this later."

I bite my lip, liking the idea of later no matter how he plans to make me pay.

On the ride home, I lean back into my seat, kicking off my shoes and dropping my feet into Brody's lap. I'm wearing his hoodie—something he insisted on when I complained about being cold—and it smells like him in the best way possible. I feel like I'm snuggled in a Brody cocoon.

I don't really expect to leave my feet in his lap—I'm more trying to tease him than anything—but then he wraps his big hands around my ankles, sliding them down until his thumbs are pressing into the balls of my feet with gentle pressure.

I let out a low moan. "Oh man, I was not asking for a foot rub, but if you're offering . . ."

His lips lift in a soft smile as he shifts both hands to one foot and begins massaging in earnest.

I let out another whimper. "How are you so good at this?" I ask, my eyes falling closed. "And how did I not know you were good at this? Is this something your twenties taught you?"

He shrugs, his hands still on my left foot. "When I was a kid, I used to give my mom foot rubs whenever she spent a long day in the goat barn."

I can't even with this man. I shake my head and let out a laugh. "Are you freaking kidding me right now? Could you be any more perfect?" I drop my head back and close my eyes, draping an arm across them like a pair of oversized sunglasses. "It's not even fair, you know that, right?"

It isn't fair. So much about this situation isn't fair. I've been eating up his attention all day, but do I truly think I can be what Brody needs? I'm supposed to get on an airplane in less than twenty-four hours for a job that's a thousand miles away. How can I be thinking about a London job while simultaneously thinking about making a life with Brody in Silver Creek?

Brody shifts my feet off his lap and opens his arms in invitation, his fingers gesturing me forward.

Fear pulses low and deep, but I don't let myself dwell on it.

I'm so tired of *thinking*.

Worrying.

For once, especially after the day we've just had, I want to lean into whatever this is and see what happens. Maybe it was all the time spent next to a raging river, or the thrill of seeing Brody conquer that river. But suddenly, I *want* to do something reckless.

I want to forget that I'm scared or that people might get hurt.

I want to let myself *feel* without worrying about the consequences.

I shift and lean into Brody, and his arms wrap around me, tugging me close. He tilts his head back and closes his eyes, but his hands never stop moving, tracing feather-light circles on my back. I don't know if he actually sleeps, but by the time we make it to Triple Mountain, fire is pumping through my veins. I am aware of Brody's every movement as he helps unload the kayaks and the rest of the gear. As he shifts his own kayak from Griffin's trailer over to the back of his truck. As he says goodbye to his friends, bro hugs and back slapping all around. Soon, he's driving me home, the air so thick with crackling tension, there's no way he doesn't feel it too.

When he pulls into my driveway, he just sits there, his hands gripping the steering wheel like it's holding him up.

I swallow the ball of nerves pulsing in the back of my throat. "Walk me to my door?"

He closes his eyes, and his jaw tenses, and I almost regret asking. But then he cuts the engine and climbs out. I sit still long enough for him to make it around the truck and open my door for me. I don't expect him to. Normally, I'm out as quickly as he is. But my heart is pounding in my ears, my skin prickling with anticipation, and it's making my movements slow and unsteady.

I climb out of the truck, and we walk side by side up to the porch. I'm halfway up the steps, my keys in my hand, when I realize Brody stopped at the bottom. The evening light is fading fast, and his face is shadowed, so I can't quite make out his expression. "Do you . . . want to come in?"

He lifts his eyes to mine, desire flashing behind them before he runs a hand across his face and sighs. "Are you sure this is what you want, Kate?"

I know what he's asking. I was the one that, only a week ago, said I shouldn't have kissed him because I *didn't* know what I want.

I drop back down a few steps so we're only one stair apart, bringing us eye-level. "I'm tired of resisting, Brody. I'm tired of worrying about our friendship. I'm—"

He lifts a hand to my cheek, his thumb tracing a line over the edge of my bottom lip.

My eyes drift closed.

"Then stop," he says. "Let's stop worrying and see what happens." He leans forward, the tip of his nose brushing against mine. "Do you have any idea how beautiful you are?"

His words sound like a prayer, and they fill me like one, curling into every corner of my heart.

He kisses me softly at first, the pressure light, but that's all it takes for me to explode with desire.

Goose bumps break out across my skin, and heat flows through my veins as my hands lift to his chest. He is warm and solid under my palms, his pulse pounding against my fingers. His free hand wraps around my waist and pulls me closer as he brushes his tongue along my bottom lip. It's an invitation, and one I willingly accept as I tilt my head to deepen the kiss. Somewhere in the distance, July fourth fireworks explode into the night sky, the sound bouncing across the mountains until it reaches us. I have been kissed in a lot of different cities by a lot of different men. But I have never been kissed like this. Soon, even the fireworks fade into silence. I only hear Brody. My name on his lips, his breath as it skates across my skin. I drop my hands to his waist, sliding my fingers under his t-shirt and pressing them against the warm skin at the small of his back. His muscles tense under my touch, and he pulls me even closer.

Slowly, we stumble up the stairs, still kissing as I scramble to get my keys into the front door. I drop them and they clink onto the wooden slats of the porch, but I don't even care. We are wedged in between the storm door and the heavy wooden front door, and I'll happily stay here forever, pinned against the wood with Brody's big body hovering over me.

I watched him do incredible things today. Marveled at his strength, his control, his bravery. And now my hands are on him, sliding over those same muscles, feeling them flex under my touch.

A pulse of desire roars through me, quieting just slightly when Brody breaks the kiss and takes a step back, his hands resting on his hips as his breath comes in ragged gulps. He stands there a good ten seconds before he comes back and bends to retrieve the keys.

He unlocks the door, leaving the keys dangling in the lock while he places his hands on either side of me, just above my shoulders. "I'm only going to kiss you tonight, Kate," he says gently. "I need you to know that." He closes his eyes for a beat and takes another steadying breath. "And I need you to not ask me for more."

I nod, warm relief unfurling in my chest. I wouldn't have asked. But I'm not sure I would have been able to stop, either. Not if *more* was what he wanted.

We might survive the uncertainty of a kiss. Even a thousand kisses. But more than that? *No.* There would be no coming back from that. Not unless we're ready to make a commitment. Unless we know there will never be anyone else.

Brody pushes the door open, and I intertwine my fingers with his, leading him into the living room where we drop our hands so we can both slip off our shoes. He places my keys onto the coffee table, then moves toward me with the grace of a giant jungle cat, agile and smooth. His hands cradle either side of my face, and he kisses me again.

The potency of the attraction that overwhelmed us on the front porch has dimmed to something more tender, but it is no less intoxicating. He sinks onto the couch, pulling me down beside him, his movements measured and intentional. There is nothing frenzied about his kisses, and I recognize this as his way of maintaining control. Of heeding the boundary he's drawn for himself.

My respect for him only grows, tugging my attraction right along with it. Minutes or maybe hours pass. I have no sense of time when I'm in his arms, only a desire to freeze it. To suspend the two of us in this moment forever.

The old mantel clock that sits above Grandma's fireplace sounds the hour, and I count the chimes, my head resting on Brody's chest. He's fully reclined on the couch now, a throw pillow behind his head, and I'm leaning into his arms, wedged in between him and the back of the couch.

"It's midnight," I say softly.

His hand brushes up and down my arm. "I could sleep here," he says lazily. And I hope he does. A part of me senses the magic of whatever is happening will diminish in the daylight, taking us back to a reality full of jobs and families and uncertainty. But I won't dwell on that now. Right now, there is only us. And it's enough.

I lift my head up and prop my chin on Brody's chest, my arms tightening around his waist. "Can I ask you a question?"

His eyes flutter open. "Sure."

"Had you ever thought about kissing me before tonight?"

His hands have been tracing slow circles on my back and they still at my question, his body tensing under me. He is silent so long, I start to think he isn't going to respond. But then he leans up and presses his lips to mine. The yearning in his kiss is so potent, so charged, it nearly takes my breath away. At first, I think it's the only answer he's going to give me. But then he closes his eyes again and folds his hand over mine, pressing my palm to his chest just above his heart. "Every day, Kate," he whispers. "I've thought about kissing you every day."

His words are a live wire to my skin. I take a steadying breath. "Since I got back?"

"Since . . . forever."

Intense longing swells in my chest. I could give in. Let it take over and whisk me away to a world where Brody and I might actually be happy together. But even sharper than the longing is the same visceral fear that's been chasing me all week.

What if I hurt him?

What if I end up leaving?

What if I try to stay, and it doesn't work?

It's easy to imagine all the traveling my work requires driving a wedge between us just like it did my parents. I'm not sure the volatility of my traveling life is something Brody would even want in a relationship. Honestly, it's not something *I* want. Leaving is always easier when there isn't someone you're leaving behind. There are so many uncertainties, so many possible outcomes, and too many of them end with pain. Especially if Brody has had feelings for me all this time.

A few hours ago, I wanted to be reckless. I wanted to *feel*. And for what? Will it have been worth it if it ends up hurting Brody? I could tell he was hesitant to get out of the car. He was probably trying to protect himself. But I pushed for this. I asked him to stay.

Tiny pinpricks of pain explode across my chest.

If I do leave Silver Creek, and odds are pretty good that I will even if I don't take the job in London, tonight will have been a terrible mistake.

It will mean I *used* him. Took advantage of his feelings, and for what? Because I wanted his arms around me? Because I think he's sexy, and I'm impressed with the way he handles a kayak?

I feel the falsity in my words even as I think them. There is so much more to how I feel about Brody than that. But I am also no closer to figuring out what the next chapter of my life is supposed to look like. And until I know, I can't toy with his feelings. I can't risk hurting him worse than I already have.

I fall asleep still curled in Brody's arms and don't wake up until weak sunlight filters through the front windows. I'm alone now, a blanket draped over my shoulders. I don't have to look out the window to know that Brody is gone.

A dull ache fills my heart, radiating outward. I already miss him. But the longer I'm awake, the more I remember. And the more I remember, the more the ache shifts into sharp discomfort.

My phone buzzes beside me, and I look over to find it charging on the console table beside the couch. I didn't plug it in last night, which means Brody must have. Found my charger and left my phone where I would be sure to find it. My heart squeezes behind my too-tight ribs.

There's a text from Brody waiting for me when I pick up my phone.

Brody: Had to go feed Charlie. Call me when you're up? I was thinking I could make us some breakfast. We have a lot to talk about.

Does he remember I'm supposed to fly out today? Does he think I won't go after last night?

Should I not go after last night?

When I'm cocooned in his arms, it's very easy to imagine giving everything up. The London job. All of my traveling. I could just stay here with him. Let him take care of me. But for how long? The novelty of our new relationship will eventually wear off, and then what? I can't *only* be Brody's girlfriend. And I don't know how to be anything else in Silver Creek. If I stayed, could I still be a writer? Could I still be me?

Somewhere in the back of my mind, a tiny hope pulses to life. *You can, Kate. You can make it work.* But the thought only wakes up the fear I can't seem to escape.

I pull the afghan Brody draped over my shoulders a little tighter. It still smells like my grandmother, and tears suddenly pool in my eyes. Grandma Nora was stern, like my mother. She ran a tight household and had high expectations, but her edges were always a little softer than Mom's. No matter the state of things between me and Mom, Grandma Nora always found ways to make sure I knew I was loved.

Then I left her.

I ran away because it was easier than dealing with Mom. Because

I was so terrified of turning into Mom and was too selfish to put anyone else's comfort over my own. Even when Grandma Nora died, and it felt like one of my guiding stars had fizzled out, I still didn't come home.

A fresh wave of shame washes over me.

I am not very good at loving people.

Brody might not realize it yet, but everyone else who is close to him does. That's why Olivia and her mom seem so worried about me being here. His family doesn't trust that I won't hurt him.

I look down at Brody's text. I don't want to hurt him. And I wouldn't. Not on purpose. Never on purpose. But if I can't love him like he deserves, wouldn't that be hurting him too? Brody doesn't deserve to compromise. He shouldn't have to settle.

I pull the afghan off my shoulders and slowly fold it before draping it back over the couch. I'm still wearing Brody's hoodie, and I pull that off, too, placing it on the cushion next to me.

I sit with my hands resting in my lap for a solid twenty minutes. Breathing. Thinking. Soaking up the stillness.

When my thoughts are finally clear, my resolve hardened, I leave my phone on top of Brody's sweatshirt and go upstairs to pack.

Chapter Twenty-One

Brody

IT IS AFTER ELEVEN a.m. when I finally hear from Kate.

At first, I didn't worry. We were up early yesterday. I couldn't fault her a desire to sleep in. But as the morning stretched toward noon, I began to wonder.

Maybe I shouldn't have told her.

Maybe I should have waited.

Maybe asking her to breakfast, suggesting we talk was too forward. Too fast.

But none of that matters now.

I read her text one more time, trying to make sense of what she's telling me.

Kate: Last night was a mistake, Brody. I want to be who you need, but I'm not sure I can ever be the person you deserve. And I love you too much to ruin our friendship by trying to be.

I'm staring at my phone when a second message pops up.

Kate: I'm headed to London for my interview. I hope we can talk soon.

Her interview.

With everything that's happened, I completely forgot she was leaving for London today. I've gotten very good at the mental gymnastics necessary to keep myself from dwelling on what a future with Kate might look like. But when I woke up this morning to the orange-blossom scent of her hair, her body still pressed against mine, I finally stopped fighting. I closed my eyes and let the thoughts come. And they did—like water rushing through the dam at Lake Summit.

A wedding on the farm. Buying a house together. Starting a *life* together. Then ordinary stuff like shopping for groceries. Going on hikes. Planting a garden. I saw us raising a family. Taking the kids up to the farm to ride on the tractor or feed the goats or eat strawberries straight off the plant. I even thought of ways I might adjust my schedule so we could spend summers traveling or living in Europe so Kate could be closer to the parts of the world she's written about most.

Five minutes ago, I thought I would fix her breakfast, tell her I'm in love with her, and ask her to stay.

And now she's gone.

I run a hand through my hair. I have made a colossal mistake.

Monumental.

An earth-shattering, soul-splitting mistake.

Because even if I never see Kate again, she has ruined me for anyone else.

I should have agreed when she said she shouldn't come with me to Robbinsville. I should have arranged for Griffin to do her second kayaking lesson. I should have avoided her. Avoided *this.*

I pace around my kitchen feeling like a bomb about to explode. Perry warned me this would happen, and it didn't even take all summer. Kate's only been around a month, and I'm already here, desperate for her, overwhelmed by the reality of her leaving, furious that she won't stay.

That she won't . . . *choose me.*

I grab the keys to the Gator and push out my back door. I take off down the narrow path that leads to the farm, driving fast enough that I can hear my mother's voice scolding me in my head. When I reach the farm, I keep driving, flying past the farmhouse and out toward the orchards. When I hit the east pasture, I cut right and head into the forest, winding through the trees until I reach the spring-fed creek we used to swim in as kids. But even this doesn't feel like an escape. Kate swam here, too. Everywhere I turn, there's something that reminds me of her.

I need to find my brothers. At least one of them is probably around somewhere.

I turn the Gator around and head toward Lennox's restaurant. Or, *almost* restaurant. Renovations still aren't finished, but Lennox is there most of the time anyway.

I pull to a stop right outside the back door. Would he be here on a Sunday morning? As far as I know, he's still living at Perry's place. If he isn't here, would he be there?

Before I can question further, Lennox appears in the back doorway of the restaurant. He's barefoot and shirtless, wearing a pair of sweatpants and eating a bowl of cereal. His hair is sticking up in so many directions, I have to assume he's only been awake a matter of minutes.

"I thought you might drive straight into the side of the kitchen," he says dryly. "Feeling a little blustery this morning?"

"It's almost noon."

He shifts his bowl to one hand and pulls his phone out of his pocket, glancing at the screen. "So it is." He holds up his bowl. "Cereal?"

For making some of the most incredible food I've ever eaten, when he isn't working, Lennox has a surprisingly simple pallet. Cereal. Fruit. Ham sandwiches.

I shake my head. "What are you doing here? Are you living here?"

"The apartment's empty. So yeah, temporarily. I was tired of living with Perry, and I still haven't found my own place."

"Julien moved out? Did he quit?" Julien has been the catering chef at Stonebrook as long as we've had a commercial kitchen on site.

I finally climb out of the Gator and follow Lennox inside.

"Didn't quit, but he's retiring at the end of the summer. He bought a house on Lake Summit." I follow him up the stairs to the small apartment above the kitchen. "Where were you last night?" he asks. "I thought you might bring Kate."

Kayaking was a convenient excuse to miss the family Fourth of July gathering, but I'm not sure I would have wanted to go regardless. Not with the way everyone has been watching and worrying about me and Kate. "I texted Mom. I was kayaking."

He moves into the kitchen and drops his cereal bowl into the sink. "Sounds like a convenient excuse. Why did you leave early last Sunday?"

I slump onto the couch in the living room. "Olivia was being dumb to Kate."

He sits down on the chair opposite me and leans onto his elbows. "She's worried about you. And based on how you're acting right now, I'd say she's justified."

"I'm fine," I say. "I don't want to talk about it."

"Except you're here, so you clearly want to talk about something." He reaches forward and slaps the side of my knee. "Want me to call Perry? The fence at the back of the east orchard needs some posts replaced. Want to help?"

There are plenty of farmhands at Stonebrook who could handle this sort of thing. But this wouldn't be the first time we've found something to do around the farm just for the sake of doing the work. When we were kids, whenever Dad wanted us to talk, he always found some chore for us to do, said working with our hands made it easier to work out our thoughts.

I sigh. "I could fix a fence."

"Good. Perry was planning on showing up at your place in half an hour anyway. I'll call him and tell him you saved him the trip."

"You were already planning this?"

"How else would I know there's a fence that needs repairing? I don't pay attention to that kind of crap." He disappears into the back room and emerges a minute later wearing jeans and a dark gray t-shirt, a pair of work boots in his hand. The image makes me grin. Lennox created a sleek and shiny existence for himself when he was working in Charlotte. After winning an episode of *Chopped* on Food Network, he turned into something of a local celebrity. He even did a few cooking segments on the morning news. He ate up the attention, his life—and his wardrobe—getting fancier by the minute. But all that glitz and glamour doesn't change the fact that he grew up on a small-town farm, mending fences, feeding baby goats, and fishing in the creek every Sunday afternoon. He might look like he belonged in that fancy life—and maybe he did. But he belongs here too.

He drops into a kitchen chair to put on his boots. I look down at my own shoes. I'm dressed more for working out than I am farm labor, but I'll manage.

"Perry and I worked it all out last night," Lennox finally explains. "You've been dodging our calls, cutting out early on family meals, skipping annual family traditions. We figured somebody had to save you from yourself."

"Why do I feel like I just walked into a trap?"

He grins. "You did. But don't lie to yourself about it. You know you need us, or you wouldn't have come over."

Chapter Twenty-Two

Brody

HALF AN HOUR LATER, the three of us are driving a Stonebrook Farm truck out to the fence at the east edge of the apple orchard that separates the fruit trees from the rolling pastureland where Mom's goats graze. Perry is driving, and Lennox and I are riding in the back with the fence posts, rails, and tools we'll need to replace the rotting posts with new ones.

Perry pulls the truck to a stop, and Lennox tosses me a pair of work gloves. "Let's get to it."

We work in silence for close to half an hour, the sun beating down on our backs. It's nice to feel like I'm doing something productive. This one small thing—fixing a fence line with my brothers—is something I can control. At least for now.

Perry and Lennox don't push me, but I don't miss the looks passing between them.

I finally drop the mallet I'm using to hammer a fence post into the ground and prop my hands on my hips. My brothers stop what they're doing as if sensing I'm finally ready to talk.

I use the back of my wrist to wipe the sweat from my forehead. "I kissed her," I finally say.

My brothers exchange a glance I can't interpret, then look back at me. "Okay?" Lennox says.

"I kissed *Kate,*" I say again. "Last night. Pretty much *all* night."

Lennox frowns as his eyes dart to Perry who is looking unusually . . . smug? Why is he smug?

"And I guess this is a big deal because you've never kissed her before?" Lennox asks dryly.

My brow furrows. "Of course I haven't." Technically, *she* kissed *me* a week ago, but that feels like a minor detail after last night.

"I told you," Perry says. "I *told* you." He reaches out and shoves Lennox, his lips curving in a smile we almost never see. Lennox shoves Perry back, elbowing him in the gut, but it only makes Perry laugh and wrap his arms around Lennox from behind in an attempt to knock him off his feet. The only thing that keeps me from interrupting the scuffle is the fact that Perry seems to be enjoying himself. We haven't seen too many signs of life in Perry the past couple years. It's nice to think he might be waking up.

Then again, he can wake up on his own time, because right now, we're supposed to be talking about me.

I clear my throat. "Can someone please explain what's happening here?"

Lennox gives Perry one more shove before they finally drop their hands and stand next to each other like civilized adults. "Lennox was convinced you and Kate have had more of a friends-with-benefits situation going on."

"What? *No.* Never. We've never—we're just friends. We've only ever been friends."

"Well, right," Lennox says, "but sometimes friends—" He gives his head a shake, like he can't make the words line up in his head. "Are you honestly telling me you've been best friends with someone that hot for all these years, and you've never even kissed her?"

"I told you, man," Perry says. "Brody isn't like you."

Lennox rolls his eyes. "Come on. Every time she shows up, he drops everything for her." He looks at me. "The only time I ever saw you in Charlotte was when she was passing through. And you've never had a serious relationship with anyone else. I mean, I guess I just figured . . ."

"Is that seriously all you think about?" I say. "*Friendship*, Lennox. You should try it sometime. Have a relationship with a woman that doesn't involve sex."

"That's not what my relationships are about. You don't know near as much about me as you think you do. And what, you think I should be more like you? Fall in love with someone who isn't ever going to love me back? Waste *years* waiting for something that's never going to happen?"

Perry holds out a hand. "Hey," he says to Lennox in a voice that sounds so much like Dad, it almost pulls me out of the moment. "That's enough."

I move toward the longer fence rail that will stretch from one post to the next and pick up one end, waiting as Perry moves into position on the other end. "No, he's right," I say bitterly. "I *have* been waiting for something that's never going to happen. Because right after I kissed her, she left for London." We drop the rail into the pre-cut notches on the fence posts, settling it into place.

"Is she coming back?" Lennox asks. "Or is this it? She's just . . . gone again?"

"No idea. I didn't even see her in person. She sent me a text."

"Ohh, ouch," Lennox says. "That can't be a good sign."

"Why London?" Perry asks. "Did she just randomly pick a city, or—?

"Who cares what city she's in? She left. I kissed her, and her reaction was to flee the country."

I'm not really being fair. Kate didn't necessarily *flee*. She went on a trip she's had planned for weeks, for a job interview she told me about. But somehow, after finally admitting my feelings, I hoped things might be different. Kissing Kate sent my brain all the way to *and now I ask you to stay with me so I can love you forever.* But for Kate, the opposite happened.

"I'm just trying to understand her motive," Perry says. "Didn't you say she came home to get her grandmother's house ready to sell? Is that done yet?"

"That's not—" I reach for my phone. "She's not gone for good. She'll come back to finish the house, but that's not the point." I scroll to Kate's latest text and hand Perry my phone. "She made her feelings pretty clear."

Perry tilts the phone so he and Lennox can read her message at the same time.

Lennox winces. "That sucks, man. I'm sorry." He pulls his t-shirt up to wipe the sweat off his forehead, then moves to the next rotten post. I step in beside him, and together we shift it back and forth until the ground around it loosens and it slides free, splintering and breaking apart where the wood is rotten.

Perry hands me my phone while Lennox shovels the broken chunks of wood out of the soil.

"Maybe it's a good thing," Lennox says while he shovels. "Now you know, right? Nothing is ever going to happen between you two, so you can put all this behind you and move on."

"I don't know, man," Perry says. "How was the kiss?"

I shoot him a look. I don't know why he thinks he even needs to ask.

"And she was into it too?"

I think of Kate in my arms, warm and responsive. "It definitely seemed like it."

"I recognize this isn't the advice you expect from me, but . . ." Perry shrugs. "Maybe you shouldn't give up."

I lift an eyebrow. "What?"

"That text message doesn't say she doesn't care about you, Brody. It says she's scared." He gives his head a weary shake. "Listen. I know I'm the last person qualified to give relationship advice. But if my divorce taught me anything, it's that people have to do things for their own reasons."

Lennox's eyes dart to mine. Perry doesn't talk about his divorce. *Ever.*

"Let's say Kate didn't leave for London this morning," Perry says slowly. "Let's say you asked her to stay. For you. To be with you."

He's surprisingly close to exactly the conversation I imagined.

"If she loves you," he continues, "she might have said yes. She might have stayed because staying is what *you* want her to do. And it might have felt good for a while. For months, years even. But trust me, man. You don't want that. If Kate stays in Silver Creek, you want it to be because it's what *she* wants. If it takes her going to London to figure that out? Then let her go."

"But why London?" Lennox repeats the question Perry asked earlier. "Seems kinda far if she's just running scared."

"A job," I say. "She was offered an editing job with a travel magazine. She went to London for an interview."

"Ah," Perry says with a nod. "Then I mean what I said even

more. She's got choices to make, and you can't make them for her."

"You read her text, Perry. She already made her choice. And she didn't choose me."

"But she did say she *wanted* to choose you," Perry says. "That's not nothing."

"So what do I do? Just sit around and wait? It feels like that's all I've ever done for this woman. I'm so tired of waiting."

He shrugs. "Then don't. Only you can decide what's worth it and what isn't."

I grab the post hole digger and thrust it into the dirt, digging with twice the force I actually need. I understand what Perry is saying, but I still feel like Kate didn't just leave, she left *me.* Left without talking to me. Without telling me what's really going on in her head. It feels like she's giving up on something I would fight for no matter what.

Perry's hand falls onto my shoulder, stilling my frantic digging. "That's deep enough, man," he says, his tone gentler than normal.

I sigh and step away from the hole, watching as Perry and Lennox lower the new post into the ground.

Once it's in place, Lennox turns to me while Perry shovels dirt back into the hole to cover the base of the post. "All right, hear me out," Lennox says, palms up.

I can already sense where this is going, and odds are very high I will not like it.

"I've got this thing on Thursday night. Back in Charlotte. It's an awards thing, and Kitchen 704 is being honored for a few different things. They want me to be there since I was part of the team when the award was won." He waves his hand dismissively. "Anyway. It'll be long and boring, but the food will be good, and there will be a big party afterward with plenty of women in attendance." He eyes me. "You're tired of waiting around? Maybe you just need to get away for the weekend. Get a little drunk. Find a date or two." He smirks and lifts a shoulder. "Or ten." He glances at Perry. "Actually, you should both come."

Finding any number of dates with Lennox as my wingman sounds like a terrible idea, especially if he thinks plying me with alcohol first is an acceptable strategy. But I might need to go just to support him. "You're getting an award? Why didn't we know about this?"

"The restaurant is getting an award. I'll be mentioned as the head chef on staff when the award was given, but it's a more all-encompassing restaurant thing. The wine list, the food, the ambiance. I'm only going because I feel like it'll be good networking for opening Hawthorne."

"Will it help you find a new catering chef? We're going to need one of those in a few months," Perry says in his droll business voice.

"Yeah, possibly," Lennox says. "A lot of people in the industry go to these things."

"It sounds like Perry has a good reason to go with you then." I toss the post hole digger into the bed of the truck. Perry can go be Lennox's cheerleader. As long as one of us is there, that's good enough. "I hope you guys have fun, but I'm teaching on Thursday."

"You're missing the point," Lennox says. "This isn't about the award or the networking. Not for you, anyway. This is about getting Kate out of your head. And it isn't until Thursday *night*. You can teach and still come."

"Where's Flint right now?" Perry asks. "What if we called him to see if he can come out for it?"

Lennox raises a finger like he's considering. "That's not a bad idea. Flint will draw media attention, and the media will naturally mention why he's there. Might be a subtle way to get people talking about the restaurant without directly piggybacking on Flint's fame."

"Except that's exactly what you'll be doing," I say.

"But it wouldn't look like it," Perry says. "It would look like Flint's just there to support Lennox. If the media also happens to mention Lennox is about to open his own restaurant?"

"Which they will," Lennox says.

Perry nods. "Then what's the harm in that?"

My brothers have more reason to be invested in the success of Lennox's restaurant than I do. I want it to be successful, but they both *need* it to be. The farm is putting up a lot of capital to make it happen, and Lennox's reputation is on the line. "I don't even know if Flint is stateside right now," I say. "Wasn't he filming in Brazil last week?"

"Bolivia," Perry corrects. "But he talked to Mom on Friday. I don't think he's there anymore."

"Here, I'll call him." I pull out my phone. "This is not a complicated question to answer."

Despite his ridiculous schedule, Flint almost always answers when one of us calls. It's advice his agent gave him right after his first movie turned into an overnight sensation. *"Never stop talking to the normal people in your life—the people who aren't famous. They're the only ones who will keep you grounded."*

"Brody!" Flint yells into his phone so loud, I have to move mine away from my ear, and both my older brothers roll their eyes. This is classic Flint. He's been the loudest, brightest star in every room he's ever been in. Even before he was famous.

"Hey. Where are you?"

"Right now? On the beach behind my house in Malibu. Where are you?"

"We're fixing the fence in the east pasture. Me, Perry, and Lennox."

"Oh man," Flint says. "I'm so jealous."

"Yeah, I'm sure you are. How's your suntan?"

"I'm serious. I hate it when you guys are together without me." That, I can actually believe.

"That's why I'm calling. What are you doing Thursday?"

"Good question. Jonie!" he yells into the background to whom I assume is his manager. Or a personal assistant, maybe? "What am I doing Thursday?" he asks.

Even though it's been years, I'm never not surprised by how different my little brother's life is than mine.

"Jonie says I've got a photoshoot thing, but it can be moved," Flint says. "What's going on?"

I put the call on speaker and listen while Lennox fills Flint in. In a matter of minutes, we've made plans to meet in Charlotte for a weekend, just the four of us, in whatever house Flint's entourage can rent for us, which undoubtedly means something enormous and ridiculously expensive.

"But just to be clear," Flint says, "even though we're saying this is to support Lennox, the real reason we're all getting together is so Brody can talk to us about Kate, right?"

I breathe out a sigh. I should have known better than to think Mom or Olivia hadn't already filled him in.

Lennox eyes me, his expression smug, as if challenging me to back out now. "Smart man," he says to Flint.

He knows he has me. I'll go on Thursday. I'll spend the weekend with my brothers. I'll probably tell Flint everything. But it won't change anything.

Kate will still be gone.

I'll still be alone.

I want to believe what Perry said. I want to hope.

But I'm beginning to wonder if the price of that hope is just too high.

Chapter Twenty-Three

Kate

It's rainy in London, and even though it's July, I wish I'd grabbed Brody's hoodie when I left the hotel this morning. Yes, Brody's hoodie. The one he loaned me a couple of days ago on our way home from Robbinsville. Yes, I still have it, and yes, I brought it with me to London, and no, I will not be judged for that fact, thank you very much.

Of course I brought his hoodie with me. The thing smells amazing. Trouble is, now everything else in my suitcase smells amazing too. Honestly, if I could figure out how to bottle *essence of Brody,* I could make millions. I can already picture the advertisements. Half-naked kayakers, rippling muscles, raging whitewater in the background.

Forget journalism. I should go into marketing. Women of the world wouldn't know what hit them.

That's how I'm feeling walking around London enveloped in Brody's scent. No matter where I am or what I'm wearing, I'm thinking of him, which is the exact opposite of what I wanted this trip to be about. I wanted to clear my head; instead, I can't get him out of it.

It doesn't help that every free moment I've had, I've been

working on my article about Brody's whitewater kayaking program. So I'm not just smelling him all the time, I'm also thinking about how amazing he is. Writing about his altruistic heart. The way he cares about each of his students. His dedication to their growth even while making their safety his top priority. Add in the pictures Griffin sent me of Brody kayaking the narrows in last year's Green Race? *Not* thinking about Brody is about as likely as saying no to a drink of water in the middle of the Sahara.

The article is finished now, which is a feat considering how much time I've spent at *Expedition's* offices. But I had to write fast. If this thing is going to matter, it has to be published sooner than later. It sped things along that there is so much scholarly research on experiential education, particularly regarding outdoor experiences and the positive impact these kinds of activities have on student performance.

And Griffin was an absolute lifesaver. With his help, I was able to network with several of Brody's former students, all of whom were happy to share their thoughts about Brody specifically and his program generally. Even the guy I called at two in the morning, not realizing he's stationed at Ramstein Air Force base and is on Central European Time instead of Eastern Time, had positive things to say.

I sent the finished article to James Wylie, an editor with *Beyond*, a national publication based in the US, early this morning. He's published my stuff before, and James has told me more than once he'll always be happy to read anything I send his way.

I'm done for the day at *Expedition,* but I still have two hours to kill before meeting my dad for dinner, and that's long enough for a nap snuggled up in Brody's hoodie.

I know. *I know.* I'm a top-tier hot mess.

I'm also pretty sure I'm in love with him. Sucks for me because loving him and being right for him are not the same thing.

As soon as I knew I'd be in London, I called Dad to see if he could fly over from Paris to meet me. It's been a while since we've had the chance to catch up, and with all the turmoil of the last month or two, I could use his steadying influence.

I cross the street and head toward my hotel, stopping at the corner when my phone rings. My breath catches when I see who's calling. Maybe I've managed to get one thing right, at least.

"Hi, James."

"You've saved me, Kate Fletcher."

I grin. The editor at *Beyond* has never been a guy for small talk. "Saved you?"

"I love the piece you sent over. It's different than what you usually send us, but I like your angle. The way you discuss the concerned parents in a way that makes them *not* seem like idiots even though it's obvious to anyone with a brain that they are, in fact, idiots. Very nuanced."

"Thanks? I think?"

"Did you send this anywhere else?" he asks.

My heart rate ticks up the tiniest bit. "Not yet. I wanted you to see it first."

"Excellent. I want it. We just had to pull our feature—what was that?" he says to someone in the background. "Absolutely no exceptions. There is no criminal charge that we would be okay with. No. As long as there is an active investigation, we aren't publishing anything about his brewery. End of story." His voice comes back on the line. "The nerve of these people," he says, then he sighs. "Where were we?"

"You were telling me you had to pull your feature story? James, what does that mean for me?"

"It means I get to be the hero because you've given me a story to replace the one that just got axed, and you go to press in ten days for our August edition."

I only *just* keep myself from squealing right there in the middle of Gracechurch Street. I had hoped to get something in print by early fall, but even that was going to be a stretch. August is perfect.

"Where are you right now?" James asks. "This is obviously going to get rushed through. Can you email me a list of your sources? And whomever we need to contact about printing these photos. They look professional."

"I'm in London, but I'll be stateside by tomorrow night. And I can send all of that to you right now." Assuming Griffin knows who took the Green Race photos. Or at least knows someone else who knows.

"Right *now,* right now," James says. "In the next five minutes, if you can swing it. Can you vouch for all your personal sources?"

"Yes. Absolutely. I swear they're all legit. And I'll email over links to the research I cited as well as the transcript of the interview I had with the professor at Western Carolina University."

That phone call was a shot in the dark, but it turned out to be hugely beneficial to get the perspective of someone who has made a career out of researching effective teaching methods.

"I owe you one, Kate," James says.

"Let's call it even. You have no idea what it means that you're getting this published so fast."

"Hmm," he says. "This kayaker in North Carolina. He mean something to you?"

"Off the record?"

"It isn't going to change my mind if that's what you're asking. Desperate times, and all that."

"He's a close friend," I say. "I don't want to see his program shut down, so I'm trying to get him a little bit of positive press."

"This should do it," James says. "It's good writing. Send me the address of wherever you'll be tomorrow, and I'll overnight the proofs."

We end the call just as I reach the front door of the boutique hotel *Expedition* booked for me. For a moment, I consider calling Brody to tell him about the article, but I'll be back in Silver Creek tomorrow night, and by then I'll have the proofs. Not that he'll want to see me. He never did respond to my text. But why would he? I don't deserve a reply.

My dad meets me in a corner bistro right down the street from my hotel. He stands when I approach and pulls me into a big hug. "How are you, Katie? You look good. Really good."

With Dad's arms around me, the tightness in my chest loosens. It's good that I'm here. No one understands my lifestyle better than Dad, because it's always been his too.

We settle into a corner booth where he gives me an update on where he's been and what he's up to. "I'm over the entire European division now," he says. "It's a big deal."

"Still a lot of traveling?"

His shoulders lift and he grins, but there's an emptiness in his expression I've never noticed before. "You know me. Always going somewhere."

There are deep hollows under Dad's eyes. His hair is thinning, his skin a little looser than it was the last time I saw him. For the first time, he looks *older*. "Dad, are you seeing anyone?"

His eyebrows lift. "What, like dating?"

"Yeah. Or just, I don't know. Do you have friends?"

The question came out of the blue. But it's suddenly very important that I know.

Dad waves his hand dismissively. "Ah, Katie. You know I don't have time for stuff like that."

I have always felt a certain camaraderie with my dad. We're the world travelers. The ones Mom never understood. I'm not like her. I'm not small towns and boring routines. I'm like Dad. An adventurer. A free spirit.

And alone.

Tears prick my eyes, and Dad's face falls. "Hey, hey, what's going on?"

I shake my head quickly and use my napkin to dry my eyes.

"Is this about the job? How did your meeting go with them yesterday?"

"It's not that. The meeting was great. They like me, they like my work. And I like all of them, too. If I want the job, they would love for me to start as soon as possible."

"Well, that's good news, isn't it?"

"*If* I want the job."

He takes a slow, deep breath. "And you maybe don't?"

I lift one shoulder in a half-hearted shrug.

Dad takes a deep breath. "Why don't we start at the beginning?"

Chapter Twenty-Four

Kate

I TAKE DAD ALL the way back to my last writing gig in Ireland—to the itchiness I felt there and how it made me more willing to say yes when Mom told me she was selling Grandma Nora's house and needed my help sorting through everything in it. I tell him about how untethered I feel whenever I think about traveling, and how much it's made me question whether I want to keep doing what I'm doing.

Then I tell him about Brody. *Everything* about Brody. Including our kisses and how confusing it is to feel things I've never felt before.

He looks on with kind, patient eyes, nodding in all the right places, not saying a word until I've said everything I could possibly say on the subject.

When dad finally speaks, his tone is gentle. "You've always been a woman to go after what you want. If this man is it, go be with him."

I shake my head. "But it isn't that simple. His life is in Silver Creek."

He winces. "I did always think you were meant for bigger things than that small town. But men have done less for love.

If you're supposed to be together, maybe he'll move to London with you."

The wrongness of the idea is as potent as it is immediate. I would never ask Brody to leave Silver Creek. I can't imagine him living anywhere else, with or without me. "I don't even know if I want the London job, Dad. The only reason I considered it is because I loved the idea of having a steady paycheck. I'm tired of the grind, you know? And freelancing is never *not* a grind."

"So find a different steady paycheck," he says. "Do you want to work for me? I could find a place for you, I'm sure."

I can't keep my face from scrunching up at the thought. There's no way I would ever fit in Dad's business suit world. That's not the life for me anymore than London is the life for Brody.

Dad chuckles. "Okay, let's strike that option from the list."

"Sorry. I promise it isn't personal."

"What about another editing job?" he says. "There are other magazines just like *Expedition.* And they aren't all based in London."

"Dad, I have zero qualifications. I can't just apply to be an editor when I don't even have a bachelor's degree."

"You're right. It was probably your *zero qualifications* that made *Expedition* offer you a job in the first place. Come on, Kate. You're scrappy. You want an editing job? Get yourself one. You know writers and editors all over the world. Network. Make it happen for yourself."

His advice is surprisingly simple. It also feels impossible. In my head, *Expedition*'s job offer has always been more of an outlier. It's never been something I'm qualified for. At least not on paper. The job offer was dumb luck. A one-off. But maybe he's right. Maybe . . . I could try.

"Now, you probably won't find an editing job in little old Silver Creek," Dad says with a condescending chuckle.

I am immediately defensive, and the feeling surprises me. What does he know about Silver Creek?

Then again, Mom's too-deep roots in her hometown played a part in ending his marriage, so maybe I can't blame him.

"I know you have reasons to hate that town, but it really isn't so bad. There are a lot of good people there."

"I don't hate Silver Creek, Kate. I enjoyed living there." He reaches over and squeezes my hand. "But the world is so big, honey. I want you to have it all, and I'm not sure you'll ever find it there."

Have it all? And what, be alone just like him?

It's always been exactly what I wanted, but somehow I never truly processed what it would mean long term. But seeing Brody with his family, his friends, *feeling* what it could be to share a life with him. If I'm choosing, I'm not choosing solitude.

My dad's words replay through my brain, and this time, they catch on something different. I look up. "Did you just say you lived in Silver Creek?"

He nods. "Of course I did."

"What? When?"

"Before the divorce. Just for a year or so. Almost two."

I shift in my seat, suddenly nervous to be talking about my parents' divorce. My dad and I are close, but I was so little when everything happened, it's always been a thing that was behind us. We've never truly talked about it.

"What happened, Dad? Why did you and Mom split up?"

He sighs wearily. "We were just too different people."

I shake my head. "No. That's not good enough. My whole life, Mom has been angry at me. Angry every time I leave town.

Every time I travel to see you. She has resented me. And I've blamed Silver Creek and her ties to a place that was too small for the life you wanted. I decided it was too small for the life I wanted too. But now I'm wondering if there's more to the story."

Dad presses his fingers into his eyes for a long moment before finally bringing his gaze back to me. "Your mother was not angry at you for leaving. She's angry because you *got* to leave when she didn't."

Something shifts in my brain as information tumbles and realigns. "What do you mean?" I need time to catch up, to process what Dad is telling me.

He leans his elbows on the table, a gravity to his expression that says he's about to tell me something he's never told me before. He gives his head a little shake, a sadness passing over his face that makes my heart lurch. "We were living in Atlanta when you were born."

I nod. I know this much, at least.

"About the time I got the promotion that took me to Paris, your grandfather got sick. Sick enough that your Grandma Nora couldn't take care of him on her own. So instead of moving to Paris, all three of us, like we originally planned, we moved to Silver Creek. Bought a house a few doors down from your grandparents. Blue, with white shutters."

A wave of shock rolls through me. That explains the photos of me as a baby on Brody's front porch. I *lived* in Brody's house when I was a baby.

I can't spend time on how weirdly coincidental it is because I'm too hung up on what Dad is telling me. In my head, Mom always *left* Dad so she could live in Silver Creek. Dad living there too doesn't fit.

"Why don't I know this? Why hasn't Mom ever told me?"

There is a heavy sadness in Dad's eyes, and he stares into his empty coffee cup for a long time before he finally answers. "It wasn't a happy time for your mother, Kate. I still took the job in Paris. I didn't prioritize our family like I should have, and your mother is the one who suffered for it."

Talk about having the rug pulled out from under me. I just had the whole floor pulled away. I'm standing on rocky soil, the foundation of everything I ever believed about my parents' marriage reduced to rubble around me.

"We did try to make it work," Dad continues. "But traveling back and forth—it was hard on us. I started staying in Paris more and more, and then I . . ." He meets my gaze and breathes out a sigh. "I met someone. A woman. She's the reason your mother and I are divorced."

My skin flushes hot then cold, and a sheen of sweat breaks out across my upper lip. "You cheated on Mom?"

He closes his eyes, his jaw clenched, and slowly nods. "It was only once, and I immediately told your mother what happened. We'd been growing apart for so long, she didn't even act surprised. We decided together that ending things was the best thing for us both."

I don't have words. Anger, hot and thick, coils in my gut, but it is dampened by a profound sadness for my mom. She gave up so much. And for what?

Except so many things still don't make any sense. Mom really did seem to love Silver Creek. And I didn't imagine all the times she dogged on my love of traveling, though come to think of it, it was always in the context of the traveling I did *with Dad.* Knowing what I know now definitely frames things in a different light. Especially when I remember how many times I told her I wished she were more like Dad, how much I wanted to live with *him* full time instead of her.

"I should have told you," Dad says simply. "It was so long ago, I guess I thought it didn't matter. But I see now that it does."

I sniff, at least appreciating that he's willing to acknowledge it. "Why didn't *she* tell me?"

"Why did she move home to take care of her parents?" Dad asks. "She's been putting other people before herself her whole life, Kate. It's what she does. She put your relationship with me—your *feelings* about me—above everything else."

Understanding settles in my gut with uncomfortable certainty. Mom sacrificed her own comfort to take care of her parents, and she did the same thing so I could have a positive relationship with my dad. She couldn't stop herself from being bitter about it though, and that's what leaked over onto me. Her disappointment. Her *hurt.*

It's not a wonder she moved to Florida right after Grandma died. It was the first time she'd ever been free to make a choice that only impacted herself.

"Say something, Katie," Dad says. "I know it was a long time ago, but I'm still sorry for what I did. For how it impacted you and your mother both."

A sudden desire to call Mom swells inside my heart like an expanding balloon. Which is saying something because most of the time, I avoid talking to my mother like I avoid center seats on airplanes.

But this? This changes things. I'm not naïve enough to think it will change *everything*. But I do owe her an apology.

I study Dad closely, noting the deep creases around his eyes. His irises are a watery blue, a few shades lighter than mine. In the dim light of the restaurant, they almost look translucent.

Colorless. "Dad, would you do anything differently if you could?"

He takes a long, slow breath. "I was never meant for settling down, Kate. It's not me. You understand what that's like."

Suddenly, all I can think about is what Dad missed. I loved all our traveling together. But he wasn't around when I learned how to ride my bike. He wasn't there to teach me how to tie my shoes or take pictures of my junior prom. He missed every single one of my birthdays.

I *do* understand what his life is like because it's been *my* life for the last ten years.

And I don't want it anymore.

I want a home. A family. A life with someone beside me. And I want that someone to be Brody.

Sharp yearning nearly overwhelms me. I feel trembly. A little nauseous. I'm hot and cold. Sweating and shivering. I'm . . . elated. Excited. So scared. I want to text Brody and tell him, but I don't even know what I would say.

A pulse of fear throbs in my gut.

Will he forgive me for running away?

Will he want me to stay in Silver Creek?

Will he want *me*?

Chapter Twenty-Five

Brody

I STAND ALONG THE back wall at the reception after Lennox's awards ceremony. Lennox was right. There are a lot of young, attractive women around.

Fortunately, Flint is diverting most of the attention.

Perry leans against the wall beside me. "It was a genius plan, right?"

I lift an eyebrow. "What plan?"

"Bringing Flint," Perry says. "Without his distraction, it'd be us having to entertain all the women Lennox would be thrusting our way."

Understanding dawns. "You mentioned Flint on purpose. When Lennox invited us to come. That was a calculated suggestion."

Perry takes a swig of his drink. "Yes and no. It was calculated, but only because I knew *you'd* only agree to come if Flint were here too. The fact that Flint is an attention hog and can deflect it off me? That's just a bonus."

"You know, you *are* going to have to start dating again at some point," I say, eyeing my oldest brother.

He eyes me right back. "So are you."

"I thought you were the one saying I shouldn't give up on Kate. Which, you still owe me an explanation for that. Why the sudden change of heart?"

"It wasn't a change of heart," Perry argues. "I was never anti-Kate. I just didn't like the way you obsessed over her when it didn't seem like she was ever going to return your feelings. But I also don't think she would play you. If she was willing to let the relationship progress as far as it did, it can only be because she feels something. That doesn't mean it'll necessarily work out. But it might mean the conversation isn't over yet."

I appreciate that Perry is trying, no matter how uncharacteristic his advice. But I'm too tired for his brand of encouragement. In my brain, the pendulum has already swung the opposite direction. I haven't heard from Kate since she left. Not a text. A phone call. Nothing. I'm beginning to wonder if I ought to just cut my losses and move on. No more conversations with Kate. No more reading her articles. No more scrolling her social media accounts. No more late-night video chats or racing over to Charlotte whenever she flies through for a night.

No more dreaming of a life we're never going to have.

Olivia was right. The sting of loving her and losing her is so much worse.

"I don't think I can do it anymore, Perry."

He eyes me, his lips pursed. "With Kate? Like, at all?"

I nod. "I think I have to be done."

Well, Lennox did bring us here so we could move on.

I don't actually want to meet anyone tonight. But there's a part of me that wants to prove to myself that maybe, eventually, I will.

Perry tosses back the last of his drink and sets the glass on the table between us. "All right then, let's move on."

"What?"

Perry motions toward Lennox. "Let's go. We're here, aren't we? Let' go . . . do the thing. With the women."

"Do the thing?"

He growls in frustration. "Talking. Flirting. Isn't that how it's supposed to start?"

I press my lips together.

"If you start to laugh at me, I'm rescinding my offer."

I clear my throat. "Not . . . laughing," I say. "Let's go *do the thing.*"

We make our way toward Lennox who is across the room, his back against the bar, his ankles crossed. He almost looks the part of a movie star as much as Flint does.

I loosen my tie on my way over. I've been wearing a suit for close to four hours now, and that's about three hours and fifty-nine minutes too long.

I'm five yards away from Lennox when three women approach, leaning on either side of the bar next to Lennox. Perry's steps slow beside me. "Nope," he says. "I change my mind. I'm not ready for this."

I grab his arm. "Lennox has already seen us," I say. "If we turn away now, there's no way it won't look rude."

"But there are three of them," Perry argues. "I don't care if we look rude."

"There are three of us. One conversation," I say. "You can do this. You don't even have to say anything. Just stand there and try not to frown."

Lennox introduces us when we stop in front of him, and the women shift to make room for us.

The brunette closest to me slips her hand around my forearm. *One conversation,* I think to myself. If I can make it through one conversation, maybe hope isn't completely lost.

"Lennox tells me you're a kayaker," she says.

My phone buzzes in my pocket before I can answer.

Could it be Kate?

Do I want it to be Kate?

That last one is a stupid question because of course I want it to be Kate. I may know I need to get over her, but I'm less than five minutes into this new life plan, and I'm only human.

But I'm also a gentleman, and I will not ignore this woman's question no matter what text pinged into my phone.

I nod. "I am."

She twirls her hair around her finger. "Will you tell me about it? When I think of kayaking, I imagine paddling around on placid lakes. But I'm guessing what you do is more than that?"

My phone buzzes one more time.

I run a hand across the back of my neck. "Yeah. It's . . . not on lakes," I manage to say.

She wrinkles her brow. "The ocean, then? Rivers?"

Another buzz from my phone, and then another.

"I'm sorry, can you just . . ." I pull out my phone. "Excuse me for one second?"

I'm the literal worst.

The grimace the woman offers me as I turn away confirms it.

I move a few yards away and pull up my text messages. The messages *are* from Kate. One right after another.

Kate: Hi.

Kate: That's a dumb way to start.

Kate: Is it okay if I still text you?

Kate: I know I left without much explanation. And the fact that you didn't respond makes me think you probably don't want to talk to me.

Kate: Brody, there's so much I want to tell you.

Kate: For example. You remember those pictures I showed you of me as a baby? And you said they looked like they were taken on your front porch?

Kate: It's because they WERE taken on your front porch.

Kate: Before my parents split, my dad lived in Silver Creek for a couple of years when I was a baby. And SURPRISE WE LIVED IN YOUR HOUSE.

I appreciate Kate's all-caps yelling. I can easily imagine the inflection in her voice if she were telling me this in person. But also, *WHAT ABOUT US?* There's my all-caps yelling. *WHAT ABOUT US?*

Another message pops up.

Kate: So many things I thought were true actually aren't. Example two. My dad cheated on my mom. That's why they got a divorce. Can you even believe that? And I never knew.

I run a hand across my face. I know Kate well enough to understand how much learning these things about her dad has impacted her. But I can't be the person she turns to for stuff like this if I can't be her person for everything. My heart can't take it. I can't just be her friend.

"Brody," Perry calls. "Come tell us the story about the bear sitting on your tent."

In other words: We are in this together, and you better get back over here so I don't have to handle this conversation alone.

I stare at Kate's text thread for another moment then close it out and silence my notifications so I won't even feel the buzzing if she texts me again. She can have her realizations, but she didn't have the most important one. The one I need her to have—that she loves me.

The woman who asked me about kayaking smiles as I return,

and I smile back. It's forced, but hopefully she won't be able to tell. What is it people always say? Fake it until you make it? I'm definitely faking it, but it's all I can do at this point.

The conversation has moved on past Perry's Appalachian Trail stories, so I never do tell the story about the bear, but Rebecca—that's the woman's name—seems perfectly content to monopolize all my attention.

She's very nice. She's an accountant. She has a goldendoodle named Dragon. She runs marathons. She's great at maintaining eye contact. She can talk five consecutive sentences without needing any oxygen. And she seems genuinely interested in everything I have to say.

But that's the problem. I don't *have* anything to say. I'm trying my best to answer her questions, but I'm not thinking of any questions to ask in return and as hard as I'm trying, I just . . . don't care.

Rebecca is looking at me now, like it's my turn to say something, and I can't remember what she said last. I think back through our conversation, but she might as well have been speaking a different language. "I, um . . ." I run a hand across my jaw. "I'm not—"

She stops my words with a hand on my forearm. "Hey," she says gently. "We don't have to do this anymore. Your mind is clearly somewhere else." She cocks her head. "Maybe on *someone* else?"

I sigh. "I'm sorry, Rebecca."

She shrugs. "Don't worry about it. But leave the acting to your brother, okay? You aren't fooling anybody around here."

I grimace. "It's that bad, huh?"

"What it seems like is that it's been that bad for *you.*" She smiles, and I am so grateful for her kindness. "Do you want to talk about it? I've been told I'm a good listener."

I consider her question, but it feels like all I've done is talk about Kate. I'm tired of talking. Tired of thinking. "I appreciate the offer, but it's . . . more than I feel like unpacking right now."

She nods. "Fair enough." She studies me, her lips pursed. It feels like she wants to help me, and she's trying to figure out how. "What if we dance instead?"

I raise my eyebrows. It isn't a question I'm expecting. "Dance?"

"Sure. It's a great way to stop thinking. Especially if you've got a few drinks in you."

When I don't respond, she stands up and extends her hand. "Come on. It's just dancing."

Over her shoulder, the party is picking up, the music thumping. Flint is near the center of the gathering, dancing with a blond woman who's smiling like she just won the lottery.

It's a very unBrodylike move. Which is exactly why I say yes.

Flint smiles when he sees me approach, my hand still holding Rebecca's. He lets go of the woman in his arms long enough to clap me on the back and pull me into a quick bro-hug.

Soon, Lennox is beside us too. Only Perry stays off to the side, leaning against the bar where we left him, his arms crossed, a scowl on his face. At least he tried, if only briefly. That's more than we've gotten from him before.

It takes me a few songs to really relax, but Rebecca was right. It is a great way to stop thinking.

Kate is never far from my thoughts. Every time I see a woman with dark hair pass through my periphery, I do a doubletake. When someone laughs, it's Kate's laugh I hear.

But I'm living anyway. I'm breathing. I'm smiling, laughing, enjoying being with my brothers.

I can do this.

I *have* to do this. It's the only choice I have.

One day at a time, I'm going to get through this. I only hope it gets easier.

Chapter Twenty-Six

Kate

I SIT IN MY grandmother's front porch rocking chair and stare at my phone. My mom and I have been texting back and forth since the conversation we had while I was in London.

As soon as I made it back home, I sent her copies of a few of the pictures I found, and she's been texting me stories about them. Little things she remembers. She even told me how she met Dad and what their early relationship was like.

Things still aren't perfect. Far from it. But they at least feel a tiny bit easier.

Things with Brody on the other hand?

I have no idea how I'm supposed to feel.

I pull up the news article I've visited approximately five hundred and fifteen times since it popped up in my newsfeed Friday morning. *Hollywood A-lister Flint Hawthorne returns home to North Carolina to celebrate brother's success.* I normally click on articles about Flint because it's crazy and weird to read about someone who is famous to everyone else but a childhood friend to me. But this one impacted me in ways I didn't expect. The article includes two different photos. One is of all four Hawthorne brothers, their arms around each other, their smiles wide. Lennox is in the middle, holding some sort of award. But the second photograph? It's of Brody.

Okay, fine. It's actually of Flint. He's on a dance floor, surrounded by people, but Brody is clearly the guy standing right next to him. He's in a suit, which is all kinds of hot, but he's also holding hands with a woman.

That? Not so hot.

His lips were on mine just over a week ago, and now . . . and now I don't know what. I don't know anything because he hasn't responded to any of my text messages.

He's home, at least. I know that much. It's possible I went for a long walk last night that may or may not have looped by his house multiple times, stopping only when his truck was back in his driveway at 7:04 p.m. You know. Give or take.

Honestly, I have no idea how he didn't see me. Or hear that I'm back in town.

I don't know the protocol for this situation.

I came home from London ready to tell him I'm pretty sure I'm in love with him. No, not just pretty sure. I came home ready to tell him I *am.* In love. The end.

But I can't do that if he doesn't want to talk to me. Which, obviously he doesn't, or he would have responded to my texts.

I hurt him, I know. Leaving like I did was cowardly. But I was scared. Scared and overwhelmed and . . . what if it's too late? What if it doesn't matter at all because he's already thinking about someone else? What if he spent the entire weekend with the nameless woman in the photo, and I'm not going to see him again until we randomly run into each other at the grocery store when we're both buying avocados?

I might be overreacting.

I was *definitely* overreacting when I did a deep dive into

Flint Hawthorne celebrity gossip looking for any sliver of information about the Hawthorne brothers' weekend in Charlotte.

I'm not proud of how far down the rabbit hole I fell. I think I took celebrity stalking to a whole new level. I visited message boards I will never be able to unvisit. Saw posts from women who literally know everything there is to know about Flint. And I mean *everything*. Shoe size. Favorite food. Favorite color. The name of his dog when he was a kid. They know about Stonebrook. Several of them have even been there. There were half a dozen different photographs of women standing in front of the big farmhouse or crouching in the strawberry fields, their smiles wide as they hold up the picking buckets labeled with the Hawthorne family name.

Brody has mentioned it to me before, that they sometimes have fans show up, but seeing the devotion up close and personal was disconcerting, to say the least. And completely fruitless.

In all that searching, the woman in the original photo, the one with Brody, didn't show up anywhere else.

The fact brings little comfort. They were *holding hands*.

Except, logically, I know even that could mean nothing. I've seen photographs capture the complete opposite of what's actually happening in real life. The right angle, a good crop, and the lens can easily distort the truth of a situation.

But my heart isn't feeling very logical right now.

It's only feeling jealous. Sick. Angry that I let it come to this. That I let Brody slip through my fingers. I'm the one who left. The one who *ran away*.

Can I really blame him for spending the weekend with someone else?

The proof for the magazine spread *Beyond* is publishing next month is on the wicker table beside me. It looks so great. A full-page photo of Brody surrounded by whitewater, his expression serious, fills the entire left half of the title page spread. He looks unbelievable. Like he deserves his own fan club. *Move aside, Flint. Your big brother is taking sexy to a whole new level.*

I should just get over myself and take the article to Brody. He deserves to know. And it's a good excuse to see him. Maybe having a reason outside of, say, a full-on love confession, will help me figure out what to do next.

I stand up.

I can do this. I'll go see him.

I sit back down.

No, Kate. Be brave.

I stand back up.

Clear my throat.

Grab the magazine proof and my keys from the table and walk purposefully toward Mom's Subaru. Brody is usually at Triple Mountain on Mondays. If I don't find him there, I'll probably have to cave and call him.

When I catch my reflection in the driver's side window, I pause.

I do not look like a woman getting ready to declare her feelings. I look tired. My hair is in a messy bun, my t-shirt is baggy, and even though I'm wearing my favorite jeans, they look more like bumming-around-the-house jeans than heading-out-on-the-town jeans.

I can do better than this.

I huff and head back into the house for a twenty-minute makeover. I put on a turquoise sundress with wide straps and a plunging back. It makes me feel pretty, but it also doesn't look like I'm trying too hard. I curl my hair into loose waves and put on a little more makeup, but not so much that I look like I'm wearing any.

It's ridiculous how much actual effort goes into looking *effortless.*

Still, I feel more centered now, more like I'm armed for battle instead of just running in flailing, nothing but emotions leading the way.

I give myself another pep talk as I drive the short distance to the paddling school. When I see Brody's truck in the parking lot, my heart lurches, and a wave of nausea rolls over me.

Why? *Why?* Why do emotions have to impact our physical bodies so drastically? I've been around Brody seven million times. He knows everything there is to know about me. He's seen me at my worst, snot-nosed and crying. He's seen me hungover. He's seen me with food poisoning. He's held back my hair while I've thrown up in a hotel trashcan. He knows how much I've struggled to get along with my mom. How much I wish I have as many siblings as he does. He knows how much I love tacos. He knows everything.

This shouldn't be so hard.

Except, maybe him knowing everything is precisely *why* this is so hard. Because there's so much more at stake.

Griffin is at the counter inside the shop, just like he was the first time Brody brought me to Triple Mountain. He smiles when he sees me. I owe the man dinner. At least a drink. He's the main reason I was able to get Brody's article written and published in time.

"How's it going, Kate?" he asks.

"Good. Is Brody around?"

"He's out on the water, but he's just out back if you want to go watch. He isn't running rapids today. Just helping someone work on technique."

"Great. Yeah, I'll do that. But here." I pull out the magazine proof and hand it over. "I want to show you something first."

He flips through the pages, his smile growing the whole time. "You did it."

"We did it. I couldn't have done it without your help."

"This is amazing."

"It runs next month in *Beyond.*

His eyes go wide. "Next month? How did you even pull that off?"

"Honestly, I just got lucky. An editor friend of mine got word they had to pull their feature article. Something about an arrest and criminal charges? I didn't get the whole story, but it opened up a spot, and I had an article they could use to fill it."

"Has Brody seen this yet?"

"Not yet. I just got it myself. That's why I'm here." *You know. Among other reasons.*

"He's going to freak," Griffin says. "You think it'll actually work? That it'll save the program?"

"I don't know. I hope so. But it definitely can't hurt."

He carefully tucks the proof back inside the folder it arrived in. "Thanks for doing this, Kate. Brody's lucky to have you."

I smile, unsure how much Griffin knows.

I clear my throat, willing my inner jealous voice to calm down. I can only control what I can control. My feelings are my feelings, and his feelings are his feelings, and I will approach this conversation like an adult.

"Kate?"

I look up.

Griffin is still holding the folder, waiting for me to take it.

"You okay?" he asks. "You look like you swallowed a frog or something."

I take the folder and give my head a little shake. "I'm good. Great. I'll just wait for Brody outside."

Waiting outside is not a smart move.

From the picnic table behind the shop, I have a clear view of the river. Brody is in the water, shirtless except for his PFD. There is a single kayaker in the water with him, a woman who is young and beautiful, at least from what I can tell through all her gear, and clearly enamored with Brody. She's too far away for me to really tell, but she could absolutely be the woman he was with over the weekend.

I'm just about to turn and go when he looks up and sees me. *Great.* Now I'm stuck. And I'm too far away to read his expression.

I remind myself that I'm here to show him the magazine proof. And that won't change even if he's already asked the new girl to marry him.

Plus, I'm done running.

I will have this hard conversation.

I won't let fear keep me from being vulnerable anymore.

The lesson lasts about fifteen more minutes. Brody's teaching the woman how to roll her kayak upright after flipping upside down without getting out. I saw Brody do it when we were in Robbinsville and he was in the middle of churning whitewater, but it's almost as impressive to watch him teach the maneuver to someone else. I'm not close enough to hear what he's saying, but he's using his hands, gesturing to his hips, the boat, the paddle. The woman in the kayak appears to be listening intently. She nods whenever she's ready to give it a try, and then she rolls into the water. Over and over, her hand shoots out of the water and taps the bottom of the boat, which must be Brody's signal to roll her back up. But then, finally, she does it. She rolls herself back up, her smile wide, and drops her paddle onto her lap to give Brody a two-handed high five.

I'm a ball of nervous energy by the time Brody carries the woman's kayak toward the shed on the other end of the parking lot. His PFD is draped over his arm, exposing every inch of his toned, tanned, glorious chest. I watch as he puts away the rest of the gear and says goodbye to the woman, who, based on their interactions after the class, I'm pretty sure is *just* a student and not a personal friend.

That doesn't stop me from worrying over how much Brody might have enjoyed teaching her. I'm a complete mess. One stupid picture on the internet, and I've lost my grip on reality.

But it's more than that. I'm scared about the other woman because it's a surface-level thing that's easier to worry about than all the other fears pulsing through my brain. I don't truly think Brody went and found himself a new girlfriend since last week. There are a million different explanations for the photo. I know this.

I'm just plain scared.

Scared he doesn't feel the same way. Scared if he *does* feel the same way, I'll still end up hurting him. Scared that he'll hurt me. Scared that if things don't work out, we'll lose our friendship.

I can't imagine my life without Brody in it. I don't *want* that life.

I'm still sitting at the picnic table when Brody slides onto the bench across from me. His expression is guarded—more guarded than I expect.

"You're back," he says casually.

"Hi."

"How was your trip?"

"Good. Long. How was your trip?"

His eyebrows go up. *That's right.* He never told me he was taking a trip.

I shrug. "You were with Flint. The internet knows everything about Flint."

"Ah. Right."

We sit there for what feels like an eternity, neither of us saying anything. It probably isn't more than forty-five seconds or so, but the way he's staring at me, the way the sunlight is catching on the drops of water still clinging to his shoulders, I am in literal agony, and it's making my brain jump all over the place.

"I texted you," I say.

"I saw."

He is not making this easy.

I press my palms against the picnic table and focus on the feel of the rough wood against my skin, letting it anchor me to the here and now of the moment. "Brody, I'm sorry I left without talking to you," I finally say. "I know it might not matter anymore. That maybe you've already decided you don't want to take a chance on a flight risk like me. And I understand. If the woman in the photo is someone important to you . . ." I close my eyes, suddenly unable to finish the last part of my sentence.

"The photo?"

My eyes pop open. He hasn't seen it? But then, why would he have seen it? I doubt he reads celebrity gossip articles about his brother.

"It was a picture of Flint. But you're in it. On a dance floor, I think? You're holding hands with someone."

He slowly nods, leveling me with one of those intense stares I know so well. "Would it matter to you if she does mean something to me?"

I drop my gaze, heat flushing my cheeks. So he *did* meet someone else. I force a slow, deep breath. "You're my friend, Brody," I say without looking up. "I want whatever makes you happy."

"Kate."

I look up.

"You know that's not what I'm asking." His words are careful and measured, so very Brody.

I shake my head, tears already gathering on my lashes. "What do you want me to say, Brody? Yes, okay? Yes, it would matter." My hands start to tremble, and I slip them off the table, hiding them in my lap. "It would make me feel sick with jealousy and rage and irrational fury." I wipe away a tear and bite my lip. "And it would make me so angry at myself that somehow, I let you slip away."

His voice is smaller now. "You left, Kate. I told you how I feel, and you ran away. Do you know what that felt like?"

"I know. I know, and I'm so sorry," I say, my voice quivering. "I wasn't trying to hurt you, I just . . . I got scared. This is a big deal. There's a lot on the line. But I want this. I want . . . *us*."

Gravel crunches in the parking lot behind us, and Brody looks at his watch. "I've been waiting for you for so long, Kate. I've loved—" He shakes his head. "Even when you dated someone else. Even when you stopped texting me. When you stopped coming home and ignored my messages and skipped Grandma Nora's funeral. I've been here. Trying so hard to convince myself I shouldn't wait for you. I shouldn't hope. But then every time I got close to letting you go, you showed up again, staying just long enough to keep me on the hook."

Tears spill down my cheeks. "Brody, I didn't know. That wasn't what I was trying—"

"But you did know last weekend. I told you how long I've—" His voice catches. "And you still left."

I close my eyes. How did it take me so long to truly see him?

"Hey, Brody?" Griffin says from behind me. "The group is here and ready to get started. I need your help."

Brody nods and runs a hand through his hair. "All right. I'll be right there."

"Wait." I stand from the picnic table and grab the magazine proof. "Here." I sniff and hold it out. "This is for you. It runs next week in *Beyond* magazine."

Brody stays where he is, his hands propped on his hips, his face like stone. Every ounce of him is tense. He is a caged animal. A coiled spring.

I drop the proof on the table and take a step backward. I take a steadying breath, my eyes darting from Brody to Griffin, who is watching on, his eyes full of concern. "I'm so sorry, Brody," I finally say. It's the only thing I *can* say.

And then I turn and go home.

Chapter Twenty-Seven

Kate

"You know," Kristyn says, "this would have been a much easier conversation had you not saved everything up for one phone call."

I lean back onto the quilt I dragged off my bed and stretch my arms over my head, looking up through the branches of the sugar maple in Grandma Nora's backyard. The leaves are a deep rich green right now, but in the fall, they'll turn a bright, vibrant yellow before dimming to burnished gold. "I'm sorry I didn't tell you. It just felt like everything was happening so fast," I say. "I think I knew I was falling for Brody, and I knew you'd be able to tell if we truly talked about it."

"I get it. But sheesh. You got a job offer, spent a night sleeping in Brody's arms, fell in love, and learned the true reason your parents divorced all in a month. Your friends-to-lovers story turned into a telenovela."

"Don't forget about finding a picture of the *other woman* on the internet."

"Ohh, that's right!"

"Is there a romance trope for friends that lose touch and never talk again? I think that one is mine."

"Don't lose hope, Kate. You'll talk to him again. You guys will figure this out."

I breathe out a sigh. "I don't know, Kristyn. You should have seen his face."

"Just give him a minute to process. And don't go anywhere, for crying out loud. No more spontaneous trips across the Atlantic."

I smile. "That's good advice."

"It is good advice. And I would have given it to you before had you paused for two seconds and asked for my opinion."

"Fine. Lesson learned. From now on, I'll pause all my major freakouts and consult with you before doing anything drastic."

She chuckles. "And your life will be better for it. So what are you going to do now?"

"I don't know. Finish Grandma Nora's house, I guess. Start applying for jobs."

"I bet it will be easier than you think. Just email every editor you've ever worked with and let them know you're looking."

"Not every editor," I say. "I want to be in the states. I want to see more of you. And I probably ought to see more of Mom and finally meet the husband she's had for four years." What I really want to see is more of Brody, but my heart won't let me dwell on that right now. It only took two hours after I left Triple Mountain, but I finally stopped crying. I'm too wrung out to start up again.

"I would love to see more of you too," Kristyn says. "You know, there are probably a lot of writing jobs in Chicago. You could always come up here."

I groan and roll onto my stomach. "No, thank you. Chicago gets colder than London."

Once I gave myself permission to acknowledge it, it only took a minute to recognize the home I'm craving can only be in Silver Creek. And not just because of Brody, though he's obviously the biggest part of it. But I've enjoyed being back in the mountains. When I carve away the hard parts, the tension with my mom, the uncertainty of my life with her, there is still a lot of good in this place. I haven't been very good at recognizing it. But I want to start. I'll look for a job based in Asheville. Or, if I have to, go back to my idea of freelancing the pants off of Western North Carolina tourist destinations. Whatever it takes, even if that means stocking shelves at the local Feed n' Seed, I'll find a way to stay.

But only if Brody will have me. The town is too small for us to peacefully coexist if he won't. If my future is going to require me to get over him, it will have to be living somewhere that isn't here.

"All right, I gotta go," Kristyn says. "Jake wants to leave for dinner, and he's tired of waiting on me."

"Go get dinner. I'll call you tomorrow."

"Or before if you and Brody work things out. Okay, love you, bye!"

The sun is almost fully set now, the first fireflies dancing in the yard. I could stay out here all night, but I haven't eaten since breakfast, and crying burns a lot of calories. I can't fill the emptiness in my heart, but I can at least eat.

I stand and shake out the blanket then carry it toward the house, stopping when I see Charlie ambling toward me.

My heart stutters then starts again, beating at triple speed as I bend down and scratch his ears. If Charlie is here, that means Brody is too.

Instead of going in the back door, I skirt around the side of the house to the front porch.

Brody is sitting on the steps. His truck is nowhere in sight, so he must have walked over. The magazine proof is sitting on the rough, wooden planks beside him.

I stop a few yards away from the porch, and Charlie drops to his haunches at my feet.

The night isn't silent by any stretch. Cicadas are humming in the trees, the sound rolling across the night like a wave, and frogs are croaking down by the creek. But the heaviness of *Brody's* silence is almost more than I can take.

I won't talk first though. He came here. It has to be because he has something he wants to say.

"Are you still leaving at the end of the summer?" he finally asks, his voice floating across the settling darkness.

I take a step closer. "No." My heart squeezes. "I don't ever want to leave again."

He doesn't respond for a long moment. So long that Charlie walks over and sniffs Brody's hands as if checking to make sure he's okay. "You want to live here?" Brody finally says. "Forever?"

"Honestly, the where is less important to me right now. I'm more concerned about who I'll be living with." I slowly walk to the porch and climbs the stairs, dropping onto the top step beside him. We aren't quite touching, but he's close enough for me to feel the warmth of him. To catch his scent. "Brody, I love you. I mean, I've always loved you. But now I'm *in* love with you."

He closes his eyes and huffs out a laugh. "Do you have any idea how long I've waited to hear you say those words?"

For a split second, I tense up, wondering if there's a *but* at the end of Brody's sentence. *But you're too late. But you missed your chance. But it wasn't worth the wait.*

But then Brody looks up, and his eyes are so full of love and tenderness, my fears evaporate in an instant. "So I guess you aren't taking the job in London?" he says through a grin.

I smile. "No. I don't want to live in London. I want to live here. Or anywhere, really. As long as you're there too."

He holds out his hand, palm up, and I slip my fingers into his. He tucks it close to his chest, scooting me closer so my side is flush against his.

"I didn't meet anyone else in Charlotte," he says after a long stretch of silence.

I shake my head. "Brody, I don't care. It doesn't matter now."

"She was just a stranger who led me to the dance floor. That was it."

"Okay," I say simply, suddenly sensing that wherever he's going with this, it doesn't have anything to do with the nameless woman in the photo.

"Kate, I was so close to deciding the only way I could move forward was to cut you out completely. No more texting. No more reading your articles. That's why I didn't respond to your texts. Because I couldn't be the guy you talk to about stuff like that if I wasn't—if I'm not—anyway, I was done."

I press my lips together. I came so close to losing him for good.

He looks at me, a seriousness in his gaze I'm not sure I've ever seen before. "If we do this, we're all in, all right? Right from the start." He reaches out and wipes a tear from my cheek. "I won't lose you again. I can't. And I can never go back to just being your friend."

"You won't. I'm not going anywhere, Brody. I promise." As I say the words, a peaceful certainty blossoms deep in my gut. He's it for me. He's always been it.

He leans over and kisses me, and I arch into him, my hands moving to his chest. His hands are everywhere, on my shoulders, my back, running up and down my arms, tangling in my hair. It's like he's cataloging every inch of me, and I do not want him to stop.

"Seven thousand, one hundred, and forty-five days," he whispers into my throat, his lips close to my ear.

I lean back, catching his eye. "What's that?"

"That's how many days I've loved you."

"That . . . is a lot of days."

He scoffs, a smile in his voice. "Tell me about it."

Tension drains out of me as the reality of what's happening finally settles in.

I really did get my friends-to-lovers romance. Kristyn would be so proud.

I push against Brody playfully, like I'm going to get up, but he catches my hand and tugs me even closer.

He nips at my earlobe with his teeth. "Don't even try it," he says, his teasing tone sending shivers down my spine. "You're never running away from me again."

"Is that a promise?"

His lips trace a slow line across my jaw, each kiss moving closer to my lips. "I'll promise you anything. Whatever you want, the answer is yes."

I'm not sure how long we kiss, but when my empty stomach grumbles, *loudly,* Brody is the one who pulls away. He chuckles. "Hungry, Kate?"

The familiar question immediately brings new tears to my eyes. "Oh my gosh, you have got to be kidding me." Stupid tear ducts. "That question is enough to make me cry?"

But it's more than the question. It's everything. It's how well he knows me. It's how much we've been through together and how completely I trust him to take care of me. To love me.

He lifts my hand to his lips and presses a kiss against my palm. "What are you hungry for?"

He shifts sideways so he's leaning against the stair railing, and I turn the same direction, settling against his chest. He pulls his phone up in front of both of us and pulls up a food delivery app.

I gasp. "Silver Creek has DoorDash?"

"We're moving up in the world," he says. "But we only have three choices, and there's only one guy in town who delivers, so honestly, it's pretty hit or miss." He scrolls through a few more screens. "How do you feel about burgers and fries?"

My stomach grumbles, this time even louder than the first time.

"Burger and fries it is," Brody says. "Oh hey, look at that. Rosco's delivering tonight. We're in business."

"His name is Rosco?"

"Are you really going to judge our only source of sustenance right now?"

"I was just . . . going to say how lovely the name is."

Brody chuckles and pulls me more tightly against him.

We stay on the porch while we wait for our food. My ankles are mosquito bitten, but I don't even care. I could stay like this, wrapped in Brody's arms, the warmth of his solid chest behind me, forever.

"What are you going to do?" he asks. "About your job."

I lift my shoulders. "I don't have a clue. I'll figure something out. Or maybe . . . we'll figure something out? Honestly, I'm kinda tired of figuring stuff out on my own."

"We will," he says. "I promise we will. I want to do this right. I want to take you on real dates. I want to hold your hand and walk you to your door and kiss you senseless whenever I get the opportunity. But I also want you to have whatever career you want. I don't want you to choose me at the expense of all your other dreams."

"I know. I'm not. I promise. I *would* like to find something more permanent, even something similar to the job in London. But there are magazines in the states. Maybe I'll find a place that will let me work remotely. In the meantime, I've got a long list of things in Western North Carolina I can write about."

He's quiet for a beat before he says, "I can teach anywhere, Kate."

I shake my head. "You can't teach kayaking anywhere."

"No, but there are other rivers."

I turn in his arms so I can look at him. "I've never had a big family. I know you never thought you'd hear me say it, but I want to be close to yours. I want to live in Silver Creek."

He responds with a kiss, this one potent with promise and hope.

Our food arrives a few minutes later and we eat it right there on the porch, Charlie lounging at our feet, eating the French fries that Brody drops and the ones that I toss at him when Brody isn't looking.

And Brody wonders why Charlie likes me so much.

While we eat, we talk about everything I learned about my parents and their divorce. Brody listens patiently as I process—*again*—working my way through all the ways my erroneous beliefs influenced my feelings about Silver Creek and my desire for a relationship.

Uncertainty still pulses through me as I talk. Trusting myself with Brody's heart feels like a giant leap of faith, but the alternative—living without him—feels so much scarier. I don't deserve him loving me. But I'm not sure anyone possibly could. That doesn't mean I won't try though. Every single day, I'll try to love him as well as I know he'll love me.

"We'll be okay," Brody tells me. "We'll move forward together. We'll work through everything together." And when he says it, somehow, I know we will be.

"So the woman you were kayaking with today," I say as I crumple up the wrapper to my burger.

Brody smirks. "Is my girlfriend jealous?"

Ohhhh. That felt good. I need him to call me his girlfriend again.

I raise my eyebrows. "Does your girlfriend have reason to be?"

He leans forward and plants a brief kiss on my lips, which is good because the intensity of his eyes on me was about to make me melt in between the slats of the porch.

"Her name is Jessica," he says. "And she was very excited today because she just learned how to roll her kayak, and her fiancé is going to be *very* impressed."

"I . . . am so happy for Jessica," I say through a wide smile.

"Kate, you managed to hold my heart captive when you were twenty countries away and not even trying. You really think you need to worry? I'm at your mercy. All of me is yours." He tosses a French fry at me. "Not that I mind you being jealous. It's only fair. I did have to watch you with Preston for two agonizing years."

I gasp. "Oh my gosh. I made you listen to all the gritty details of my first kiss!"

Brody nods, his expression solemn. "Worst hour of my life."

I drop my head onto his shoulder. "I'm sorry! I swear I didn't know. I never would have said anything if I'd had any clue how you felt."

He pierces me with his steady gaze. "I know. And as ridiculous as it sounds, I'm glad you didn't know. I think we both had to grow up a little bit. Figure out who we were before we were ready for this."

"Is that why things have felt so different this time? Because they have. Right from the start, things have felt different."

He shakes his head. "I don't know. I just know I never really believed you'd love me back until I saw you standing there on Siler, waiting to surprise me. I guess it felt like you were looking for something you've never looked for before."

I smirk. "Honestly, it's the abdominal muscles, Brody. Once I saw you naked, I—"

"That's it." He stands up, not even grunting as he picks me up and leans me over his shoulder. He goes down the steps and heads around the house, Charlie up and nipping at his heels. "You're going in the creek."

I squeal and shift, trying to force him to put me down, but he only hoists me higher. I beat on his back, laughing until he finally drops me right beside the edge of the water at the back of Grandma Nora's property.

"You would never," I say as I back away.

His eyes sparkle in the moonlight. "I might."

"Even after I went to all that trouble writing an article about your program."

"Oh my gosh!" His eyes go wide. "I forgot the article!" He turns and jogs toward the house. I follow behind him, watching as he reaches the porch and retrieves the proof. He turns to face me, the folder pressed against his chest. "I can't believe you did this for me," he says.

I shrug. "Griffin helped."

He opens it, flipping through the pages. "How long did this take you? And how did you possibly manage to get it published so quickly?"

I give him a quick rundown of all the tiny miracles that led to the article being published. His eyes move over every page, his fingers tracing the photos. "It wasn't a miracle that made this happen, Kate. It was *you.*"

He holds out his hand, and I move to his side, settling next to him as he wraps an arm around my back.

"I don't know if it'll make a difference," I say into his chest. "Maybe nothing will change. But I had to try."

He squeezes me a little tighter. "I love you for trying." He leans back and tilts my chin up. "I love you for so many reasons."

"I love you too," I say. "For so many reasons." My hand snakes up to his stomach and slips under his shirt. "One," I say playfully, digging my finger into his abs. "Two. Three. Four."

He squirms away, yelping loud enough to make Charlie bark.

I laugh as he lunges for me and dart out of his grasp. I take off running into the house, hoping he'll follow me, knowing he will.

I have no idea what tomorrow will bring. I don't know what I'll be doing for work. I don't know where I'll be living. I don't know anything.

But I know who will be standing next to me.

And that makes anything—*everything*—seem possible.

Epilogue

Brody

SIX WEEKS IS NOT a very long time by *general* relationship standards.

When your relationship is with someone you have known for nineteen years? Six weeks feels like a lifetime. Especially since we've spent every spare moment together, bouncing between Kate's house and mine, plus Sundays up at the farm for family dinner.

To say my family is excited for us would be a vast understatement. Mom cried. Olivia breathed a huge sigh of relief. Lennox wrapped Kate in a huge bear hug. Even Perry nodded his approval, making sure Kate knew he was the *only* Hawthorne sibling who never encouraged me to move on and put Kate behind me.

Kate only laughed. "Well, you're more generous than me. I would have given up on me long before Brody did."

Only Dad seemed unruffled when we walked in holding hands. He watched on silently as everyone else reacted to the news. Finally, he shook his head and grumbled, "I don't know what the big deal is. I always figured they'd get together in the end."

I stop and get tacos from the stand next to Triple Mountain, a celebration of sorts, since today I found out that an anonymous and incredibly generous donation was made to Green River Academy—one to be used exclusively by the whitewater kayaking program.

My little brother will never admit it if I'm right, but I'd put money on it being Flint's doing.

Either way, the program will be up and running as soon as school starts, with the school board's official blessing and enough funding to pay Griffin and one other instructor for their time on the water.

Victory is sweet. Even sweeter because it was Kate's article that made all the difference.

I pull up to Kate's house, tacos in the seat beside me, but I forget all about them the second I see Kate sitting on the front porch, her phone in her hand. She looks . . . stunned. Confused, maybe? Whatever is going on, she isn't smiling.

My heart rate ratchets up as I race out of my truck. "What's wrong? What's going on?" I ask as I reach her. I crouch down in front of her, and she finally offers the smallest smile.

"Hi," she says faintly.

"Are you okay?" I reach forward and cup her cheek, needing the reassurance of her skin against mine.

"I'm okay. Sorry," she says, giving her head a tiny shake. "Everything is fine. I just . . ." She takes a deep breath. She looks at me, her eyes brightening, like she's finally stepped out of a fog. "Do you want the big news, or . . . the bigger news?"

I shift so I'm sitting on the stairs beside her. "Um, let's start with the big news?"

"I was hoping you would say that." She lifts her hands and presses them to her cheeks like she's still surprised by what she's saying. “I got the job.”

My eyebrows shoot up. “With WNC Magazine?”

She nods and smiles. “I have to be in the office in Asheville once a week, but other than that, it’s completely remote. It’s perfect, Brody. I’m really excited about it.”

I lean down to kiss her, still marveling, even all these weeks later, that I get to do this. That she’s mine. “I’m so proud of you. And . . . I can’t imagine what news is bigger than this.”

She blows out a breath. “Oh, it’s bigger. About two thousand square feet bigger.”

“Um, what?”

“How do you feel about this house, Brody?”

“This house? Your grandmother’s house?”

She nods.

Does she want to buy it? Maybe her mom offered to sell it to her? “I . . . think it has the best lot on the street? The backyard is great, and I like the creek. And I think the kitchen remodel looks really great.”

She bobs her head in time with my words. “Right. Yes. All good things.”

“Kate? How do *you* feel about this house?”

She bites her lip. “Well, um, it’s mine now. So I think I . . . like it?”

I blink. “You bought it?”

She shakes her head no. “But I just talked to my mom.” Another deep breath. “Grandma Nora wanted me to have it.”

“Whoa.”

She laughs. “Yeah. Whoa.”

“How are you feeling about it?”

“Um, weird? A little conflicted? It’s why Mom worked so hard to make me want to stay. You remember? The way she left her car and bought the groceries and had the bed made up? It's also the reason she kept it even after she moved to Florida."

"She was saving it for you."

"Exactly. But Grandma Nora only wanted me to have the house if I decided to live in Silver Creek. It was never in the will, but she told Mom what she wanted. So Mom just hung onto it, waiting to see what I decided to do. She finally told me today."

"That feels weirdly . . . manipulative? You only got the house because you decided to live in town? That's why you're conflicted."

"Yeah. Because I actually think that's what Mom *thought* she would do at first. Lure me here, then, I don't know, bribe me to stay? But things have gotten so much better lately. Our relationship has gotten so much better. She told me I can do whatever I want with it. We can keep it if we want. Or we can sell it."

My heart squeezes at the sound of her saying *we.* But this is her decision to make. No matter how perfect I think the backyard would be for a garden, or how easily I can imagine sitting on this front porch with Kate until we're eight hundred years old and wrinkled and gray, I'll support her no matter what.

"What do you want to do?"

"Do you want the unfiltered, I'm-not-worried-about-what-anyone-is-going-to-think truth?"

"Well, I'm nervous now, but yes. Lay it on me."

She reaches over and squeezes my hands. "I want to marry you. And then I want us to live here so we can make this house our home."

My lips fall on hers even as I'm laughing, my hands moving from her face to her shoulders and back again. "Did you seriously just propose to me?" I say in between kisses.

She laughs. "I'll take it back if you want to be the one who asks."

I kiss her again, this one longer, a little deeper than the last. "I don't care who asks."

"So you're saying yes?"

"Kate, I've had a ring since the week after you got back from London. Of course I'm saying yes. Today. Tomorrow. As soon as we can. Yes. Let's do it."

She pushes me away from her, hands pressed to my shoulders. "You've had a ring all this time and you haven't asked me yet?"

I squirm, suddenly feeling a little sheepish. "I was trying to be reasonable. It's only been six weeks."

She shakes her head, her hand moving to my cheek. "Brody, it's been nineteen years. You could have asked me that first night when we talked about everything, and I would have said yes."

My eyes drop. "But it hasn't been nineteen years for you. I was trying to give you some time to, I don't know. Make sure you really want this."

She looks at me, the intensity of her gaze suddenly making me feel vulnerable. Exposed. She leans forward, kissing me softly at first, then with increased pressure. "I love you, Brody Hawthorne. I want this," she whispers against my lips. "I want you."

We kiss for another long moment before I finally pull away. "I guess it's a good thing I said yes then, huh?"

She rolls her eyes and stands up, holding out her hand. "Come on."

"Where are we going? I have tacos in the truck."

She pauses. "Mmm. Okay, fine. We can eat tacos first. But then we're walking to your house."

"What's at my house?"

She scoffs like she can't even believe I'm asking the question. "You did say you have a ring. You can't expect me to know it exists and not want it on my actual finger."

"I love a woman who has her priorities in order. Tacos first, *then* diamonds."

"This feels perfectly reasonable to me." She pulls me to my feet, and we walk together to the truck.

"What will you do with your house?" she asks.

"Let Lennox rent it, probably. He's looking for a place."

"Oh, I love that. But he's looking *now,* isn't he? That means you'd have to move in here pretty quickly."

"True." I shoot her a look. "After we go get the ring, we should probably head up to the farm and see how quickly Olivia can plan us a wedding."

She rolls her eyes. "Olivia is less than two months away from having her baby."

I blow out a sigh. "Then we'll have to work even faster."

"You're ridiculous, you know that, right?"

I hand her the tacos. "Nope. Just been waiting a really long time to get what I want."

"Says the guy who waited six agonizing weeks without proposing?"

"Agonizing, huh? I'll just take back the dinner I bought you and go—"

"No! I'm sorry. You're forgiven. Please don't take my tacos. You can even keep the diamond an extra day."

I let her have her tacos.

And then we walk, holding hands, down to my house where I pull her ring out of my nightstand, get down on one knee, and propose properly like I should have six weeks ago.

We get married the second weekend in September. School

has already started, so we don't have time for a honeymoon, but honestly, just coming home at the end of the school day knowing Kate's waiting for me feels like honeymoon enough. I sometimes wonder if the novelty will ever wear off. If I'll ever stop marveling that I'm the man she chose.

When I hold her in my arms or fall asleep with her breathing beside me. When I find her in the kitchen making granola bars, her hair piled on top of her head, or stretched out on a blanket with a book under the sugar maple out back.

When she reaches for me in her sleep, her hand sliding over my chest like just feeling me next to her is enough to soothe a bad dream. When she waves goodbye or kisses me hello or smiles for no reason except that we're together.

These ordinary moments with her, they are all I have ever wanted.

She is all I have ever wanted.

And not a day goes by that I forget it.

Acknowledgments

I love learning new things. When I started this novel, I didn't know a single thing about whitewater kayaking. There's no way I could have turned Brody into such an expert kayaker without help, so special thanks to my brother-in-law, Brian Davis, a whitewater kayak instructor, for sharing all of your knowledge and know-how. It was so incredibly helpful!

And to my sister-in-law, Misty, Brian might have helped with the technical details, but YOU were the one who helped me make all those details sexy. I'm so grateful for you. For your heart, your friendship, and your support! I love you both.

It is universally true that behind every novel, there is an army of people who support the author and process. I can't think about my army of people without getting emotional.

Kirsten, you are an extraordinary critique partner and this novel would not be what it is without you. You make me bring my A-game every time, and I'm so grateful for that. But also, I just love you. Thank you the most for being my friend.

Emily, my first reader, my brilliant sister. I never have words. Thank you for sharing your smarts so generously.

Melanie, Becca, Brittany. Every time one of us publishes a new novel and I realize how far we've come, how the collection of our books has grown, I legit get teary. I'm so proud of us for hanging in, for learning new things, for writing words. I love you all. Thank you for reading so fast. I ask ridiculous things of you and you drop everything and do it, and that will always mean the world. I have the very best friends.

Josh, you will always be my favorite love story. Thank you for believing in me, so much that you were willing to pause your dreams to help me realize mine. You're my favorite.

About the Author

Jenny Proctor grew up in the mountains of North Carolina, a place she still believes is one of the loveliest on earth. She lives a few hours south of the mountains now, in the Lowcountry of South Carolina. Mild winters and of course, the beach, are lovely compromises for having had to leave the mountains.

Ages ago, she studied English at Brigham Young University. She works full time as an author and as an editor, specializing in romance, through Midnight Owl Editors.

Jenny and her husband, Josh, have six children, and almost as many pets. They love to hike and camp as a family and take long walks through the neighborhood. But Jenny also loves curling up with a good book, watching movies, and eating food that, when she's lucky, she didn't have to cook herself. You can learn more about Jenny and her books at www.jennyproctor.com.